I0592603

EDEN'S PROMISE

SUMERIAN CHRONICLES PREQUEL

DANIEL PHALEN

Creston Hall Press

For Sue again

This prequel sets the stage for Daniel Phalen's historical trilogy set in ancient Sumer: *The Sumerian Chronicles*. Part 1, *Eden's Bride*, is available now!

MAP OF MISHA'S JOURNEY

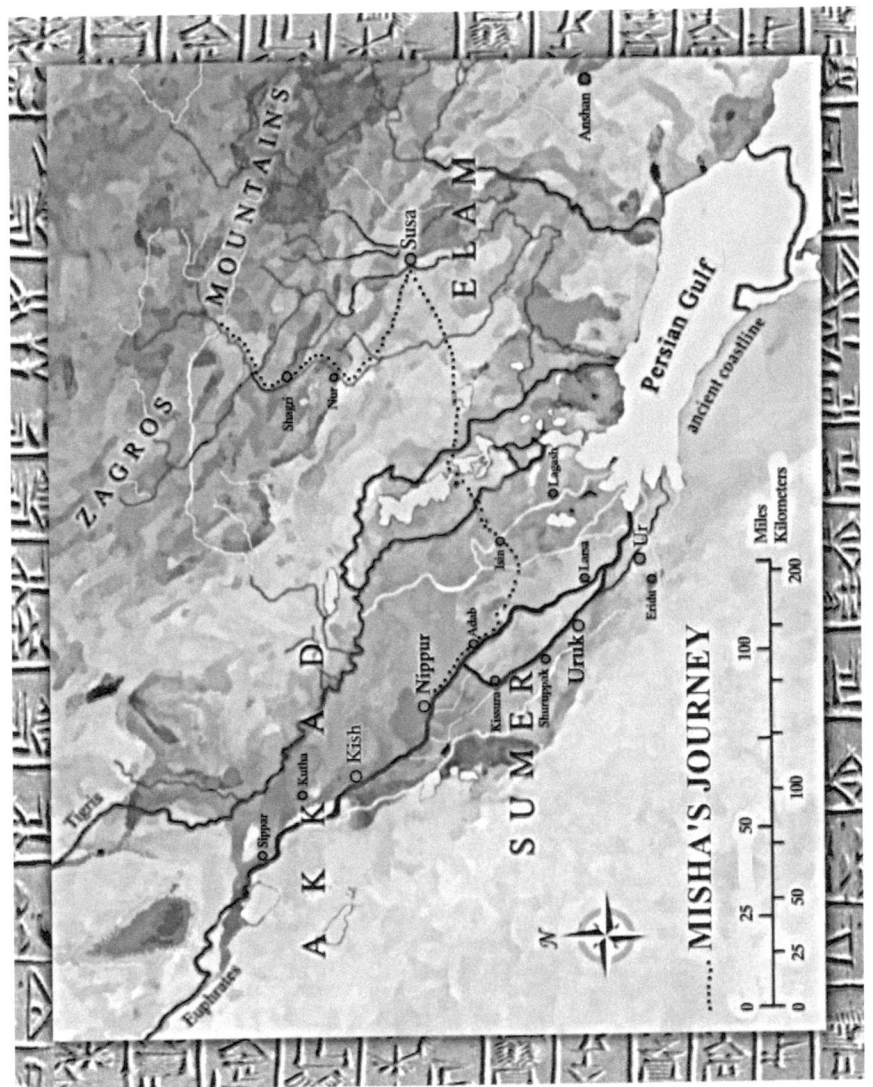

ii

CITY OF NIPPUR

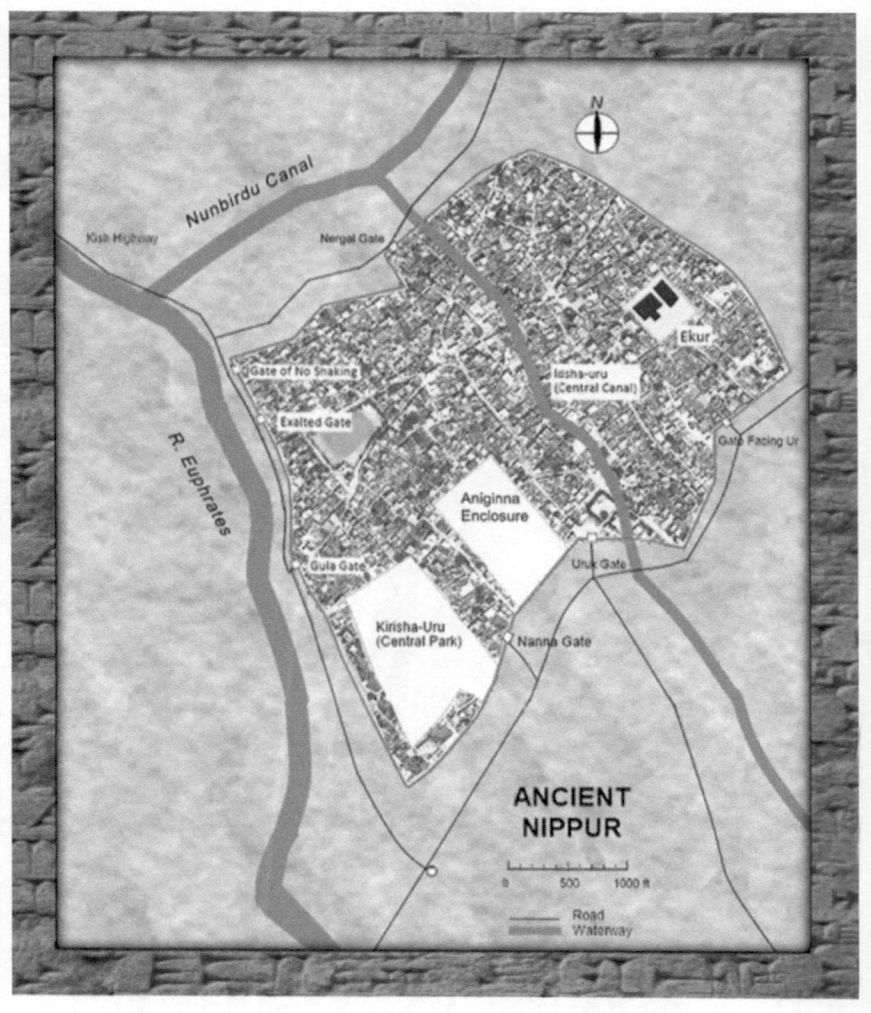

ANCIENT
NIPPUR

0   500   1000 ft

Road
Waterway

Character Brief

Misha	(MEE-shah) main character as a child
Uruna	(oo-ROO-nuh) queen of Nippur, seeker of the Sight, keeper of Serpenthood; also Entu, or high priestess
Gudamma	(goo-DAH-muh) first mentor, prophet seeker
Ashur	(ASH-er) hunting mentor
Nebur	(NEE-ber) reformed thief, beneficiary of first healing
Kinar	(ki-NAHR) best friend and mentor
Memet	(mem-MET) cobra companion, conduit for godly communication
Niccaba	(NICK-uh-buh) Uruna's mentor and mother figure; stalwart keeper of tradition
Mena Ramush	(MAY-nuh rah-MOOSH) Nippur's sitting queen, Misha's first mentor
Lubna Seddua	(LUB-nuh SED-oo-ah) temple politician and would-be queen; Uruna's nemesis
Suba	(SOO-buh) Uruna's first love, rescuer, half-Nord student of hunting, combat
Zug	(Zoog) planter; overseer and advisor to Uruna during rescue mission
Retha	(RETH-uh) Gar's half-Nord infant daughter
Nabi Gahn	(NAH-bee GAHN) master of stealth, weapons, combat

Heganna	(hay-GAH-nuh) from Sumerian *heĝal* [PLENTY], richest woman in Sumer, Anu's mother
Anu	(AH-noo) Heganna's renegade teenage son who aspires to hunting
Khufu Mahut	(KOO-foo mah-HOOT) Uruna's first consort, Egyptian royal
Nippur	(ni-POOR) Sumer's sacred religious center
Ekur	(ee-KOOR) Nippur's temple
Aniginna	(ah-ni-GHINN-uh) Nippur's civic center of government
Uruk	(OO-ruck) Nippur's southern rival city
Eanna	(ee-AH-nuh) Uruk's temple
Mada Ghin	(mah-dah-GHEEN) refugee village
Enshiggu	(en-SHIG-oo) god of Serpenthood and prophecy
Jebbut	(JEB-but) Heganna's Egyptian house man
Kissura	(KISS-er-uh) a town on Euphrates
Euphrates (Greek)	(yoo-FRAY-teez) major river feeding Sumer (Iraq today)

* See also GLOSSARY in the back of the book.

JOURNEY

Chapter 1

Fateful Union

Elam, ca 3,230 BC

In her first year wandering the Zab road alone, the child from Anshan learned to tuck the cobra out of sight before begging food. Mountain folk were an insular bunch. Many wouldn't answer the door at all, and if they did, a dust-caked urchin might be a shill for lurking brigands. And even the most forgiving? What would they do when faced with a huge snake draped about her shoulders?

A few hungry nights made it clea--r to the girl that others did not hear the serpent song that abided in her soul. By sparing them needless fright she kept herself fed.

She was her adoptive father's niece, Misha by name, the offspring of deposed royalty from a forgotten land, a detail which accounted for her striking beauty but not for her uncommon abilities.

She interpreted dreams.

She detected sickness in others.

She felt their sorrow and their pain, knew their innermost longings—often before they did.

But another lesson must be learned, and in all haste, for no one, especially grown-ups, wanted to hear such things from a child. In fact, a truth spoken would as likely earn a switch to the leg as a pat on the topknot. It seemed older people hid the black things from themselves. Some even husbanded a bleak prospect as the only meaning to a drab life.

Such a dreary lot might have destroyed so sensitive a soul, had she not come upon the old woman at the well in Shagri. Misha took out her small gourd bowl for a drink. Memet rode her shoulders as usual, but she waited until the square had emptied before she made her approach. When the gray-head across the well noticed the cobra, her expression brightened.

"Oh, what have we here? One of Enshiggu's own?"

Misha could only stare in disbelief. Never had she heard the god's name spoken by a human. Always it had come from the whisper-soft voice inside her head, speaking encouragement, counseling patience, forbearance, compassion for those without serpent sense.

The lady inclined her head. "How is this one called?"

"He is Memet."

"Is he kind to you?"

"Yes. He tells me everything."

"And with great love, I'll wager, m-mm?"

"Yes, of course, but this you knew before asking."

"Oho, indeed. You have a name, child. Please speak it."

"Misha."

"Have you traveled far, Misha?"

"It's been two summers since my *adda* died." She no longer felt sorrow or pain to tell it. Only a lingering curiosity about what became of the dead.

The old one seemed to understand. "I am Gudamma. I too am a traveler, my whole life, it seems."

Misha sensed she might confide in this woman as she had no other. "You set out from a big city before I was born. You are a seeker of some kind."

Gudamma's face brightened. "Perhaps no longer, for I may have just found what I seek. But I expected a grown woman, not a child. Such is the whimsy of Serpenthood. Do you know what that means?"

"Enshiggu speaks of a prophet. But I'm only six—I think. My mother didn't really know because—because..."

"She did not bear you herself. The one who did was called Itani. Very beautiful, most kind, and wise beyond her years."

"How do you know these things that even I do not?"

"Ah, but you do know, Misha, for you just told me." Gudamma tapped her own head. "And if that makes no sense, be glad for the mystery and seek not to know all. Now tell me, why do you travel?"

"Memet says I have a family waiting, but he hasn't told me where yet. I just go without much thought for where my feet take me."

"Perhaps our two journeys in solitude have come to an end. Can you imagine further travel halfway across the world?"

Misha had dreamt of a house that rose like a mountain from a vast, unbroken land where a great river cut a path through green grasses.

Gudamma must have read her thoughts again. "The land is called Sumer, and the house is a great temple called Ekur, which means 'mountain home.' I shall take you there myself, so that you may rule it one day."

Misha could not answer, for in her mind's eye she saw Gudamma laid in the ground soon after their journey's end. She would not speak of such a dream, but instead walked around the well to take the woman's hand.

Gudamma looked down and saw a darkness in the child's eyes.

She then took the small hand in her own and gave it a firm squeeze.

"It is always so," she said. "As one path ends, another begins."

⟨◦⟩⟨◦⟩

A wine grower put them up the first night in a one-room storage shack. They dined on sweetbread until Misha realized what they were eating, and said she suffered greatly from eating animal innards. The farmer found an overripe squash, which the child devoured with relish.

Misha wished to take advantage of her first shelter in many days and so removed the cobra from his basket and placed him on the floor. She then squatted on a bed of straws and waited. As Gudamma watched, quick death rose slowly on the powerful stalk. The broad breast plates flared, steady and powerful, as the round lidless eyes homed in on the target.

His mistress responded with a light shrug of casual indifference.

"Oh, you are so curious tonight, Memet," she chimed in her soft voice. She then bent her wrist toward Gudamma. "Welcome this lady from across the mountains, who takes us to our new home."

Memet was interested only in the child. Nevertheless, Gudamma remained in the doorway a safe distance away. Had her long search truly ended in the make-shift shelter of a snake-bearing nymph? Misha's youth only added to Gudamma's earlier impression that she was the lucky witness to a marvel of startling significance.

"We are studying how one earns passage to the Fourth Door," the girl explained as she wiggled her bottom on the floor to address her companion more squarely.

The Fourth! According to lore, six Doors must be passed to attain Sight, and this babe was already half-way home! How could she possibly know of serpently doors at all, if not directly from the god himself?

Gudamma stilled her heart lest she disrupt the proceedings. Serpents were acutely sensitive to human emotion and she dared not risk the god's displeasure.

She was forgotten, however, as Misha entered a private realm with her guide to cosmic mysteries. Memet remained motionless, erect, his mind and will oblivious to mundane shadow passings, while he and the object of his intent communed in a soundless world of their own.

The attraction of the two for each other was sensual, almost sexual. Secrets of utmost intimacy passed between the locked pairs of eyes. A god was at work here. The power in the room was profound, undeniably vital. You couldn't be Lukur and not feel its message fairly shake you with the affirmation that this was the seer Gudamma had pursued for the last sixteen years of her long life.

The temple sisters would be astounded. Gudamma herself would not have dreamed the outcome had she possessed foresight of her own. Yet, the small bundle of humanity trilling happily to a deadly viper was a reminder that the wisdom of the gods transcended mortal sense. For reasons best known to the younger wives on Nippur's council, it was aging Gudamma who had received the god's sacred trust to find and bring home a serpent seer. Now in her sixtieth year of life, she must add to that burden the responsibility for a safe return passage through two hundred miles of wilderness, and once there make a convincing argument why Enshiggu-god, jealous guardian of human fortune, had chosen to instill his most precious gift in a child of six.

But as she watched, the subtle insinuation of "Him" crept into her thinking. This she knew to be the god's way of rapping for the attention of those lesser mortals permitted to approach the First Door but never to enter. She raised the latch of her mind, and attended the whisper-soft voice of Enshiggu.

Behold my child! he said with proud satisfaction. *See her devotion to the serpent. Watch how nimbly she balances between student and master, control and attention. But note also her physical perfection, her self-possession. Here is my chosen one. Here is the princess you seek, in whose willing heart lives the salvation of humanity. Cherish and protect my little queen, for she is my gift to your world.*

Through tears Gudamma watched Misha's shiny black locks sweep forward as she crossed her slender arms over her chest and bent to attend some inner communication from the cobra. She was indeed the picture of graceful feminine perfection. But what absolutely fascinated the old priestess from Nippur were the eyes, great luminous grey orbs rimmed with long, dark lashes and set wide in a small oval face. As the eyes followed you with a child's ingenuous candor they also enfolded you, gathered you up with mother-bird wings to drink the deep love catchments in her timeless soul. Gudamma felt safe in those eyes, and thus experienced none of her old terror of serpents as she watched the scaly executioner from a mere two paces away.

Gudamma took little pleasure in her own victory. She knew well the arduous life ahead for the child, the sacrifices demanded by public life, dangers waiting at every turn. Misha held such promise as none before her in two hundred years, but she might fail to reach the pinnacle for any number of reasons before she was sufficiently practiced in Serpenthood. The Lukur ladies partook in a monstrous gamble, conspiring for control of a young life. Misha's success would introduce a skew to the world's fortunes, with unpredictable consequences. Whether mankind would survive the little queen's impact or die of it remained for others to see.

Gudamma would take her to her new home, see to her safety and comfort, and await the babe's achievement in her dotage. Long ago she had been told thus...

...A soft rap on the wall brought her awake. Gray light from the doorway spelled dawn's arrival. She'd fallen asleep!

"Nana," said the melodious voice from across the room, "are we ready to go to Nippur? Memet would like to get started. He says Great Mother is waiting."

Chapter 2

Desert Guardians

Gudamma and the child had not quite reached the Zab's lower stream when winter's early advance set in. Two days short of the river, the first icy wind swept down from the north in unusual haste, making travel in the open a hazard. They put in at a cluster of mud hovels called Nur and found lodging for the night in a hut behind a tavern.

Misha would need a woolen wrap sized for her small frame. The tavern keeper, a woman in late age herself, said the wool merchant wouldn't arrive for another week or more, and advised Gudamma to either cross the river without delay or head south. An early frost did not bode well.

"This one promises to bring a nasty chill. You'd best cast your lot with the stick people down Susa way."

Years ago, Gudamma had spent a short winter among the wood harvesters on the alluvial pan west of the Zagros foothills. They traded oak limbs for Sumerian barley and emmer wheat. She and her small charge might spend a short time there, but the grueling trek would lengthen their journey by weeks, possibly months.

"What's between?" she asked, dreading the answer.

"Open plains, a river stop or two if the ferrymen haven't already gone south. There's aught but the one road the whole way down. Wander too close to the river and you'll get stuck in a bog."

The next day they set out on the Susa road. Misha caught a lizard for Memet and avowed it would keep the cobra sated for several days. That night they sat without a fire between two hills and chewed dried meat in the dark. Gudamma worried about wolves until Misha sensed her concern.

"None are about tonight," she said. "More to fear from the wind."

They spent the night shivering on the cold ground, Misha giving her body warmth to Memet.

Gudamma was slow to get up at first light, but she willed her feet to climb the slope from the draw and press on toward the unbroken line of earth and sky to the south.

Toward evening, they came across a boar hunter and his son standing where an animal track intersected with the road.

"Saw you coming, figured you might be in a speck of trouble," said the hunter, and when Gudamma sang her praise for his deed he simply shrugged. "Out here, we take care of our own. Come sit, Mother, I've some tea left in the flask."

The hunter's name was Ashur and his son Kumir. As they shared pig meat over a fire, the four determined they were all headed for Susa. Ashur vowed they must continue together, and when Gudamma demurred, citing her slow pace would hold the hunters back, he scowled his disapproval.

"I won't hear that again, madam. That's not the Elamite way."

By noon two days later, they stopped in the dappled shade of a scrawny mimosa, the first tree Gudamma had seen in a week. She rested her back against its trunk and closed her eyes. Ashur came over and squatted beside her.

"She has a gift, hasn't she?" he said.

Gudamma's eyes blinked open to stare at him. "How did you find out?"

"Told me things about my wife before she died. Things no stranger could know, not even my son. But she said it without prying. Rather assuring me that my memory was correct. As I said, she's a treasure."

Gudamma nodded. "Worth more than silver and gold. She goes to Nippur, my friend. Therein lies not just her future, but the way for all mankind. But it's a long trek. We could stand some menfolk for company."

He looked away. "I have my own son," he began.

"And a fine youth he is, with his father's kindness. And his father's will and strength. I can pay."

He stared at her as if she'd uttered an insult. "I would not do it for money, if I did it at all. See here, Mother, I know nothing of the city. I would be a danger to you both."

"Nonsense. But think also of Kumir. He has his whole life ahead of him. Will he live as a boar hunter or something else? Does he have a say in his own fate?"

"I have always tried to do right by the boy. Now that he's a man, he'll find his own place."'

"Where is your home, Ashur?"

He lifted his gaze to scan the horizon. "What home I had is gone. There's just the two of us now. We bed down wherever we find ourselves."

"Then come and make a new place. Ashur, think of it! We are blessed, you and I, to be chosen for this path in her life. Together we'll see her to Nippur, give her to the Mothers there. They will be her family and you can return to your home and rest a wealthy man."

"I'm not sure about that snake..."

"He'll honor your protection. Take heed of the child, though, and learn from those eyes, Ashur. Learn from the depths of her sacred soul."

"You speak as if I've already agreed."

"But Ashur, your heart has spoken. For this you and I were chosen. To serve Inanna is the highest gift."

Chapter 3

Bringer of Gifts

If Ashur was merely a boar hunter with reward in mind, he certainly did not show so little character. With money from his own tote he purchased a woolen cloak for Misha's shoulders and, at her pleading, the same for the cobra's basket. After a day's provisioning at Susa, he led Gudamma and the girl onto Road to the Setting Sun, and sent his son Kumir to walk point a half mile forward. Both men were armed with boar lance and arrows, for Gudamma's tote made a target for brigands.

For the first day, Misha skipped along at twice her normal pace in an effort to keep up with the longer adult strides. The flat pan was warm beneath the sun but went frigid at night. Memet's basket rode the backs of the men in alternating stages. Neither Ashur nor Kumir complained. Their lives had been elevated by good fortune. The serpent was part and parcel of the gift. Their simple minds regarded such as their lot and moved on to the more mundane rhythm of travel, rest, eat, sleep.

Misha was taxed to keep up, but she never complained of her struggle. Four days out of Susa they came to the broad Tigris. Misha slept through the entire river crossing, so Ashur decided to slow their pace, that they might deliver the girl well and whole. This was brought forcibly to the attention of all the next morning as the wasteland fell behind them on the first fringe of plantation.

The approaching brigand band numbered only three, but as they leapt up from the ditch where they had hidden, they had the advantage of surprise and used it to close fast upon Ashur's troop.

"We'll take it all," said the apparent leader. "Lest you want a knife to your gut."

Before Ashur could form a rejoinder, Misha stepped forward with her hand outstretched.

"Give it to me."

The bearded rascal stared at the small, wide-eyed face that answered his demand with calm rather than the fear he had expected. "Give you what? I'm taking, scuttle dog. Nebur gives nothing to nobody."

"Give me your pain. I can help."

"My what? Only pain I got is you, brat. Hand over that basket."

"Your left side only aches after a long day, but it will grow worse unless you let me take it."

Nebur glanced at his cohorts. "Which of you told her?"

His smaller cohort shook his head. "You're doing all the talking, as usual. I haven't said a word."

Nebur squinted at the small child who spoke of the thing he feared. "You can't do nothing. Nobody can. Not the healers, not the witch down in Lagash. You gonna mumble and toss coins in the air like them? Forget it."

The girl set her basket on the ground. "I cannot help you unless you ask."

"Nebur don't beg for nothing! You hear? Nothing!"

"To ask is not to beg."

Before any of the men could stop her, Misha stepped close to Nebur and took his hand.

"This will do," she said, and then she reached her other hand under his shirt and pressed his side.

Nebur gasped and stepped back, but Misha moved right with him, keeping both hands in place.

"You have nothing to fear from me. Let it go."

The thief stared bug-eyed at the girl. "I can feel it."

"Yes, it wants to leave you now. Let it go."

"You're a witch!"

The girl's eyes squeezed shut. "Let go of it, Nebur. Now!"

The air cracked with the sound of a snapping whip. Nebur fell backward and landed on his buttocks in wide-eyed amazement. The other two brandished their knives, but Ashur stepped before them with one hand upraised, the other on his knife.

"Behold a miracle, or it'll be the last thing you see."

Nebur scrabbled in the dirt. "It's moving! The thing's moving in my gut!"

Gudamma stepped in at that point. "Give it to the child, Nebur, give it up. It's the blackness that torments you and makes you hate. We are not your enemy here. Blackness is the enemy."

"I-I'm going to die! It'll kill me!"

Misha spoke again. "You are greater than this thing. You are its master. It can harm you no more. Give it to me."

Her hand remained outstretched in the space between them. Nebur shot a questioning glance at the small palm, empty and waiting.

"Can't give it to you, can't give this demon to no one."

"You are no longer its home. Let me send it where it belongs. Take my hand."

Nebur looked up at the child who stood as erect as any temple woman before an altar stone, placid, assured, controlled. His eyes could not leave the face that glowed like the sun. Grey eyes that gazed back at him with the love and forgiveness he had known from a full-grown woman long ago, but had forgotten.

He felt a welling up in his belly, fought to stifle it, lost the battle, and a cry burst from his throat like the howl of a new babe. In a trice, the pain fled.

As tears streamed down his face, he rolled onto his hands and knees and stared ahead like a bullock facing the slaughter. But the killing did not come. No axe fell, no arrow pierced, no blade sliced.

He was alive.

The thing was gone.

He slowly got to his feet and found all four men staring at him, their faces locked in stupor. Gudamma stood with gnarled hands covering her mouth, tears streaking her wrinkled face.

He swung around to face the girl. She had slumped to her knees, her eyes closed, her head shaking with a violent tremor.

He snatched her up and pulled her to his chest. His mind sought words for what tore at his heart, but his lips had gone too long without saying them.

Her tiny hands dug into his shoulders, drawing him closer. They clutched each other for a long time until he realized he was getting her shoulders wet.

"Are you better now?" he asked.

She nodded silently against his neck, so he gently set her down and turned to the elder Elamite. "Wherever she's going, we're going too."

Ashur answered with a wry smile. "All the way to Nippur?"

Nebur's face stretched in a smile it hadn't known for a long time. "To the end of the world if that's the doing of it."

He and his two thieving companions spent the next few days taking turns carrying Misha on their backs. Who went first was often a contest Ashur settled only to avoid violence—a facet of their nature that dissipated with each step in the greater presence of a wonder.

Chapter 4

River Goddess

Misha's first sight of the great river came shortly after sunup on a warm spring morning. Her travel party had reached Euphrates at its widest flow, where their westward track met Sumer's main thoroughfare a mile above Lagash. To the others the river marked a turn onto the last leg of their sojourn, a path each had trod often in times past. For the child, the view was a life-altering event.

The river's flat berm had occupied the horizon from the moment they'd left camp. But when she crested the levee on Kumir's shoulders and caught sight of the river's wide sweep, with boats of all sizes and shapes gliding up and down its course, clusters of travelers treading its banks in both directions, she cried aloud and leaped to the ground before Kumir could stop her. She stood on the riverbank transfixed, her tiny fists pressed to her face, tears streaming down her cheeks, as she beheld the greatest wonder of her life.

She turned to Nebur, bouncing on her heels with excitement as she reached for Memet's basket. "Put him down, please!" she cried. "I want him to see too!"

Nebur checked with Gudamma first, and the old woman

silently nodded her assurance that the sight of a cobra-clad urchin would not disrupt the rivergoers' activity.

Memet climbed the short distance to his mistress' shoulders and she carried him to the water's edge, pointing out each wonder as it passed. Foot travelers slowed to take in the unusual sight of a child talking to her cobra like a farm girl with a pet goat. Expressions on their faces ranged from wide-eyed shock to mild alarm to open delight, but once they realized the serpent attended the river and not themselves, they continued on.

Ashur turned to Gudamma to speak. During the long trek together they had formed a close friendship.

"Look at Memet!" he said. "See how he cranes his neck this way and that. He's as fascinated as she is!"

The old woman hugged her arms about her ribs, a blush of purest pleasure lighting her face.

"Mark this day in your memory, Ashur," she said. "See how she bonds with the river, with the people. It all begins right here, right now. This is her homecoming, her first and greatest love affair. In this moment she is already leaving us in quest of her heart's desire. Mark it well, my friend, and count yourself blessed to partake in it."

The first travelers to come to a full stop were a farmer with a tall boy at his side. The farmer spoke to Misha as she crouched on her heels, and she stood and forthrightly presented the cobra. Snake and boy regarded each other at arm's length for several moments, while Misha watched first one, then the other. Just as Gudamma began to worry, the travelers took their leave and moved on toward Lagash.

"He had no fear," Misha said in reply to Gudamma's concern.

"Just curious, I suppose."

"More than that. He said he liked the smell."

A twinge of alarm broke Gudamma's calm. "What smell is that?"

"You know, Memet's skin. He said it was like swamp mud only cleaner. Isn't that beautiful?"

"Misha, I don't think you should—"

"Memet was very pleased. Shall we go now?"

Misha was disappointed to learn that the swamp she so badly wished to see was in the wrong direction and too far to visit. Nebur explained that it was home to the Hani people, or Old Ones. When he described the animals abiding there she felt a restlessness in Memet, not quite a longing, but more like a wistful memory. When she queried him, the cobra would not discuss it.

She asked to walk on her own a while, for she wanted to feel the dust of her new home, to touch the roadside hibiscus and lissum, embrace the wide trunk of a date palm. Her "family" indulged her until, eventually, she tired and went back atop Ashur's shoulders.

Toward noon, the clusters of travelers had thinned, as some peeled off for other routes and others lagged or quickened the pace or transferred to water transport.

At irregular intervals, river flow and tree shade permitting, vendors would set up small tents to offer food and drink. You would first see their skiffs pulled up on the bank in haphazard array, and then the tents and awnings clinging to feathery shade if it was to be had. Atop one or two a pennant might be seen to flutter in the soft drift of river breeze.

Ashur pulled over at the first tent for a chat over a beer bowl, and Kumir began sifting through a cache of obsidian blades offered by a woman who asserted they were newly brought from the mountains above Susa. Rather than argue that he knew better as a Susa native, Kumir moved on to the next stall.

Gudamma took Misha in hand to join a few ladies sipping from the same bowl through long straws. Misha soon grew tired of grownup talk and wandered over to a stall run by a dark-skinned boy who seemed about her own age. She had just begun to pick over his collection of earrings when she heard a commotion farther downstream.

Nebur had gone down to the river's edge to wash his face. Two black-headed Sumerian farmers detained him. Misha smelled trouble and decided to see what she could do.

The taller farmhand was jabbing a finger at Nebur's chest.

"...know your face, poacher. Seen you down Lagash way climbing up the canal bank with a fresh goat. Grower was lying in the rushes where you laid him out."

"You got me confused with someone else, friend."

"No confusion on my part. These eyes can catch barley rust before it's even set."

"Look, I got friends up there at the stalls with me. We been traveling clear from Shugur, and just got here."

"Maybe you should just turn around and go back."

Misha saw dark anger cloud Nebur's eyes, the old hatred returning. The knife image started in his head and moved toward his hand. She jumped beside him and grasped his knife hand in her own, smiling up at the farmer.

"This is my Uncle Nebur. He carried me all the way from Shugur on his shoulders 'cuz I'm too small."

The farmer scowled at Misha, gritted his teeth, confronted Nebur again. "Hanging around kiddies these days, are you?"

Misha spoke before Nebur could form a retort. "We're going to Nippur. Where are you from?"

"None of your business, little girl. Now go back to the tents."

Misha started jumping up and down excitedly. "I saw some rings for my ears, Uncle Nebur. Come see, come see!"

She tugged on his hand, wishing away the black anger forming in Nebur's heart. Wishing, wishing. *Let it go! Please make it go away!*

Suddenly a beatific smile lighted Nebur's face. "Why, of course, dear. Show Uncle Nebur what you found." He looked up at the farmer again. "Such a beautiful child, don't you think? Her eyes tell the whole story."

"I ain't interested—"

Misha gazed up at the farmer and hunched her shoulders in an impish grin. As the farmer looked more closely at her face, she felt his heart, saw his fear, saw the woman crouched in the hut, leaning over the cradle. She reached out her other hand and touched his arm.

"You have a new baby at home, don't you?"

The man jumped away, his eyes bulging. "How-how do you know?"

Nebur placed a hand on the farmer's shoulder, kept his smile on, the ugliness shrinking like a dying coal. "Inanna's blessing on you, friend. Boy or girl?"

"G-girl. But how—?"

Nebur just nodded. "When did she arrive?"

Misha blurted the answer without thinking. "Four days ago." Then, before the farmer could react, she touched his arm again. "In the field! How beautiful! She was born in the barley rows, Uncle Nebur. That's the best sign."

"Is it?" said the farmer. "A sign? What's it mean?"

"More children to come, a big harvest. And a strong girl at your wife's side."

The farmer faltered. "Sh-she's not my wife—yet. But I'll marry her, and soon."

Nebur's grin radiated good will. "Of course you'll marry. You're a good man. Now, Misha, show me what you found, but remember I've not a lot of money."

The farmer plunged a hand in his pouch and pulled out a coin, bending down to Misha as he handed it to her. "For the little queen."

"Oh, I'm not a queen yet," she said.

The farmer straightened up and spoke to Nebur. "She's royal to me."

Each man gave the other a curt nod before parting.

Over a campfire that night, everyone watched as Misha fitted a small ring of gold to her newly pierced ear. When it was in place, she dropped her hands to her lap and smiled at Nebur.

It was a simple gesture, that fitting of adornment to mimic an adult, but devastating to Nebur, who returned the girl's smile, then sobered at once as he caught Gudamma's scrutiny. His haunted expression startled her, for she beheld in it the familiar scourge of unrequited attachment she knew would henceforth be repeated hundreds of times over.

The child, now approaching her seventh year and ignorant of her effect, was in some ways fast becoming a woman. And the man, despite the difference in their ages, was hopelessly, helplessly smitten.

Chapter 5

Cold Welcome

The following day at Adab, Gudamma engaged a runner to convey a simple message to the high priestess at Ekur, one he couldn't possibly get wrong:

Gift found, Gudamma.

"Then tell her we'll arrive tomorrow evening by barge."

She then treated her male retinue to such entertainment as poor Adab had to offer, and was surprised by its favorable effect on their moods.

As for the child, Gudamma sat her down and spoke to her as an adult.

"Your gift of healing will meet the same resistance you found with Nebur at first. Do not let their doubt discourage you from your path, Misha. Listen and watch. These are powerful ladies well-trained in the art of persuasion."

"You're saying they lie a lot."

"Good heavens, child, must you be so blunt? M-mm, I suppose anything else would be contrary to your nature."

"A silent tongue sometimes helps such people find a straighter path themselves."

"Indeed it does, but you must also learn how they use others to their advantage."

"I will ask Enshiggu for guidance."

And pray their boisterous clamor reaches his ears, little one.

The following morning, as they set out on the river, Misha turned to Gudamma and took her hand.

"Kumta spoke to me last night," she said.

"Who is Kumta?"

"He's the other god, the one I was born with."

"I see. And what did Kumta say?"

"You are to introduce me to the ladies by another name."

"Why, how strange. What in the world for?"

"I don't know. He just told me."

"I see. And what name has he chosen for you?"

"Uruna."

"Hm-mm, doesn't sound Sumerian, or Elamite, but what matter? It has a lovely ring."

"Yes, I like it too."

"Then so you shall be called. Uruna."

"I think it was my name before."

"Perhaps so. Given by your mother at birth?"

"No, before that. You know, in the other place."

"Yes, of course."

Gudamma found the girl's remark no more bizarre than any other during their trek together. She had learned long ago to render unto the gods things mystical. At her age, she might be nearer the answers to such matters than she suspected.

Besides, what more could there be to a name?

Uruna could not believe the wonders before her. She stood on the quay in solitary awe, spellbound, while the grown-ups around her busied themselves with landing stores and arranging for this and for that.

Ashur caught her gaping and looking a little lost, so he hoisted her onto his shoulders to point out the sights, a marvel to his own eyes.

"There sits the temple," he said, pointing to the enormous ziggurat that towered above all else. "And there, the gate to the city, do you see it?"

"I see, I see!" Uruna shouted. "And another gate over there—and there! But see all the people streaming in and out. Ashur, I've never seen so many in one place."

"Me neither. Look here, that fellow carries baskets on his head."

"Like the women do in Anshan, but he has four!"

One of the fine ladies in white dresses approached Ashur and tugged on his arm. "This way with you now."

Ashur turned with Uruna still astride his shoulders and stepped off.

"No, she stays," said the woman.

Ashur objected. "But we go everywhere together."

"Not here, you don't. Men to the old city, women in the new until we get things straightened out."

Ashur put Uruna down as ordered, and she immediately spoke to the woman in white.

"If you please, we're a family. We've traveled weeks together, and—"

The woman cut her off. "That's enough from you." She then raised her voice to address a younger woman in a gray smock. "Take the girl and don't let her out of your sight. We don't know anything about her yet."

Gray-smock was actually a young girl. She wore a frown above a surly face that plainly said she did not care for her task or her charge. She grabbed for Uruna, but too late, as Uruna ducked away.

"I have to fetch Memet," she called over her shoulder, and ran for his basket.

"What? Another road brat?"

The girl made to chase Uruna down, but Ashur held her by one arm. "She's no urchin, that one, and best you remember it. And neither is her companion."

The girl wrenched her arm loose. "Brigand! Do not be insolent with me! How dare you try to pass yourself off as decent."

Ashur regarded the girl coolly. "I'm a hunter, as you could tell if your eyes had ever left your city refuge."

"I am a priestess of the Lukur!"

"No you're not, you're a *kadishtu* acolyte. Now stand like a good little wench and wait for Uruna to fetch her cobra."

"C-cobra? Which cobra?"

"The one who judges us all."

The priestess twisted her mouth in smug disbelief. "You can't scare me with talk of serpents."

"Good. Then we've settled the most important matter."

Uruna found Memet coiled in his basket, a gleam of alarm cast in his eye. She assured him they would soon be in their new home. When she returned to Ashur and the girl in gray, she handed the basket up to the hunter, but the girl stepped between them and blocked the way.

"Let me see what you have in there, little missy."

"He'd rather you didn't," Uruna began, but the girl snatched the basket from her hands and flipped it open.

Memet's head popped up with a loud hiss, his fangs bared, black irises flashing anger.

The girl shrieked and dropped the basket, backed away several paces, and broke into a run.

Uruna got Memet back under cover, hoping no one had

noticed.

"That's why I keep him inside," she said to Ashur. "People like her. Always putting their nose where it doesn't belong."

"What's going on here?" The officious Lukur had returned.

"Nothing much," Ashur replied in his easy manner. "Just introducing Uruna to your great city."

"Well, you'll have to introduce yourselves to that fellow over there—you men, not the girl. She stays."

"So we were told, but—"

"You'll be together again soon enough. This is how we must do things for now."

Uruna looked up at Ashur, then back at the woman. What was wrong? Did Nippur have rules against welcoming travelers?

The temple woman glanced about. "Where's Adana?"

Ashur frowned. "Can't say. Just up and ran off."

"Hmph! Silly little *kadishtu* goose. Now both of you wait right here until we make arrangements."

Gudamma fretted. Only three white-clad ladies had met her boat at the quay. No others, no bearers, no offering of tidings. She knew not one of them. She had hoped at least one friend from her days at Ekur might still be alive, but her first impression dashed those hopes.

"The herald spoke of a gift," said one of the matrons—young by Gudamma's measure but graying at the temples and showing crow's feet and creases of brow. Was Gudamma at sixty such an anomaly?

"We'll talk about it later," said another Lukur, before she addressed Gudamma directly. "I'm Lubna Seddua," she said. "Don't remember you from before. Anyway, we'll get you settled into quarters in town and then after you've rested a few days we can arrange an audience."

Why not her old room in Serpenthood House? And what audience? With whom?

"Do you know who I am?" she asked of Lubna.

"Yes, I've heard of you," she replied. "From the elders. Long time ago. I didn't enter temple service myself until late. Been about ten years now. To be honest, everyone thought you were dead."

"But as you can see, I am quite alive. I have traveled from—"

"Here we are—Shedu! Take this lady and her granddaughter to the inn called Shepherd's Walk." Lubna turned to the larger of Gudamma's male companions. "You men will have to find quarters in the old city."

Gudamma was shocked. "There must be some misunderstanding. This gentleman is Ashur, and his son Kumir, and Nebur here. These men have shared our burdens and protected our lives with their own. They deserve Ekur's gratitude. I sent word two days ago..."

"Well, we're quite busy with temple affairs right now. You'll have to consult the Entu about these men. Perhaps tomorrow."

Had the woman been raised in a sheep fold? Or had Lukur kindness disappeared with the sisters of an earlier day?

"Tomorrow isn't soon enough. I have traveled sixteen years at Council Kemdu's request to find the visionary they seek. Now I have returned with the one meant to—"

"Kemdu? They're all dead."

"That's impossible. See here, Lubna, I have hastened here from the far side Elam. Three months across river and desert. You must appreciate the urgency of our mission."

"Do not speak of urgency to me! I am Chief Udalla counter for the nine provinces. I have stepped aside from my own duties to replace the priestess who was supposed to arrange visitor accommodations. My presence is now required at court. You may bring any further needs to the attention of Shua Kinar, here. Come, Leda."

"Please keep us under the same roof, Lubna, we are like a family—"

"Good day to you, madam!"

Uruna stepped forward and took Gudamma's hand.

"She fears for her post," she said.

"What are you saying?"

"Another wants her place and says bad things about her."

"Augh! Temple politics! Misha—no, it's Uruna now—Uruna, I'm sorry this was your first brush with Ekur."

"The other lady is nice. Her brother is one of the big men with spears."

"Yes, yes, let's do the best we can now." She turned to Ashur. "I'm terribly sorry for all this."

"Gudamma, have you forgotten how you found us in Elam?" he replied. "We slept on the ground. This will be no problem."

Shua Kinar stepped forward and crouched before Uruna.

"Sometimes the greatest gift comes in a small package. Give us your name, dear."

With that remark, Gudamma realized the side of Lukur hospitality she remembered was still intact, if subordinate to a more severe power.

Accommodation more befitting their company was arranged. But Gudamma had seen and heard enough to understand that the world she had known here had passed into dust. Her friends and allies, the sacred trust with which she had been sent, all meant little to the new elite. She wondered what else had been lost to time, and whether her small charge might survive the ponderous march of human ambition.

Chapter 6

End and Begin

The answer to Gudamma's question was not long in coming. And it crept upon her like a thief in the night.

She wakened at first light on her sixth day in Nippur and felt death's cold touch in her bones. The change came upon her so suddenly she had no chance to call the child to her side, no last words to prepare the blessed one for life's hardships, for Uruna was already far across the city at temple worship.

The girl had taken to Morning Call like a draught animal to drink. Acting completely on her own, she had learned a quick route through the city to the temple's shadow. Somehow she had wangled her way past sentry and matron to post herself where she could watch and listen to the rites without being seen. She had caught the litany and learned the entire Alla Manna melody and lyric on first hearing. Gudamma had witnessed all of it firsthand.

On the second day of their arrival, shortly after noon, Gudamma had caught the child proceeding the length of their room in stately measure, a "gown" of shawl linen tied about her waist, a tray of rose petals in hand, trilling the song until she reached her tiny altar—a salt cellar and creamer laid out on a cutting board. Gudamma could only stare in wonder as the babe recited the entire Honors ritual that called upon Inanna for another day's favor. She then watched transfixed, as Uruna lifted the sacred chalice—her water gourd—to her lips for the libation of ox blood—Gudamma's tea dregs. The girl then expertly gave the gourd a half turn and held it aloft in the direction of the rising sun, chanting the *sema siddah* in flawless imitation of the most venerable temple practitioner.

Uruna's memory was astounding enough, but what filled Gudamma with awe was the earnest love pouring forth from the girl's heart. Her face radiated joy, even in solemn dignity, as she made a neat pirouette on heel and toe and paraded back to the foot of the bed.

"I was learning *disikku* today, too," she said, referring to the midday ceremony, "when they tossed me out. I got the part about the altar march, but I was too short to see those things they spread on the altar for the priestess to pick up.

"See, she crosses two sticks before her chest, but I couldn't see what else she did with them because some lady grabbed my arm and pulled me away and down the stairs. She told me never to go back or I'd catch a thrashing."

The fools! Pride and rectitude ruled the day, while they missed the treasure walking among them in grace, eager to serve, *able* to serve in full measure.

Finishing that recollection, Gudamma realized she had risen from her bed and donned her robe. As she tottered to a nearby chair for support, she heard Uruna's shout through the open window and looked out to see the girl running hard down the street toward Shepherd's Walk, her black hair flying, her long, unbroken wail filling the air.

She already knew. Had known before Gudamma herself felt the end coming.

Gudamma turned, intending to open the door for a great welcome, but her feet refused to move. She saw the floor tilt crazily and thrust her arm toward the bed for support, but missed and fell onto her side. The room went suddenly dark.

Had she closed the window shutters herself and forgotten? No matter, here came Uruna, bounding through the door in a burst of breathless energy, her feet pounding the boards, her voice coming from far away.

"Nana...love you...my nana..."

Gudamma's thoughts turned inward, toward another room, where figures waited in softening shadows. So quickly, the crossing to the other side. No time for a last word with the babe.

Did we finish the task, Mother? So much needs doing for the child—the precious child...

Chapter 7

Rescue

No one came for Gudamma. Uruna huddled in a corner with her grief, sobbing until she was spent in body and spirit.

She'd forgotten her Nana. Caught up in her own delight, in learning the sacred songs and vows and celebration of Great Mother's love, she had neglected the dear one who'd brought it all to her.

But everything was so full of wonder and so new. She couldn't get enough of the splendor and majesty wrought as graceful ladies in beaded finery lifted gleaming bowls and swept the temple hall with long strides in a slow dance to the Goddess. All was glorious, the magic had filled her days and she'd wanted more.

Until she felt that cold breath upon her neck.

There, inside the temple, she had turned and sensed the darkness rising swift and sure upon Gudamma. She had raced through the city, struggling against the tide of living flesh, hoping, hoping, then bursting through the door.

Too late.

Now beloved Gudamma was gone. No farewell kiss, no promise to remember, no gratitude for a life of sacrifice and toil. Only memories, little more than she carried of her Adda and Mama, whose faces she could no longer see. Would Gudamma's wrinkled love-gaze fade as well?

She had this life of losing others. For some reason, the gods saw fit to deny her the family and affection she craved. Only a taste from love's cup, then the quaff was jerked away in wrenching confusion. Why so much pain? Why no enduring comfort like others enjoyed? Why so many days of isolation and solitude?

True, she had Memet's devotion. She had Enshiggu's abiding trust. But those were intangible. She longed for more moments of surprise, like when she saw the river's smile and knew she belonged to every thing and every soul in Great Mother's heaven. It was beautiful and precious, and she longed for that connected feeling to come again and stay.

She wiped her cheeks dry and stretched her legs. They'd gone stiff from crouching so long. She was no use to Nana like this. She might be no more than a child, but she must not be a selfish one.

Yes, really, she must do something for Gudamma. Couldn't just let her lie sprawled on the floor.

She got up and went to the bed and drew the cover over her dead Nana's still form, as she had watched Mama do with Adda long ago. Then she grabbed her tote from the wall peg and went out in search of help.

There were things you were supposed to do for a dead body, things for the spirit too, but she knew none of them. When her *adda* had died, people from the village had come and taken him away, then set her on the road with aught but dining knife and gourd, after making sure she took the serpent with her.

She had asked the town elder what would become of her *adda*, and he had shooed her away, telling her such work was not a child's concern.

Years had passed since. She wasn't a child anymore, at least not the aimless, irresponsible tot who had left Anshan. A corner of her mind unraveled the skein of counts it always kept: Sixty-three and six hundred days wandering, then another four and one hundred since the well in Shagri. Was that enough time to grow up?

The sound of the mid-afternoon crier brought her up short. She didn't think it was proper to leave Nana back in the house much longer. But whom to tell? The ladies at the temple were always too busy for her, and she wasn't sure where she might find the nice one, Kinar.

Maybe Ashur and Kumir, or even Nebur. A lady had sent them to a nameless place everyone called "the old city."

She asked directions of a man selling pots in the shade of a tall building. He warned her the place was unsafe, but she took the river bridge anyway, struggled to keep pace with the throngs jamming both ends, then nearly got lost in the crowded streets that seemed incapable of forming a straight line in any direction. When at last she came to the market square, she appealed to a woman selling apricots.

"I'm looking for my uncle Ashur. Have you seen him?"

The seller merely shook her head and moved away to serve a towering hulk of a man. Uruna moved to his side and tugged on his leather skirt.

"Please, sir, I'm looking for my uncle Ashur. Nana died and I have to find him."

The big man looked down at her, from the sky it seemed, blinked, and knelt before her. Everything about him was huge, his head, his hands, his broad shoulders. And his hair was as red as a carrot.

"You say a woman died?"

His booming voice was big, too.

"She's my Nana and she brought me all the way from Elam. I tried to reach her before she—before she fell. Now I have to find

Ashur."

The man took her arms in his immense hands, a gentle grasp for one so huge, and at once, a massive surge of power rang through Uruna's entire body, shaking every limb in a single, pounding blast.

She fell back, her mind reeling as she saw the man splayed on his backside in the dust. His large blue eyes widened and his mouth made a large "O" of surprise.

"Sorry, I d-didn't mean to hurt you," he stammered.

"You have such power!" she exclaimed.

"So do you!"

The plum seller came around the end of her table, shaking a finger at the big man.

"See here, we'll not have any Nord trouble at my stall!"

Uruna quickly got to her feet. "Oh, he's no trouble. I slipped."

She reached forward and took the Nord's great mitt in her tiny hand to reassure the grocer. Instantly, a tide of gentle kindness washed through her, and a soft rasping voice spoke in her head.

Arn-Gar.

The words stilled her distress with peaceful calm. She repeated the strange sounds aloud, and received a second wide-eyed stare in return.

"How do you know my name?"

"The god spoke it. Mine is Uruna. Can you help me?"

"Take me to your Nana," he said in a deep rumble.

"But my uncle," she protested. "I have to find Ashur. He has Memet, and Enshiggu will insist on bringing him."

"Little chance of finding anyone in this pig's poke. Most don't want to be found. Besides, I never heard of those fellows you just named. First things first. Let's get you home."

"It's just a room at Shepherd's Walk. It's way over—"

"I know where it is."

"I don't have any money to pay you."

"And I don't ask for money from a queen."

There it was again, another grownup calling her queen, when she was not yet seven. Had everyone in this new land forgotten the meaning of the word?

Arn-Gar rocked forward and stood in a single fluid motion. Then he took Uruna's hand and swung her up to his shoulder. She looked out upon the heads of the market throng and, for a fleeting moment, truly felt royal.

Chapter 8

New Home

Gar's mind failed to register the ensuing confusion of events. He was sure he'd taken care of the dead lady properly, having gathered the girl's few belongings and, at her insistence, sent the dead woman's effects to that Serpenthood place in the Aniginna. The temple woman at the Aniginna gate had answered Uruna's questions about snakes with a rude insult, and he had swept away in a black mood, nearly forgetting his charge until she skipped up to his side.

He knew of only three innkeepers in the old city, and two ran places no self-respecting man would tolerate. That left but one possibility, and he found Uruna's men there.

Bala Sua ran a sparse but clean household. She had inherited the two domiciles adjoining either side of her own, and rented rooms in all three by the day. She would cook for guests only if they couldn't find a meal elsewhere. One street repast was enough to send any tenant back to her table, and so Gar found Uruna's three "guardians" supping at a tiled earthen slab beside the hearth.

When he appeared on her door stoop asking for Ashur by

name, Bala Sua glanced up at the girl on his shoulders, shook her head in resignation, and led the way back to her cook room.

Gar wasn't prepared for the tearful reception from two burly huntsmen and a hard-looking reformed thief. One would think they'd been separated six months, not six days, but the genuine affection each man displayed had Gar convinced he wasn't alone in his feelings for the girl.

The meal was extended to accommodate the two late arrivals, and Gar listened to a disjointed tale of road adventure while Uruna sat quietly and busied herself with a lamb shank. At length Ashur beckoned Gar away from the table to Bala's tiny parlor and closed the door.

"We've nothing left to care for her with. Kumir and I can hunt for a living, keep her fed, but the wild is no life for the likes of her. The old lady spoke of money put away someplace, treated us well while we shared company, but who knows if there's any of that left for Uruna's care. Gudamma expected more from the temple women, but Gar, they're a rude and lofty lot."

"I know, got a taste of it myself today, and it wasn't all about my being Nord."

"So, what I'm saying is, we'll do what we can for her here for a few days, but she needs a woman's care, a home and family."

"I have an idea."

"Good, 'cause I can't come up with a thing."

"You and your son, you're good hunters, right?"

"When we can find boar, we usually take 'em."

"I'm Nord. You know what we do?"

"Wring necks?"

"We're smiths and draymen. Temple won't allow us weapons on account of our forefathers who came down from the north and nearly sent this land to hell. Sumerians said never again. Put us before the plow where oxen used to pull, or at the forge. So we pay the temple to put meat on our table. The thing is, we can forge knives and plowshares and trace rings, but nary a weapon. Been that way so long we couldn't shoot a deer even if one walked up to us."

"Wait, you're telling me you forgot how to hunt?"

"That's right. Now, if we were to stumble across someone who knows how to sneak up on a deer or rabbit or a grouse, that might change things. Better still if that someone were to show how it's done."

"But you'd have to know archery. You know, how to fletch an arrow, how to shave a spear haft to fit a head and wrap it—oh, I see where you're going."

"My home's Na Purna. The whole village is Nord. We got ten forges, twenty smiths, thirty ploughmen, wives and kids. A couple hundred mouths to feed. Menfolk are big like me, need meat to keep strong, keep going."

"But if you could squeeze in a few more mouths, with able arms and legs to boot, you might make a few changes."

"Might. Depends on how well we solve both our problems together."

Ashur's eyes glowed. "Been wondering where Kumir and I might put down. Been looking for a place that could use Kumir's skills, chance for him to make a life, start a family of his own. There's nothing waiting for us back in Elam. As for Nippur? I made two calls on the temple huntsman, and he just laughed. Said no stranger would learn the hunt on his grounds. Said our skills aren't matched for these parts."

"I'd say it's time to put your skills to the test."

"And I'd say it's time we gave our little queen a home of her own. One more thing, though."

"Yes?"

"Her serpent companion."

"A snake? She has a pet snake?"

"Yes, a cobra she calls Memet. Carries him around her shoulders."

"In the house? With other people?"

"Don't know. Only saw him on the road with her. Lately we keep him in a locked shed, toss him a mouse or two."

"Around her shoulders. Under the bed. In the coat cupboard. One bite and you're dead."

"Maybe not. Three months with the two of them and never a close call."

"Real gentleman."

"Needs care and feeding, is all. 'Course you don't want to get on his bad side."

"There's a good one?"

"He's docile enough when she's around. Six days in that shed has put him out of sorts…what I'm saying is, we'll have to find a suitable place for him *and* the girl."

"Together."

"Yes."

"In the same room."

"Usually."

"A household pet."

"Fellow minds his own business."

"Toth's beard!"

"Who's Toth? You got a landlord in mind already?"

"Toth is a wrathful Nord god. Come to think of it, probably as suitable a host as any, if he can abide snakes."

"She's worth the trouble."

"That's what I was afraid of."

The two men locked elbows chest-to-chest to bind the pact and returned to the dining room. Uruna glanced up from her soup and greeted both with a vexing smile only Ashur had seen before.

"Toth's beard!" she said. "How shall I learn to cook and sew properly from a smith's wife?"

ARRIVAL

Chapter 9

Royal Outrage

Ekur's ailing High Priestess summoned her council members to her bed chamber, where she had held court for the past three months. She was in the habit of taking her tea at the same time. Her adjutant, Lubna Seddua, had just divulged Gudamma's arrival and demise all at once and for the first time, and Entu Mena Ramush was livid.

"How long has she lain dead?"

"Buried a month ago, maybe two. It's not of great importance."

Mena slammed her cup on the table so hard the drink sloshed out. The council ladies jumped, eyes widened in shock at the queen's first sign of animation in months.

"By the gods, Lubna! I am the judge of what's important here, not you, not anyone in this room! Unless, of course, you think I already have one foot in the grave?"

"Not at all, madam. It's just that none here had heard of her before."

"Of course you hadn't. I'm the only one old enough to remember the day Gudamma set forth on our quest. And you say she found an adept? A serpently woman?"

"Not a woman, madam. She brought with her a tot who mutters to her pet cobra. With all due respect, I believe the deceased had lost her mind."

"A child, you say? With a cobra?"

"Indeed, no more than seven years in age. She has no line, no family. A road urchin found wandering the hills above Elam. This woman claimed she took the girl—"

"*This woman*? Do you know of whom you speak? Gudamma once sat this very seat, ruled as I do now, and better. She commanded all Lukur throughout the provinces. Gods! Have we lost so much that our most blessed go to the grave forgotten?"

"I assure you we did not know."

"She must have asked to see me?"

"She did ask to see the Entu, but we thought it presumptuous under the circumstances. A stranger just entering the gates in dust-ridden company. One look at her male companions and we knew them for ruffians."

Mena turned her head toward her message keeper, Shua Kinar. Her snapping black eyes bore her outrage.

"Her first words?"

"'Gift found, Gudamma.' That was the extent of it."

"Oh, good heavens! One message, a quick glance, and you missed the prize! Where is the child now?"

Lubna folded her hands at her sternum in pious rectitude. "She abides in the Nord settlement with outliers of her kind. She is happy there learning the ways of honest toil."

Mena Ramush closed her eyes and gripped the arms of her chair with hands wrinkled and spotted with age. She gathered herself, curbed an impulse to consign her adjutant to six days in the scullery, and expelled a deep breath. This was the way of things today, a slow downward slide from a peak of greatness that had begun its decline before her own time. But the blame for this travesty fell on her shoulders alone. The matrons now skulking about her bedchamber had known only the easing of discipline begun at her predecessor's word. Mena had failed to check the descent into complacency.

And oh, the injury done to faithful Gudamma! *My dearest sister! May thy pledge be honored, and thy faithful service find just reward in Heaven.*

"Bring my litter," she commanded.

Lubna stepped forward. "Mena, dear, we've been through this before. The physicians counsel rest to prolong your days. If you wish to meet with the girl we can have her brought here."

"Help me up!"

"Madam, please…"

"Do as I say! I must go to Na Purna without delay."

Lubna turned to Shua Kinar.

"Do as Entu commands. The royal litter and four bearers. And roust out that lazy *galla* squad from their beer bowls. The queen must have an escort, or at least the appearance of one."

Kinar's glower showed her unspoken disapproval. Council had already agreed. She might be no more than twenty-three, but she knew folly when she heard it. Lady Mena could barely get about in her own apartment. She was in no condition to travel. The further from Nippur's walls she ventured, the longer it would take for medical help to arrive, should she suffer another attack. But ambitious Lubna would willingly risk her queen's end and in so doing elevate herself to temple power. She had raised her token objection before all assembled, so that none could deny she had performed her adjutant's duty.

Kinar took a bold step, the first of many in the years to come that would define her approach to temple service. She moved past Lubna, past the bobbing heads of her superiors, directly to the Entu's side.

"If thou please, Mother Mena," she said in the old tongue, and lest Lubna raise an objection, hastened further. "The proper place for Enshiggu to view thy first encounter with his chosen is not among the Nord heathen, but in his most sacred tabernacle, within Serpenthood itself. For the god so spake unto those gathered for Gudamma's departure six and ten years past: 'Leave Heaven unto the heavenly and the earth to mortals, that my blessings may abide with the true in spirit.'"

Lubna stepped forward, her features drawn in irate fury. "Most insolent woman! You presume to know sacred words spoken while you scrubbed your mother's floor?"

She had worse castigation in mind, but Mena brushed her objection aside with a wave of her hand.

"The god did indeed speak thus," she said, aiming a rueful eye at Lubna, "if you yourself would remember, for you were present. Kinar, explain further."

"If the child has heavenly merit, Enshiggu will show his approval not in the soot and clamor of a forge, but among the devout, who hold high the light Gudamma carried into the world. We, who follow in her footsteps, who trust the divine promise of a prophet, must bear witness on holy ground and in sacred accord, as we honor His blessed gift."

Lubna continued to glower her disapproval. "*If* a street urchin is anything more than the answer to an old bird's cry for affection."

Mena turned to her adjutant with narrowed eyes. "We've already heard your assessment, madam. See that the tabernacle is prepared to please divine favor. And you, Kinar, fetch that child out of the smithy warrens before she catches a heathen spirit. I'll see her properly at *disikku*."

"Today? But Mother, that leaves only a few hours before midday!"

"Then you'd best stir your sticks." She raised her voice. "All of you!"

Her eyes followed the bustling Lukur as they crowded through her chamber door and out into the hallway. When only her *kadishtu* attendant remained, she turned to the girl with a brisk jerk of her head. "That ought to put things in order."

"Indeed, madam."

"What did you think of it?"

"I? But I'm only—"

"Answer the question."

"If you mean Shua Kinar's appeal, I think it right sensible."

"No, I expected as much from her. I mean the adjutant."

"Oh." The girl's face went crimson. "She seemed—reluctant to agree."

"Hah! Reluctant, you say? I believe if she hadn't so many ladies to bear witness, she might have choked the breath out of me right then and there."

"Madam! Lady Lubna wouldn't dare do such a thing!"

"Oh, child, such charity for the wicked. It was in her eyes, I saw it for myself. She's ruled by ambition. But she'll have another to contend with now. Be assured, Kinar the Lovely may be pretty and pleasant and full of grace, but she has backbone, that girl has! Backbone!"

"As you say, madam." The girl lifted a silver tray toward her queen. "A lemon for your tea?"

"Lemon? Tea? Fetch my robes, Pu Abi. I must prepare. We have an assignation with the almighty serpent god. Indeed, yes! And fetch my pearl brooch and signet ring. Let us put aside mere hope for the occasion and boldly expect the best!"

Chapter 10

Fetched from Na Purna

Six eggs today! Such a feast the master would enjoy! Uruna put the egg basket on the table and was about to head back to the garden when she heard a commotion outside at the gate. Visitors? No one came to Na Purna except for rare occasions to buy farm tools.

Several of the giants—that was what she called the Nord men when she was alone with Memet—had gathered at the fence to attend the arrival of a large company of men and women. The men were the soldiers everyone made fun of. The women came from the temple. She clasped her hands at their high beauty and thrilled to the sight of their brilliant white smocks with the strap gathered at the shoulder by a gold clasp. They moved with smooth grace and always seemed so happy and smiling.

The master's tall wife entered the cook room to remove her apron.

"You wait right here, girl," she said as she fussed with her hair. "And mind those eggs are still here when I get back."

She then smoothed her skirt and drew a deep breath before she pushed the door aside and went out to greet her guests.

Uruna stood in the half-open doorway to watch. Master didn't open the gate right away, but stood like a stout oak while he listened to a woman who had to tilt her head back like a child appealing to a grown-up. He then spoke to one of the men with spears, pointed at a grassy spot beside the path. The man argued once, then shrugged and stuck his spear where he was told. The other spearmen did the same, and then Master opened the gate and started for the house. His brow was low over his eyes, like he disliked his company. Leta, his wife, followed right behind him, and then the ladies from the temple.

Oh, feathers! Uruna thought. She was still wearing her mud clogs and the spattered wool shift a village girl had outgrown. She hadn't enough time to run outside to the barn to change. She plunged her hands into the wash bucket and scrubbed her cheeks and chin as clean as she could get them. She was drying her hands when Master's heavy feet clomped over the threshold.

"'Runa!" he hollered, although she was only a few steps away. "Come see these ladies as wish to talk to you."

As three women and four men tried to squeeze into the cramped Nord abode, Uruna's first impression was how small they all seemed. One woman was no more than a head taller than herself. The men looked like boys beside Master. She realized that for the last eight weeks she had seen no one but Nords.

The three ladies took Uruna aside, and the prettiest one, with the stripe of silver in her forelock, knelt and took Uruna's hands in her own.

The same lady from the quay on her first day! The kind one!

Immediately, a wave of soft, warm energy surged through Uruna's arms. Her sharp intake of breath surprised them both, but instead of recoiling, the lady smiled and put both arms around Uruna and drew her close. Uruna sensed in the woman a need of some kind, a longing unanswered, yet she herself felt enfolded in that soft warmth. They both stayed like that for several moments before the lady pulled away and blinked with a light shake of her head.

"What was that you just did?" she asked.

Uruna shrugged. "I did nothing. It must be our spirits."

"Whatever it was, we must always remember this moment, Uruna."

"I shall. And you are Shua Kinar? I like your name. It comes from a land far away, beyond Elam."

"How do you know such a thing?"

"Your mother tells me."

A tear crept down Kinar's cheek. She wiped it aside with her fingers and stood to address Master.

"We'll arrange payment for your trouble, sir."

"No need. Already been paid."

"How? I don't understand."

Master turned and pointed through an open window. At the far edge of the garden outside stood four men, one obviously a Nord, taller than the other three by head and neck. Each worked a small knife on his own arrow shaft. Ashur and Kumir were instructing Nebur and the giant in a task Uruna had heard called "fletching."

Master answered Kinar's question with a glower.

"These fellows as 'Runa brought with her have taught us hunting skills. We'll no longer need to hire it done for us at temple wages."

Kinar began an objection. "But according to law—"

"—no Nord may carry spear or mace or enter the battlefield," Master finished. "We know all about your fears, madam, duly passed down from every Nord father and grandfather for six generations. But that law says nothing about the deer arrow or the boar pike. We've broken no law, unless we're forbidden to feed our own bellies."

A small smile played about Kinar's lips. "Indeed not," she

answered with a quick nod. She then took Uruna's hand, craning her neck once more to bid farewell to the towering Nord.

"We'll take our leave if you will take our thanks."

"What're you thanking us for?"

Kinar glanced down at Uruna with a grin and started for the door.

"For safekeeping the gift of ages," she said over her shoulder.

The Nords were left scratching their heads in confusion.

Chapter 11

Primped and Prepped

Uruna's confusion began the moment Kinar left her in the big room with brick walls and fancy blankets hung to either side of a huge window. A tea set decorated a lacquered tray painted with flowers in a delicate design too precious to believe. A gown of softest linen had been laid out on a bed that squished under her weight.

Further confounding her were the three big girls who entered the room moments later, all chattering at once. Without ceremony two slipped Uruna's smock over her head and then proceeded to bathe her in an enormous pot big enough to boil stew for a whole village.

Still gabbling, the girls applied ointments to her face and touched their fingers to her neck and underarms, leaving a delightful fragrance. They then swept her hair upward from her neck into a pile atop her crown and fastened it with a nacre comb studded with glistening gems. Finally, they fitted a slender gold collar round her throat and stood her over a water basin.

Uruna peered into the water, saw her reflection, and shrieked in shock at the sight.

They had cast a spell! Transformed her into a princess encased in riches! The half-woman, half-child in the basin was another being!

The shortest girl kissed Uruna on the cheek and murmured a soothing reassurance in her ear.

"You are perfection itself," she crooned, then turned to her companions. "Don't you agree?"

"The eyes, the mouth!" exclaimed the pretty one with the soft voice. "By the gods, she needs nothing further done."

The tall one stooped before Uruna and took her hands. "You are about to absolutely crush a thousand hearts, beloved."

Uruna wished no harm to any heart, but before she could speak her concern, the girls whisked away and were gone.

She returned to the reflecting basin for another look. What did they see that so enthralled them? She had never viewed herself as others did. Was this costume someone's idea of beauty?

A soft rap at the door announced the next step in her journey. A stocky, older woman in a white gown and bejeweled arms entered, preoccupied with a hem caught in her heel. When she looked up, she stopped in her tracks and stared open-mouthed at Uruna.

"Great Mother in Heaven!" she cried. "Beloved child! Look at you! Just look!"

Uruna turned around to see for herself the vision that so caught the lady's attention. No spirit stood behind her, only the same fancy window cover, the glowing copper brazier, the soft cushiony bed.

She turned back and was nearly smothered as the woman threw her arms about her and drew her to her bosom in a prolonged embrace.

"Come to Mena, oh, come to me, my darling!"

Uruna was sure she couldn't get any closer.

Kinar reappeared at the door and moved to the old lady's side, proffering a cane.

"Madam?"

Mena shooed her away. "Not now, I'm busy. So, it's Uruna, is it!"

She bent at the waist and slapped both thighs. "My dear, you've no idea how long I've waited for this moment."

"Six and ten years."

"So you were told by Gudamma? May she rest forever in Inanna's lap."

Uruna felt this woman's unreserved love, sensed her frailty and impending death, but overriding all was a jubilant elation, a joy at having recovered something believed lost on the eve of a sad departure long ago.

"No, you were thinking about your—induction, is it called?—as queen five and twenty years ago, and you counted forward to your ninth year in temple service, when all the ladies were gathered at the quay. Nana was on the boat. She was going away for a long, long time. You loved her."

Mena straightened, reached for her cane and gripped it hard, her eyes gleaming bright with an almost youthful glow. She turned to Kinar and pointed a finger at Uruna.

"From this—" she began, but just then a third woman stepped into the room.

Haughty, arched brows above snapping black eyes, austere and grim, with a harsh beauty hardened further by middle age.

She regarded the other two ladies with severe contempt, her brows furrowed in consternation, her thin-lipped mouth turned down at the corners. Her name came to Uruna as Lubna Seddua. The forbidding one, again from that first day on the quay!

Uruna swallowed hard to stifle a surge of panic. She could feel nothing further from this woman! Nothing! A name and a hardness of spirit. That was all.

Mena pivoted around to face the new arrival.

"What are you doing here?"

"I came to see the girl." Blunt, devoid of emotion.

"Why?"

"It's important to do so."

"For two months you did not deem her worthy of consideration. Mere hours after my rebuke, you decide otherwise?"

Lubna crossed her arms in a defensive posture. "I find her appeal to the others worthy of examination. What is she? Curiosity or spirit? Is her story fact or fable? And why a child of seven rather than a woman full grown?"

The woman's cold detachment drove Uruna to quiet caution. She withdrew her innermost lights, what she termed her "touches," shut them down one by one, like snuffed candles. It was a willful act, a rejection she had never before undertaken. Lubna Seddua gave no warmth to any quarter, had none to give. She did not hear the serpent song, and therefore must be denied its secrets.

Such quick judgment brought Uruna up short. Where had all that denial come from?

As if to underscore her decision, her inner serpent quickened and recoiled. The warm Enshiggu space inside her core cooled as the god withdrew in sullen retreat, leaving the slightest breath of a curse on the air.

The dearth of feeling spread to the other women in the room. Uruna could see it in Kinar's eyes, startled wide at first, then half-closed, shrouded in distrust. Mena drew a long breath with closed eyes, as if gathering strength before a storm.

And the storm was Lubna.

At once Uruna knew for certain she was indeed no longer Misha. Serpenthood had changed, and she was transformed with it. In a trice, in the blink of an eye, she had left childhood innocence to view the world as a woman might—unforgiving of treachery, judging all with suspicion, defensive, wary of giving away too much.

The three women commenced talking at once. Adult things about tokens, and shares, and rites of blood and ascension, all spoken in a tumbling rush of emotion and fear, and somehow centered on Uruna, but not in any way she could understand.

They seemed to be arguing what to do with her and how to keep her away from another girl. Shandra would do this, and Shandra had always shown that, and Uruna had no this or that, but only a snake, which alone wasn't worth much in the balance.

She tuned out the harsh rebukes and retreated to the softness of the bed, where she lay her head on a pillow. The god's familiar warmth returned to enfold her with a softness that covered her like a shroud. She listened as a simple melody assured her all was well, she was protected. The voice in the song was memorable, but whose?

Gudamma! It was Nana singing to her! But—singing from the grave?

She took her thoughts to an inner place and saw Gudamma through a haze, restored to youth, a dark-haired beauty with flashing eyes. They walked together through a garden, and then Gudamma stopped and Uruna knew they must proceed separately.

Another voice broke her reverie.

"Now see what you've done! She's frightened by all this bickering!"

It was Mena, leaning over as Uruna lay upon the bed. Uruna felt the woman's heavier weight tug the bed mat downward as Mena sat.

It was only at that point that Uruna realized the room had filled with more ladies in white. Mena was queen, but the others were part of a large and important group.

"Out!" Mena demanded. "We must be alone. Now! I mean it, all of you!"

Mena was addressing the others now, shouting at them as if they were a flock of bothersome crows.

When the room had emptied, Mena got to her feet and took Uruna's hand. Her wrinkled flesh felt warm and soft and—was it strength she felt in that hand?

"Come to Inanna with me, Uruna," the old priestess said.

She led Uruna across the room to a small niche set in the brick wall. Within, a spray of roses set upon a small clay platform freshened the air. A single brass oil burner gleamed in the window light. Mena struck a flint and touched the flame to a slender stick. Immediately the sweet aroma of cinnamon drifted across Uruna's face, and she closed her eyes to savor the rare essence.

Mena gave Uruna's hand a squeeze before placing a strange object on the altar. Then she and the child from the East who hovered at the edge of womanhood withdrew together to sacred Serpenthood's holy center, as Mena intoned:

"Let us pray."

Chapter 12

Beloved Tutor

For Uruna, the next hour sped by in a rush of one discovery after another, each accreting onto the next until the whole became a giant ball of wondrous new understanding.

Mena comprehended at once Uruna's uncanny ability to retain facts and figures, and she quickly moved to unqualified acceptance that she was in the presence of a divinely inspired instrument for change. All this was conveyed in a single breath.

"You are an ancient soul," she declared.

Uruna responded with a confused frown, and so Mena went on.

"I haven't much time left to impart what little I know of Serpenthood. The others here in Inanna's service have scant faith and not a grain of serpent sense. They view prophecy as a tool for power. I have tried to retain what little lore I was given, but it is incomplete. You will learn far more from Enshiggu yourself.

"I speak to you now as one woman to another. You are said to be seven years old, but you are a child in body only. In truth, you have traveled the world over long ages. You possess riches of knowledge surpassing those of any now present. For that you are cherished in Heaven. You are the sword by which Inanna will smite all darkness. You are strong of will, you live and move above the pall of fear. Realize and accept your power, for you will be called upon to resist the wicked and heal those who have lost heart, and they will parry with the only weapon they know—fear. Now, attend my words, and learn how the faithful practiced the Sleep of Serpents in ages past."

Most of what Mena dispensed in that hour was lore, passed down through the ages, usually from mother to daughter, but now from Ekur's venerable queen to her adopted acolyte. The rest was simply a blissful confirmation of timeless truths Uruna had suspected but never affirmed for herself.

When Mena was finished, Uruna rocked back on her heels, stunned.

She had expected a small measure of kindly advice, but never had she imagined such an avalanche of Sumerian culture and history. And coupled with torrents of praise? What was she to think? No one had ever spoken to her as a grownup. Mena spoke with such authority about so many godly things that the sheer weight of it all sent Uruna's mind reeling.

But Mena Ramush strove on with steady voice, aware of her purpose and ardent in her intensity. She seemed driven by every saint in the Sumerian pantheon, and heedless of Uruna's difficulty grasping so much.

"Above all, remember this always, Uruna. Even as you are beloved by Heaven's host, so must you give your love to the world. For you possess love in abundance, light in abundance. Your blessings are without limit, surpassing all mankind.

"Therefore when darkness surrounds you, when it smothers all those about you and your own pain seems more than you can bear, remember to let your light shine. Let your love be a flame to drive away darkness. Let your constant courage waken others and quicken them to bold action. Be thou a strong arm to uphold the good and right in this world. Be a loving mother to the people. For this measure of grace art thou chosen."

Mena abruptly ceased her monologue and grew silent. She stared at the altar flowers for several long moments, so long that Uruna feared age might have taken its final toll. But then Mena drew herself up to her feet with a single swift motion belying her infirmity, and stared straight ahead with tears streaming from both eyes.

"I am blessed to partake in this most sacred moment."

Uruna stared into the incense smoke, shaken by the overwhelming magnitude of Mena's words. She felt the rightness of what she had just heard, but despite Mena's assurances, she could not shake off the burden of doubt.

Mena must have sensed her hesitation.

"Let it be so, for each misgiving is but a small proof of our humanity. Always remember, Uruna, you are mortal, but only a little lesser than the gods. You will never be tested beyond your ability. Now sing with me."

She then lifted her voice in homage to Goddess Inanna, and when Uruna recognized the chorus of the Alla Manna, she joined in. The old woman's chant broke just once, as emotion overtook her. They then proceeded in unison to the end.

When they turned to leave the altar, Uruna was shocked to see Shua Kinar weeping in the open doorway, her cheeks bright with tears, her lips pressed tight against her teeth.

"Forgive me, Mother," she said to Mena.

Mena leaned heavily on her cane and hobbled to the center of the room to glare at the younger woman.

"I told you we were not to be disturbed."

"But I thought you would want to know. The men brought the serpent from Na Purna."

"And why is that sufficient to interrupt us?"

"They ask where to put him. I didn't dare trust the other ladies with his fate. The bearers are waiting with his crate out in the concourse."

"Very well, we'll discuss that in a moment. How much did you hear?"

Kinar's face went white. "I-I heard the two of you singing."

"Before that?"

"Nothing. I was over in the hall—"

"That's all? You're sure?"

"Well, of course I'm sure. I only just now got here."

"In time for the Alla Manna."

"Yes. I was simply astounded."

"Indeed. Prepare yourself to be further amazed. It is only beginning." Mena turned to a nearby chair and sat. "She knows the verses, Kikki. The sacred songs and rituals, and now the first lore. The rest will remain a matter of confidence between Uruna and me."

"I understand. Um, the serpent?"

"Lam-dulla Sector. The Silver Room."

"But that's Serpenthood."

"For Uruna's personal use, yes, and the adjoining garden for Memet."

"Mena, she's seven. The other girls are twelve and older. It could prove quite difficult for her."

"You will recall Silver has its own hallway, which separates it from the Gipar dormitory. That should be sufficient to allay concerns about her mixing with female adolescents."

Uruna understood they were discussing her pending accommodation and Memet's. What she couldn't comprehend was why she shouldn't live with the other girls.

"Just because they're older?" she asked.

Mena gave her an indulgent smile. "They're going through

drastic changes. At times they can be unkind to one another."

"Oh, you mean their flow? I heard all about that."

Mena's eyebrows shot up. "From whom? I hope not the Nords."

"No, way before I left Elam. Some girls at the well in Densar were saying they got cramps and others said they didn't, and they were arguing about it when this boy came over and told about his sister—"

"I see, that's quite enough, Uruna."

"I just want you not to worry."

"Thank you, dear." Mena turned to Kinar. "You see, in many ways she's still a child, but not in all."

Uruna walked over and took Mena's hand. "I walked the Zab road alone for four and twenty months. A lot happens to road people."

Mena covered her eyes with one hand. She was still disturbed, so Uruna went on in a happier note.

"I watched a baby get born."

Mena smiled to herself. "Of course, a birth. It stands to reason that you would."

"And I saw them bury my *adda* in the house of his ancestors. Well, under the floor of our hut." She smiled to make Mena feel better. "Then they burned it all down. No more *adda*."

"Oh, good heavens!"

Kinar hastened to explain. "That's how they do it, up along the Zab."

The room grew quiet. Uruna struggled to find a more reassuring story that might explain how much she knew about grownups.

"There was a man in Shar-lush sold his daughter for a lot of money. She was only thirteen, so she was lucky to have a husband, because if she wasn't married by fifteen they would sell her to be a slave. I saw a slaver once. He was mean like Nebur used to be, only worse."

"Uruna, I think you'll do just fine in Silver."

"I just want to tell you one more thing."

"Uruna, that's enough stories."

Uruna threw her arms around Mena's neck. "I love you."

"Oh, dearest, and I love you too."

Mena then beckoned across the room to Kinar. "I'm rather tired. Would you kindly take Uruna to find Memet and show them both their new home?"

Uruna would have enjoyed her new abode more if she hadn't glimpsed, in the instant she hugged the Entu, a moment in the times ahead.

The queen's bed chamber lying still and cold—as cold as the body of Mena Ramush herself.

Chapter 13

River Conspiracy

Hours after Mena had dismissed the new light in her life, river gloss made a black mirror for the star-studded night sky. A traveler approaching from the south paused on the road less than a mile below Gula Gate. A robed figure emerged from a crumbling roadside chapel and gestured for the traveler to step no closer.

"You have news of the boy," said the voice from inside the cowl.

"He's back with his family," answered the man with leathery skin and hands that killed.

"Tell me something I don't know. You were supposed to keep him away. You had him every day for two years."

"He's too young for it, not yet ten years old. Good with small game, but he's not ready for the lance."

"He took his first boar. There will be others. You were wrong about him. You underestimated the strength of the blood line."

The hunt master bristled with outrage. "I do what you cannot! When he's ready, I'll get him out of here again, and not before! Meantime, he won't get closer to her than to pass by out there on the river."

"Well, he's back from Demshalla. The family petitions are

starting all over. We can't allow it."

"Maybe nothing will happen. He's different already, not like the pretty boys roving temple halls."

"He's got you scared. That's enough for me."

"I fear no man, much less a child. Do not talk fear to me."

"Then do what you do best."

"What, kill him? No lad deserves the sort of death I deal out."

"Then you prove my point. You're not fit for the job."

"I am not in the habit of destroying what I create."

"Then be destroyed yourself, you and all the carrion you marshal for the fighting field! My gods, you teach men how to kill their brethren and then you exact payment for the atrocity! Your greed is as appalling as your blasphemy! I won't haggle, do you hear? The bargain was sealed the day that girl showed up. The job for which you were paid is not done."

"It's not a matter of price, or fear, or anything you can possibly understand, because you and yours aren't made like we are."

"A difference for which I am thankful every day of my life. What is it then?"

"Honor. Find yourself a street rat for this work. I'm sure they abound in Uruk's catacombs."

"You realize that if I find another—and I shall—I cannot simply allow you to remain upright and talking."

"I knew that much when I came here. But don't send any after me—not any you care to use again. Those who've tried are buried where they will never be found. I'm the best at what I do, and I make sure it stays that way."

"We do not require the lad's death, only his removal, once and for all. Find a way. Our work is nearly finished and we simply can't have him getting involved. It's the worst possible time."

"He's not the pliable boy he was before. At best, I can distract him only for a short time. A year, maybe two. Once he gets his size, that headstrong heritage will take over."

"A short time is all we need. Soon it won't matter where he is or what he does. For now, give him some animals to shoot or a brawl to win—whatever his venturesome heart desires. Just keep him away from *her*!"

Chapter 14

Mentor Nashi

Uruna's eighth year of life was rich with experience. She developed a routine for each of the two endeavors most important to her.

The first was religious instruction. She sat with the older girls during their preparation for priestesshood. Temple ladies coached them in cosmic lore, in sung appeals to the gods, how to nurture various grain crops, how to read the river, how to divine weather signs, the use of symbols in clay for commerce.

But Uruna's favorite was the law, an enormous body of oral history detailing matters of every human kind, from birth to marriage to death; from matters of property, crime, and commerce to sensitive issues regarding moral responsibility. The litany eventually drove the other girls to sleep, whereas Uruna stayed rapt throughout.

As an acolyte, she partook in every worship ceremony and rite she could get to. She learned Sumerian reverence through prayer, song, story, and chant. She became adept at wielding objects of holy tradition. She fed upon the very basis of belief that constituted Sumer's moral backbone.

To her, each acquaintance, old or young, was a teacher in some respect. Every experience became a lesson for the future. Her prodigious mental capacity drew in every morsel to husband for the right moment.

And yet, she heard no mention of serpent rites. Here she sat at last, residing in the very fundament of serpently tradition, and none could speak the precepts of Serpenthood with authority. She reasoned at first that the Lukur couldn't possibly be so lax, so uncaring, as they appeared. The ladies must be holding the sacred tenets secret, for while there was talk of prophecy in many quarters, it was always described as a figment of the past, a venerated body of mysticism beyond explanation.

In short order she concluded none had serpently wisdom at all.

Awakening one morning to a commotion outside her room, she went into the hallway to see for herself.

"There she is!" someone shouted.

Several *kadishtu* girls rushed to her side and propelled her toward a strange-looking old woman in peasant garb. The girls continued to chatter excitedly. It was *Nashi* this and *Nashi* that, and oh, how long since *Nashi* had last come to the city.

The woman pushed the crowd aside and stepped forward. She stopped before Uruna with raised arm and pointed a finger straight at her.

"Here's the one I came to see."

"No, no!" they all objected.

"She's just a little girl."

"Only just got here."

"They found her on the road."

"Comes to every class and just sits there."

"Silence!"

Nashi's voice rang through the hallway and struck all dumb. The girls stepped back, hushed. Uruna felt a familiar essence fill her deepest center. The sort of sound Enshiggu might make, if that god ever again deigned to speak to her.

Nashi extended a hand to Uruna's face. The calloused touch of a workwoman brought back memories of her earliest childhood, of the woman whose fingers had brought her into this world, whose palm had stroked her to sleep as a babe, as Misha.

"So thou art Uruna now," Nashi said in the old tongue nearly forgotten. A sweet smile cracked the seams of sun-bruised flesh. "Thou hast journeyed long to thy destiny, child of promise. A nation awaits thy hand."

Uruna couldn't speak. Beyond skin folds dried by time and hardship lay beauty from a far-off memory. Familiar contours welcomed her—the line of jaw, the arch of brow, the very sound enveloping her. Nashi's deepest spirit reached across countless years to soothe her mind, warm her heart, enrich her soul.

Uruna fell to her knees, her eyes blinded by tears, her voice stuck in her throat.

"Yes," said the woman of mystery. "Yes and yes and yes."

She reached down and drew Uruna to her feet again, then stepped to her side and turned to face the small crowd of young women.

"I present your future queen and faithful servant as one. Remember today, even as the world bids you to forget."

She then addressed Uruna. "To chapel with us, where we shall resume our discourse."

Uruna didn't remember any prior talk with this woman, but she led the way anyway through the catacombs to her most sacrosanct place of worship. Little more than an alcove, the tiny chapel barely had space for the two of them, but Uruna didn't care. She knelt before the altar, picked up the stemmed yellow rose bud that appeared there daily, and offered it to Nashi.

Her new-old companion took it up, and with closed eyes brought the tiny petals to her lips. She gently placed the flower on the offering surface, chuckled at Uruna's makeshift altar, a converted grinding stone, and heaved a long and contented sigh.

"Madam," she said, "how shall we begin?"

The former road urchin from Anshan replied in her customary forthright manner. "Let us sing the Alla Manna."

"First verse or third?"

"All of it."

For the rest of that year Uruna's studies with Nashi were a scant few, but provided lessons that enriched the days between with profound significance. The desert crone made clear from the outset that her sole purpose was to divulge to her earnest pupil as much of agrarian lore and practice as she could.

"Only Inanna knows how much time I have left. I would be remiss if I didn't impart as much as I can."

The strangest part of it, and the most delightful, was that each session began a new journey to Nashi's tiny home in the country. Uruna never knew when she might "feel" the call to go, but her overnight forays were never refused. Kinar would escort her to a canal barge at Nergal Gate one morning and pick her up at the same spot at noon the next day. She took pains to assure Uruna that each unplanned notice was her pleasure and did not intrude on her own affairs.

If Mena's gift was Lukur wisdom and tradition, Nashi's was planting and the river. She was herself a planter's daughter, and had spent her entire long life with the soil.

"We have ministers abounding in knowledge of seeding, planting, the harvest, the stores," she explained one day. "But they all rely on the river. *Buranun* sends her waters hither today and thither tomorrow. Her ebbs and flows bend to Nanna-moon's will. The irrigator watches her edges with his keen eye and sounds her depths with drag and pole, opens and closes weirs to accommodate her whims. If he grows careless, the canal waters will not reach the field—or will flood it beyond use. One mistake, just one, can kill a ton of barley before it is born, or invite the red rust after the grain attains life, or cause any of a thousand other things to go wrong."

"Am I to become planter or irrigator before I am queen?"

"As far as I can see, that work is not yours. Rather, you must understand the planter's work, his way of life, if you would guide an entire nation. We who work the land love it as we do our children. Those who follow the river love her in the same way. Together, we bring forth bounty year upon year, generation upon generation. Each does his or her part, trusting Inanna to impart wisdom through her most reverend queen. But rite and ceremony alone cannot withstand the wrath of wind and rain upon the misguided. This we have learned in times past and passed down from mother to daughter, father to son. All must continue without fail if Sumer is to survive and prosper."

Uruna's thoughts turned to a passage from ancient lore Mena had related to her just days before:

There came a time of great heat, and the waters upon the earth drew back, and the waters above the earth fell not. The land between the two rivers shriveled and died, and every living thing therein perished.

For the sons of man remembered not how to store up grain, and they cried out to Inanna, Restore thy bounty, Mother Goddess. But she heard them not, and a great famine swept the land, and death reigned unto the third generation.

"Do the Mothers expect a prophet to warn them of a dry spell or a flood?"

"That is their hope, but they cannot shirk their own duties the way they have done lately."

"How is this so? They don't seem to have forgotten their

prayers."

"But they continue to ignore the people who carry out Inanna's orders. Farmers are a sturdy lot, not much given to wit or idle conversation, but committed instead to skill and hard labor. They deserve your respect and considered attention, now and later on when you become their regent, even when they might commit a social slight. I say this not from pride of being one of them, but rather as an observer myself. I served five years at temple, you know. Came to know a good many who've served and gone since. Knew Gudamma just a few weeks before Council sent her off in search of a prophet."

"You knew my Nana!"

"Not well enough, I'm afraid. I can tell you nothing about her you don't already know for yourself."

"What was she like in those days? I mean, she had four and forty years already."

Nashi lifted an eyebrow at yet another example of the child's uncanny gifts. "She always seemed younger than her years, strong of body and eager to embark on her quest. I never heard from her afterward myself, although I was told she returned a few times without success. I believe the last failure diminished her status at Council. The ladies then running things were persuaded more by their own abilities than by divine inspiration. They still are, by my estimation, but that will change."

"How do you know of this change, Nashi?" Uruna asked. "Have you already seen the days to come?"

Nashi's eyelids dropped in a slow blink, and she spoke to her earnest pupil in the old tongue.

"I have seen *thee*, Uruna. For thou art the bringer of gifts of the spirit. Thou shalt return this land and its people to their rightful place in Great Mother's heart. Neither wicked nor slanderous deeds shall stay thy hand, though they strive a hundredfold in vicious fury. For all the woes of mankind shall be as nothing before thy wisdom and power. Be thou sure of purpose. Be thou strong. Be thou loving and true in heart. Be thyself."

Chapter 15

A Case For Prophecy

On a winter day near the end of her eighth year, Uruna's prayer for a strong sign of her purpose was answered. Instead of their usual session at Serpenthood Chapel, Mena told Uruna to fetch her tote for a foray across the Aniginna compound where a surprise awaited.

"Today, we take our first step into the unknown. Have you been to House of Safekeeping?"

"In class we were told not to cross the threshold without an elder present."

"No matter, as I am overqualified in that regard," Mena said with a wry twist of her mouth.

The concourse was filled with women going hither and thither on various errands. House of Safekeeping stood halfway down the concourse, a good three hundred paces from Serpenthood, and so Uruna was treated to the pleasures of gardens and pools and towering palms. The journey was short but Mena seem to tire as they took the steps to the entry. When Uruna offered her arm for support Mena shook her head and insisted she would continue on "my own stumps."

Her stubborn self-reliance continued with their journey down the long colonnade leading to a pair of barred double doors. Mena heaved the bar aside with a great explosion of breath and stepped inside, waving Uruna in behind her.

Immediately upon entering, Uruna's nose was assaulted by the musty odor of the unlighted interior.

"Relics of the past," Mena explained. "Some have lain here untouched for centuries, more's the pity. But you and I are here to rescue a few from idle rest. Come, I want you to see this, but first we must light a few lamps."

To Uruna's surprise, the oil basins were filled and ready for her flint. When she finished the first she looked up and saw the ceiling twenty feet overhead. She and Mena stood between rows of shelves that marched away into the darkness in either direction. Mena produced a candle and touched the wick to a nearby lamp flame. Without another word she struck off to the right.

Uruna wondered aloud how many racks of goods stood in the room. Mena's terse reply illustrated her low regard for their contents. "Four and twenty. Should have buried most of it."

As Mena penetrated the darkness, Uruna realized she was aware of more than the patter of her own feet. Ancient voices called out to her, sounds of the past struggling to reach new ears, all vying for her attention. They seemed to know her heart and how to play upon her emotions. She nearly stopped in her tracks before she grappled with the din and wrested her attention from their clamor. The voices softened and withdrew as quickly as they had appeared, leaving her shaken but newly attuned to her strange surroundings.

They soon reached a wall with an open doorway leading out of the big room. Mena passed through, made an immediate left, and stopped to touch her taper to another oil lamp.

"The rest of this place is a maze of corridors and small rooms.

Mark our path well in your mind, my dear. I may not live long enough to do this again. Gods, it's been so long as it is."

After a few more twists and turns, Mena paused before a closed door.

"You'll notice it's unmarked," she said.

"Because the contents are sacred?" Uruna guessed.

"Well, that's true enough. More like their secret must be kept from the unworthy. Grab that oil lamp from the wall and light it. This taper won't be enough."

Uruna noticed a new spring to Mena's step. As the grand lady of Ekur entered the room, she hunched her shoulders like a little girl anticipating a delightful treat.

"Oh! It's just like I remembered. There's the Shining Bowl and Ladle, for Song of Utu-gahn. I used to know the verses. And over here Ezzub's own, the Wand of Tears. So many treasures, so long since I was here last with these beloved…"

The time span unraveled in Uruna's awakened senses: two and thirty years! Mena must have been just a young woman, maybe a girl just a few years older than herself. Was it possible that Serpenthood's mysteries had lain dormant like this, for lifetime upon lifetime? No wonder the Mothers had lost so much!

Mena stopped before a tall rack of shelves and began scanning the contents. What at first appeared to be a dish cupboard full of mugs and plates and vases turned out, under closer inspection, to be yet another mystery.

"They come from precious stones brought down from the mountains in farthest Egypt. No one knows who wrought them, nor how long ago. This one, I am told, was last used in Lasori's time, possibly by the great queen herself."

"What is its purpose?" Uruna asked.

Mena shrugged. "Like so many things here, its use is lost to antiquity."

"But we keep them anyway?"

"Yes, in the hope someone like you may happen by—someone for whose purpose they have been kept safe behind these walls. Which brings us to this dear object."

Mena lifted a small crystalline vial from a shelf and gently cradled it in her hands. "I herewith entrust to you the Vault of Sacred Sleep."

She then handed the object to Uruna.

The container was shaped like many others she had seen, but as it caught the light she saw Mena's face through it. *Behind and through.*

Mena pointed with her finger. "Notice the little marks on this side."

Uruna looked and found six straight lines etched into the material like rungs on a ladder. "Do you know what they are for?" she asked.

"Yes, but we'll get to that later. Here's something that you should look at because I haven't figured out myself what it means."

Mena pulled a long wooden object from the shelf and laid it out on the floor. She then pulled it apart like panels on a screen. The surfaces were painted in bright colors—crudely rendered figures of people and animals, but a scene in the center drew Uruna's attention immediately.

A man and woman sat facing each other across a low table. Behind the woman, four erect cobras looked on. A bright disk hovered over the pair, illuminating four jars placed on the table.

Uruna looked up at Mena, her eyebrows drawn together in a frown. "Is the man helping the lady get ready for prophecy?"

"I was hoping you might know the answer yourself. I was told, by one as unsure of herself as I, that it represents a ceremony for the Sleep of Serpents. Hut, before you ask, realize this is only someone's interpretation, Uruna. Someone long dead, who may not have known any truth."

Uruna shifted her gaze to the right. The scene was repeated, but the bright orb was missing and the man was facing away from the woman. She then glanced left and beheld the reverse.

Everything she had heard from the God described the process in six steps, six doors to open, six breaths to inhale, six serpents standing watch. Always six, never three, nor four. Her tendency to doubt the story depicted was confused by a feeling in her core that said this was right, the panel story was authentic.

"I'm not sure about this one," she said to Mena. "It makes me want to ask more questions."

Mena's face clouded. "You'll have to commit it to memory. That's one object that can't leave the room. Tell me, what do you make of it?"

"Well, it's the first time I've heard of a man being there. Always before it was the serpents and the god. Also, I don't know what the orb means. Is it the sun or the moon? Why is it missing in the two outer things? And look, the man and lady are turned away there. They could be special clues to part of the ceremony. Does that make sense?"

"I can't say one way or the other. I had the same question years ago and I was hoping you might supply the answer based on your communion with Enshiggu."

Uruna studied the panels again, hoping to glean more and committing as much detail to memory as she could. There was always the chance that this piece of antiquity was meant not for her but for somebody else. Still, she could not deny how grounded she felt in this place, how significant it was for her progress toward prophecy.

Mena stared at the panels for a long moment, then stirred herself. "One more object here I was told is critical for the success of the supplicant."

Again she reached to the shelf and withdrew a third object, a goblet of gold etched with runes, its rich surface gleaming in the candlelight.

"Of this I am sure," she said. "It is meant for you alone, for only you are left of those who aspire to serve in prophecy. Others may falsely claim the crown for themselves, but for their affront they will be cast down and their names stricken from memory for all time. Selah."

As Uruna turned the goblet in her hand, the markings aroused a memory. How could she have seen them before, much less known their meaning?

Mena seemed to sense her connection to the runes. "You may keep this one," she said, "in fact you must. In time, it's meaning will become clear. I cannot add more."

Uruna put goblet and vial in her tote and took one last look at the wood panel before she picked it up and put it back on the shelf. She and Mena remained silent as they retraced their steps through the maze and all the way back to Safekeeping's entrance. She barred the door herself and turned around to see Mena stepping carefully down to ground level. Uruna needed several moments herself for her eyes to adjust to the harsh sunlight. As she reached Mena's side, she looked up ahead and saw a lone figure staring across the compound.

Lubna Seddua. Watching intently while she ignored her retinue of ladies. Uruna felt the woman's eyes follow her exit from the sacred confines of the Lukur's most closely guarded secrets, marking and measuring as though appropriating Uruna's moment of discovery for her own.

Back in Mena's quarters, they sat over tea, each considering the profundity of the past hour. At length, Mena stirred to life.

"The six marks on the vial are for six potions, each for one of the six Doors to Sight. You'll notice the goblet is small, almost too small for normal drinking. That's because drink is not its purpose. Rather, it is for the milk from a cobra. You have done this with Memet."

"Yes, a few times at prayer."

"This is different. Into the goblet you collect venom from his fangs. You save the venom in the goblet. You then pour water into the vial up to the first mark and mix it with a tiny droplet of venom. You add nothing else. Then you drink it."

"I—drink the venom?"

"Daily."

"*Every day?*"

"Yes. At such time as you address your consort for the Sleep ceremony, you will mix a much stronger combination. Your daily intake before that occasion protects you from the venom's toxic effect. It is a ritual practiced by every seer and passed on to her successor, down the ages. Unfortunately, my account may be flawed. I can only tell you what I was told by my mother, and she by hers."

Uruna sat in silence for several long moments considering what Mena had just told her. This was not a matter to be taken on blind faith. She did not doubt Mena's sincerity, nor her faithful rendering of what she knew. But lore was all too easily twisted with the telling. The poison from a naja cobra could kill a small child. A single sting from a king cobra was enough to kill an ox. If a few tiny drops entered her blood, she would die within minutes. Could she imbibe it from an oil spoon without damage to her innards? Was survival remotely possible?

Such a prospect must have thwarted even adult seekers. How many women had simply quit and kept silent about it? On the other hand, dozens could have tried and perished, their disgraceful end withheld from lore to keep everybody's hopes up.

No wonder Sumer had gone two centuries without a prophet.

Those who dared not would fare the same as those who did and perished. Neither story was worth recounting.

And here she stood, no mentor, no seer guide, her only legacy a few relic artifacts and the questionable recollection of a dying matron.

Across the table, Mena's expression mirrored her own thoughts. Each understood the dilemma, each could assume Uruna's devotion to serve with sacrifice, each appreciated the far-reaching cost of failure.

Uruna got up and brushed Mena's forehead with a kiss. Nothing further needed saying. She had a lot of serious thinking to do.

She had nearly reached her own room when she met Lubna Seddua coming the other way. She felt an unaccountable discomfort under the woman's sharp-eyed scrutiny.

"What were you doing at House of Safekeeping?" Lubna demanded.

"It was a private matter."

"More about that infernal Sleep ritual, I would guess."

When Uruna said nothing in reply, Lubna felt obliged to press on.

"It's a big mistake, you know, this serpent business. If you persist in chasing phantoms, you'll put every Lukur at risk, yourself more than anyone."

"Is it your hope that I should die without attaining Sight?"

"You might die from a snake bite, but as that pain is over quickly, it would not serve me. However, if you strike for Sight and miss, as will likely happen, the pain of that failure will eat at you like a poison every day for the rest of your life. Be most careful, girl, which turn of fate you choose."

Moving on her way, Uruna took small comfort now that Lubna's intent was clear. A line had been drawn. Lubna would now confront her at every turn and would not retreat easily.

Chapter 16

Lost Touches

On another day, as Uruna sat on the Gipar steps mending a skirt, her thoughts turned to the foursome who had brought her to Nippur. She tried and failed to remember the names of the two hunters. The same with the recovered thief. Two winters had passed since Gudamma's death, and slightly less since her departure from Na Purna, or so she believed. The precise number of days eluded her. In fact, she had begun to forget quite a few such details.

Gods! she thought. *What is wrong with me?*

She snatched up her sewing and dashed through the hall to her room. Once more in familiar surroundings, she began to calm down. Forgetting must be one of the steps you took growing up. The ladies in the Gipar sometimes forgot a meeting, or misplaced a bauble.

Heavens, me! they would exclaim. *I must be getting old.*

But she was just nine. Her journey had only begun.

She left her room and went out into the hallway and down the steps to Memet's garden. She found him in the deepest shade, coiled between a large stone and a palm. He came to her call in a lethargic state, and she felt his reluctance to consult the god once more. Were they both so afflicted?

"We're losing our serpent sense," she told him. "We have to pray for its return. This is not right."

Indeed, memory loss was only a signal of the real problem: She had strayed from her course. She had filled her mind with temple affairs as she strove to absorb every detail of rite and ceremony. She had put her quest for prophecy on hold. A return to her center was in order. She sensed a mild affirmation from Memet.

After making sure he was secure about her shoulders, she climbed back into the hall and headed for the tiny shrine room Kinar had set aside for her. Many weeks had passed since her last devotion, an unforgivable lapse, and she had brought no taper for light, nor a bouquet to lend grace.

But what should that matter to a god who had counseled her amid rocks and trees in a hostile wilderness?

She stopped before the chapel door and froze.

The entrance was bricked over! A faint mortar line showed where lintel and jamb had been sealed. Her shrine was gone.

Her first thought was not to guess who might do such a thing, but where she ought to go next. She was on a mission to reconcile with Enshiggu and renew her devotion. Nothing must stop her.

She struck off up the long hallway in the other direction. The Gipar was immense, a catacomb of compartments and chambers and niches and halls—once teeming with ladies going about their daily routines, but now lying vacant and unused. She had visited every corner by day and night, thinking each exploration a great adventure, and not once had she been found out.

There was a large empty room just ahead, a place where great vats of an icky black substance had been stored far in the past. The Mothers had removed the vats, leaving behind rings of black residue on the floor. Uruna had since discovered it was the pitch used on boat hulls to keep water out. The goo had hardened. She would take just a few moments to find a clear spot for worship —

"What are you doing here?"

Uruna jumped and spun around. A woman in clogs and brown smock loomed in the wan torchlight. Uruna started to answer, but her reply was cut off by a second woman in similar garb.

"It's that girl with the snakes. Watch out, she's got one with her!"

"Girl!" the first shouted. "You get back to your room at once or I'll give you the switch!"

"We'll have to tell the Mothers."

"Got no time for such."

The first woman pointed a dirt-caked hand at Uruna. Her fingers were encrusted with dark mud, almost black. And the same smeared the grimy apron clasped round her waist. But more reddish...

Oh, gods! It was blood! They were embalmers! Tenders of the dead!

Uruna shrieked and backed into a wall.

Memet drew back with a hiss, fangs bared. She had seen him like that only once before, with a wild dog that wanted him for dinner. He lunged for the finger but stopped short.

Uruna sidled along the wall. "We're going!"

"He tried to bite me!" screamed the second.

"No!" Uruna shouted back. "It was just a warning!"

"You don't know snakes as I do, you little guttersnipe. What you doing with that thing wrapped all cozy about you like a shawl?"

"We always travel this way—"

"Well, you just travel on out of here and keep going. That thing don't belong up here in the sifting rooms, nor do you. Go on, git!"

Uruna backed away from the tirade, but the louder of the two yelled at her again.

"Not that way! Back here!"

Uruna crossed to the other side of the hallway, still facing the two embalmers. When she was past, each raised an arm.

"That's right, go on!"

"And don't come back, d'you hear?"

Uruna staggered away and around the first corner, blundering headlong down an arched passage that was little more than a tunnel. Unmindful of her direction, she sought only to distance herself from the two horrid women and their wretched business.

The tunnel ended in a hole that descended by a staircase into the black depths of a cavern. She caught a glimpse of light farther down and felt a wash of cool, damp air smelling of river. Could it be an underground path beneath the river wall?

One of her mentors, either Mena or Nashi, had mentioned Nippur's layered history. Over the ages, the original settlement had grown into a good-sized town. River silt would accumulate, filling the streets with each year's floods until, in a generation or two, the clay topped door sills and thresholds, forcing the townspeople to rebuild. The easiest approach was to construct new walls upon the old. Today, proud Nippur rested atop countless such tiers, her legacy streets and alleys forever buried beneath her monumental sprawl.

Uruna drew back from the stairs. Curiosity drove her to pursue further, but her better sense cautioned against further exploration in the darkened rubble. Besides, it was no place to take Memet.

But the cavernous depths called to her, and she vowed to return one day and explore the depths of Old Nippur's secrets.

The return to her quarters took longer than she'd thought. Serpenthood's maze of passageways was fraught with wrong turns and dead ends. By the time she reached her room, the midday meal was over and she barely had time to put Memet away before rushing off to class.

As she took her place with the older girls, she went back over her path through the catacombs. She could remember the familiar passageways once she had reached the Gipar, but she grew confused when she tried to retrace all the backing and false starts, and soon the whole track became just a twisted muddle.

As the instructor opened with a prayer, Uruna lost as well the sense of importance she had ascribed to the catacombs earlier. So be it. She would leave the underground city's secrets to themselves. She would allow Old Nippur's past to dissolve into dust, the same as any other.

The same as her own.

Chapter 17

A Voice For Kinar

Another year passed, during which Uruna devoted so much attention to learning that she barely had time for anything else. As she approached the end of her ninth year of life, she became aware that her prospects, although she was years from receiving even the lowliest *kadishtu* induction, enjoyed high regard among the religious.

A large amount of that attention was Mena's doing. The Entu set policy, and where that policy pointed toward prophecy's eminent return, Uruna's potential rose to the forefront. It soon became apparent that secular matters might be set aside for the newer focus to receive its due. And where that priority conflicted with agendas of the empowered, conflict arose. A small number of ladies in Kinar's circle undertook Uruna's education as their top priority, with the unfortunate result that concern for her welfare overshadowed attention to the older girls. Feeling abandoned for a pretty child who hadn't yet begun her own path of toil and privation, the acolytes were on the verge of rebellion when the situation abruptly reversed itself in a single night.

The queen's manner of death took no one by surprise. Mena

Ramush simply failed to rise one morning, having passed in her sleep. Of course, there was a great hustle and bustle over the funeral proceedings, the eulogy, the songs to be sung, the burial. Uruna first heard about it from Kinar on the morning Mena Ramush was to be interred in House of Spirits.

She clenched her cheeks in her hands as tears blinded her.

"We didn't say goodbye," she said in a voice choked with regret.

Kinar drew her close. "None of us did, dear. She passed alone in the night, resting in peace."

"We—we didn't finish our talks."

"Uruna, we are never finished upon our final breath. The work goes on, love goes on, life goes on without us. She knew it was coming. She was ready. You know that."

"Oh, Kikki! I loved her so!"

"And she loved you just as much. You made her final days so happy. Someday you'll understand how much."

"I want to go see what they do with her."

"It's not a place for children. Certainly not the way you want to remember dear Mena."

"Take me, please, Kikki. I didn't get to see my Nana, either—or Adda or Mama."

"Uruna, I would do many things for you, but not this time. Someday you'll understand. Soon enough it will be you, as a woman, telling another young girl to wait. In our journey through life we all get our fill of burying loved ones. Now, do you know the best thing you can do for her?"

"What? Tell me and I'll do it!"

"Go fetch Memet and take him across to Serpenthood sanctuary. And the two of you sit down at the shrine and light a candle, and pray to Inanna, pray to Enshiggu, and ask them for peace and love. You know how to do that better than anyone else, better than I do. Mena would love to hear your prayers, to feel your voice reaching to her in song. That is your gift, sweet girl. She's waiting to receive it now."

Uruna wiped her tears and threw her arms around Kinar's neck. They stayed that way for several moments, until Uruna drew back, sobered, and looked her best friend in the eye.

"Remembering is never without pain, is it?"

Kinar pressed her lips together and shook her head once. An understanding passed between them, one woman to another this time. Uruna would no longer question the source of Kinar's abiding pain. She knew.

The rest of the day was a whirlwind of obligation—rites and elegies and pomp—and for Kinar, as well, the sticky business of preparing a human body for its last voyage. Sticky because although she was well-practiced at the unpleasant details, she would never grow used to it. The incisions must be done right or not at all. Needs for the afterlife must be wrapped thusly and placed just so, as directed by the deceased in strictest confidence months beforehand. The dead deserved as much, particularly one so honorable in life.

When at last the crypt was closed and the ladies had dispersed, Kinar succumbed to fatigue and dragged her feet across the mall and through the big double doors of Serpenthood. Perhaps she would leave a final taper at Mena's shrine, just a symbolic gesture to bring the day to a close and try to ease her mind.

As she started down the hallway, a voice rang out from behind the chapel door, clear and high-pitched, in measured cadence akin to spoken verse, every sound distinct.

Kinar understood not a word of it.

The sounds were not Old Dingiru, nor did they fit her scant knowledge of marsh dweller dialect. Who could be responsible for such gibberish?

Who indeed, as she peered past the half-open door, but the child?

She crept into the chapel and stepped to one side, hoping not to disturb what was clearly a dialog with the divine.

For there sat Uruna, cross-legged before the brazier's flickering shadow, her cobra companion erect at her side, both heads swaying slightly as the pair attended a voice meant for their hearing alone.

Kinar was infringing on a private matter. Her taper and her homage could wait. She started to back away when Uruna interrupted herself.

"It's all right, Kikki, come on in."

Kinar hesitated. "I don't want to intrude."

"We're at the Fourth Door. I'm always stopped here, I don't know why yet."

Fourth Door? What was that? Some kind of arcane ritual?

Kinar advanced on tiptoe until she stood directly behind Uruna.

"Come sit, there's room next to Memet."

She? Sit beside the cobra? But she knew nothing about snakes. He would detect her shortcomings and understand her dearth of serpent sense. And then...

Uruna broke into her thoughts. "...then he'll do what to you, Kikki? We're in *semtu* right now. A state of no fear or anger, only hope."

"I—I suppose I could."

She stepped cautiously to the right, edged beside the cobra's coils, and stopped.

Memet stared straight ahead, undisturbed. She smelled his flesh, resisted an urge to touch the flared back with the twin eye pattern. She sensed an abiding peace and sank to her knees, immersed in the strangest sensation she had ever known. An indescribable presence. New, young, and poignantly vital.

"He's talking to you. Can you hear him?"

"Memet? Talking to me?"

"No, your boy, Wardum."

"Oh, gods!"

"He comes to you as you drop all cares. Listen, feel his love."

Kinar could no longer hold herself together. She broke into sobs and bowed forward with her face in her hands.

Wardum! She didn't care how Uruna knew his name, a sound her baby hadn't lived long enough to hear from his mother's lips. She didn't need anything but the abiding presence now giving her comfort in a way she hadn't felt for ever so long. The tears flowed on, great torrents blurring her view of the shrine and cascading down her face. Some part of her, a part she had hidden deep within her soul, burst with unrestrained joy and a jubilant shout. Solace found her, an abiding unspoken peace settled about her shoulders, warm assurance that all was resolved, all was well, and she was forever part of him and he of her, in a bond that could never be broken.

The presence began to withdraw, but left no pain of loss. One moment was enough. One forever promise she would carry with her on the rest of her journey through life.

Her sobbing stopped without her willing it so. A healing peace took its place. She opened her eyes and beheld the shrine wall three feet ahead.

I could sit here forever, she thought. *I could die here and be happy.*

To her left, Uruna stirred and stretched, and in an offhand manner reached for Memet and gathered him to her chest.

"Hm-mm, I'm tired, how about you?"

The girl's gaze wandered to the cobra's empty spot and fell upon Kinar. She jumped with a start.

"Kikki! What are you doing here?"

"You called me."

"I did?"

"And you told me to sit down next to Memet."

"Well, that's never happened before. I'm sorry if we scared you."

"No, I had the most wonderful experience. We were in *semtu* together, don't you remember?"

"I always forget after it's over."

"You forget going to the Fourth Door?"

"Did I make it to the Fourth again? Are you sure?"

"Uruna, you told me yourself."

Uruna shrugged. "Guess I forgot the whole thing. I'm hungry."

"Me too. How's Memet?"

Uruna craned around for a look at the wedge-shaped head, shook her own. "He's always groggy after. Let's put him away and go down to the kitchen. Unless you have other plans?"

For some reason she couldn't explain, Kinar felt ravenous. She had a faint recollection of having spent a nasty afternoon, followed by an energized release of tension bordering on bliss. A vestige of the strange memory remained, but the thought of food made it vanish. She got to her feet, and she and Uruna left the shrine together.

They ate pork on the bone with tea and bread. Cheese and grapes to finish.

Chapter 18

Lubna Schemes

The herald from Uruk had just left Lubna Seddua's parlor when she received her next visitor of the day. She knew Lady Amurritum to be a gossip monger of the first order, but from the elder Lukur's recitations she often gained an advantage as first to hear, and thus first to put such rumor to use.

"The *udalla* ministry are preparing Delondra Seddua for induction."

"I've known that for some time, Amurri," she replied.

"Tonight. Her mother, you know."

Oh, fishhooks and knots! Another mandate from the wealthy fool who could not reason!

"Why wasn't I informed earlier?"

"I only learned of it myself moments ago. Her mother insisted on moving it up before they depart tomorrow to winter in Uruk."

"Tomorrow? Good heavens, the woman treats us like household servants. She has no appreciation for how much preparation it takes."

"Actually, we're ready."

"Ah, but is the girl ready?"

"No more than usual. As you've seen yourself, she doesn't retain the verses well."

A polite way of saying dim wits ran in the family. But still the girl was a vital piece in the game. Eminently maneuverable, pliant, a willing sort whose forgetfulness played well into the designs of the more competent. As a woman, Delondra would inherit lands second in size only to those of the Hanza matriarch, Heganna. That in itself was sufficient reason to overlook today's imposition.

Heganna of Hanza was the wealthiest woman in Sumer. Her holdings rivaled those of most temples, due in large part to her uncanny mastery of commerce and legendary influence at court. Mother to three grown daughters, she'd placed each in a position of authority abroad, whereas her sole male offspring, renegade Anu, was off seeking adventure and fortune in bold opposition to her wishes.

If by some sleight of hand Lubna might one day arrange to marry off the Seddua girl to the Hanza lad, his slice of inheritance combined with the girl's would not only surpass Heganna's, the deed would extend Ekur's control of commerce from north to south over practically the entire country.

And, as a matter of course, a proportionate profit would accrue to the agent of such fortune. A smile crept over Lubna's face as she considered the prospect.

But first things first. Distasteful though the task might be, and arduous, Lubna, Amurritum, and their Lukur allies must see dunderhead Delondra safely brought into the fold. At the expense of one more qualified, if necessary.

Change at the top usually meant a drastic reshuffling for any regime, and Mena's succession was no exception. By the end of the third day after Entu Mena's passing, no one was queen, Lubna Seddua was adjutant, and Niccaba was the new chancellor. Consolidating their joint control of matters secular, Lubna and

Niccaba strove to remove opposition.

The first obstacle was also the easiest to arrange.

Rather than demote Shua Kinar, they chose to promote her— out of the way.

"We need a strong, sure hand in the provinces," Lubna declared to the assembled council on the third day. "I propose Shua Kinar as *nigenna* priestess-in-charge."

Beforehand, to avoid any hint of collusion, she and Niccaba had agreed to disagree.

"She's too young," Niccaba now objected. "And she'll be conflicted by responsibilities for her own lands. My gods, the woman is scarcely at temple service for one day before she's gone for ten."

Chief Counter Ku-Aya wasn't so sure. "That's an exaggeration. Her first thought is always for temple Ekur. She's efficient, knows how to delegate. I'd say she's the ideal candidate to oversee province-wide cultivation."

Heads bobbed in agreement. Niccaba put on a frown, moved for a vote, knowing her lone dissent would be overlooked with time.

Despite having serious misgivings about the motives behind her selection, Kinar actually looked forward to her forthcoming travels as a break from the monotony of meetings and ceremonies and courtroom appearances that so characterized her temple life. At least that was the front she put on for Heganna's benefit.

She stood in her room at Hanza House and looked around at all the finery she was leaving behind. Her extended stay as Heganna's guest had been a pleasant one, and today marked the end of their association for a while. They were as close as sisters, having shared confidences few women unrelated by blood might enjoy.

"I shall miss you terribly," said Heganna. "I suppose that's what they counted on."

"They who, the Council?"

"Don't be deliberately dense. You know I mean Lubna and Niccaba. The two greatest schemers in the city, yet I don't know what they're up to."

"You know very well. They want me out of the way."

Heganna struck a nearby table with her fist. "I thought we had the votes. I was sure of it, in fact. What am I supposed to do now? Wish you a fond farewell? My best pair of ears is leaving forever."

"Surely not that long. Probably just a year or so," Kinar tried, knowing such assignments lasted for far longer.

She folded the last farm smock and stowed it in the travel box that would be her home away from home for the next four seasons, and likely longer. The hinterland was no place for fine clothes or fine manners. After all, she was a grower's daughter, knew what to expect.

"There's another matter of greater concern to me," she said.

"What's that? The deplorable state of your constabulary at Isin?"

Kinar operated a modest barley plantation uncomfortably close to Uruk. Recent reports on her constables there held that their allegiance had shifted. Kinar would not have time to investigate herself, creating the strong likelihood those lands would fall into the hands of a competing grower, one Calla Sin.

Kinar turned and faced Heganna squarely. "No, I'm worried for Uruna."

"The girl with the cobra? I thought she was with the Nords."

"Heavens! We brought her back long ago, at Mena's request— when she was still alive. I thought you knew."

"No, I didn't."

"I'm sorry, I've let you down in that regard. She may be the most important star in our future. She lives in the Gipar now, studies with the *kadishtu* girls and prays with her cobra companion, Memet. She's—very special, very dear to me. I should have explained it to you, but I've been so wrapped up in other things, I simply forgot."

"You think there's cause for worry?"

"No, she's getting the best training one could expect. She'll do fine without me." She turned to her friend. "Now, let's try to end on a happy note without all this morose guessing. How about it?"

Heganna clung to her foul mood. "Oh, Kikki, I shall miss you so."

"I'll be swinging through Nippur often enough. You'll probably soon tire of my visits."

"Never! You know this will always be your home. Any time of day or night. And if I hear you dropped in without a visit, I'll make you sleep in Sebbu's shop with all his clay figures glowering at you in the moonlight."

"Oh, please, anything but that," Kinar mocked.

Hours later, while walking east toward Nin, she realized with a mild shock that she had thought of nothing and no one but Uruna since leaving.

Chapter 19

Gar Stews

Arn Gar set down his hammer and untied the leather apron from his waist. A half day's work lay ahead, but he was hungry, and a cold stewpot awaited him at home. He needed its fortification to finish the day.

He was tired of cold or half-cooked meals. Tired of nights spent over a game board with grouchy old men. He was off balance. Needed the company of a good woman to set him right.

As he started across the road, he heard a shout from the other end. A woman bearing a heavy basket made a feeble wave with one hand. Gar knew that basket, even from a distance. Where was Uruna? What in tarnation was going on?

The woman stopped in the road and set the basket on the ground, then arched her back and massaged her neck while she waited for his approach. She was a drudge, by the look of her. All elbows and knees on a boney frame. Hard lines around the mouth and eyes told of a life of toil.

"What are you doing with Memet?" he said without offering a welcome.

"Brung him as I was told."

"Did Uruna send you? Because we've no place—"

"First Minister's orders, I reckon. Word come down from on high, like always."

"Pestiful grub worms! Very well, fetch him over to the house."

"I done my fetchin' for the day, thank you."

Gar calmed himself before picking up the basket. He'd learned a few cobra fundamentals during Memet's previous visit.

"Why didn't Uruna bring him herself?"

The woman shrugged her narrow shoulders. "Went off with that fine lady friend of hers, I was told. Journeying about the countryside a spell, or some such. Got no place for the snake in the Gipar. Some says he been out to Nord Town before, other'n says fetch him to it anyway. This here *is* Na Purna, ennit?"

"Yawp. I got a meal ready for the coals if you care to."

"Thanks, but I got to get back quick or catch me a load of extra work."

"You got water?"

The woman shook her apron pocket, gave Gar a broad wink. "All's I need's right here."

"Who should I say brung—brought him if I'm asked."

"Tula. Tula-sin, but en nobody gonna ask. You keep good care that cobra, if you know how. Little missy fancies it."

Instead of heading directly for his own house, Gar angled off toward the hunter compound. He hoped he might find Ashur at home, or maybe Kumir, as they knew more about the snake's needs than anyone else. Or maybe even Kumir's woman—that dark-haired girl with the cow eyes. She might have a meal on the fire right now, or at least something close to a boil.

Ashes and feathers! He was town headman. A chief of his rank ought to have his own woman by now.

Chapter 20

Sent to Trades

Tula-sin dragged Uruna by the hand as she stormed across the Aniginna concourse at a hurried pace.

"I don't care what the Hanza woman promised!" she spat at the girl. "Street of Trades is where I was told to take you, and that's where you'll go."

"Let go of my hand!" Uruna shouted.

"So's you can run off and get me shown to the gate? Not today."

"I'll go with you, I promise. It's just hard this way. My arm's sore."

"More'n that's to be sore when you're put to chores as is proper."

"But what became of Kinar?"

"Your friend is gone to the countryside. Got her hands full with that lot, I can tell you. There's none left in that dandy house of hers but a watchman."

Uruna yanked her hand free and rubbed her arm without breaking stride. Tula had fetched her from her room before she could set out for temple. She had recognized the woman as a cleaning drudge from one of her daily forays through Serpenthood.

Tula grabbed for her hand again, but Uruna dodged away.

"Stop it!" Uruna cried. "You're being mean!"

"There's crowds once we get outside the gate. I can't go losing you, now."

"Good heavens, I'm nine years old. I walk those streets every day to temple as I have for three years without your help."

"Well, that'll come to a stop once you're in Trades. You'll not have time for your temple fancy, working as the rest of us do."

The sentry at the gate saluted with a smile for Uruna, then sobered at the sight of her tote. Her usual gift, a cake from the Gipar cookery, was the highlight of his morning.

"Where you off to today, Uruna?" he asked, casting a wary eye at Tula.

Uruna slowed with an apology ready, but Tula grabbed her arm again and hauled her into the street before she could answer. The sentry called after them but Tula quickly fled into the street throng with her charge.

Street of Trades was not so much a street as a broad expanse of hardpan packed with tents and benches where craftsmen fashioned wares for sale elsewhere. Uruna saw wood carvers and potters, a flower vendor selecting stems for bouquets, a tailor sewing skirts with flying fingers. Crude huts set against the city's south wall sheltered the more perishable goods. An old woman in a straw hat sat on a blanket, weaving reed baskets.

Toward the west end, a long building housed the smithy and rooftop rooms, the only residences in the compound. The tradespeople themselves lived elsewhere in the city. Tula brought Uruna to a halt before a wiry fellow in leather apron wielding a hammer. He looked up at their approach.

"Don't sell nothing here. You'll have to buy from a market vendor, same as other folk."

Tula straightened to make herself appear taller. "This here's the temple girl needing a room. You spoke to Nin—"

"Only got the stall out back with the asses."

"She said you offered a room."

"Don't care what she says, I got but the one place left. Others are spoken for. Last empty one went last night."

"But she gave money ahead for it."

"Don't know about that."

Uruna tugged Tula's sleeve to whisper her feelings.

"He was told to send you away."

"What?"

"By that man over there."

Uruna tipped her head toward a burly lout leaning against a pillar, paring his nails. The fellow returned Tula's glance with a brash, gap-toothed grin.

Tula's brow wrinkled in a perplexed frown. Uruna gave the woman's hand a reassuring pat.

"It's all right, I'll do fine in the stable."

"But what'll I tell the matron?"

Never a thought for Uruna's comfort. A paid minion fretting over shekels.

"Do as you wish," Uruna said. "If I were you, I'd go on about my day and forget the whole thing."

"I could tell her we found better over to the Way of Good Hope."

"Then she'll ask where you found the extra money."

"I bargained for it."

"Just tell her true. We found lodging in Trades, as you were told. She doesn't care what kind, Tula. She's done with it."

"S'pose you're right. Where'd a waif like you get so smart?"

"On the road, mixing with thieves and brigands."

"Ah, that makes sense. I knew you wasn't a real princess. I'll be off now."

"Thank you for all your hard work at Serpenthood. I'll remember you when I'm queen."

Tula barked a rude laugh and stalked away, calling over her shoulder: "Stable's a fine fit for the likes of you."

The tack room, as it turned out, was much better suited for living than the rooftop. The smith had to keep the forge stoked day and night, meaning its fumes wafted upward, directly toward sleepers aloft. A wall between the smithy and the stable prevented the same from reaching the animals, and likewise the little queen-to-be. There was ample fresh hay for a good straw bed. She hung her tote and spare shirt on an empty harness peg. The potter gave her a mended wash basin from his seconds pile.

Uruna considered her lot. The Lukur could contrive no privation worse than any she had endured on the Zab road. Her daily needs were simple, her stay in quarters brief. She was free to roam the city in search of less fortunate souls.

But once more she was left alone and lacking warm human contact. It wasn't Tula's fault, but it seemed no one in temple authority cared. She didn't belong to any of them, really. It would be nice to have a warm bed and her own room again, but what would be better was a lady like Mena or Gudamma to snuggle up with at the end of the day and tell her a story before dropping off to sleep.

However nice that might be, the gods had put her where she did belong. The purpose to which she was born required only the suffering. In Street of Trades she would find work aplenty.

Chapter 21

Trader's Secret

Gar could not believe the disorganized confusion that marked his dealings with temple people. First, the guard at Aniginna Gate couldn't tell him where Uruna could be found, and when he pushed his way inside and asked a temple lady on her rounds, she needed several reminders before she realized who he was talking about. It seemed nobody there knew what had become of her or how long ago she had left—if indeed she was gone.

That was before the tall vision in white spoke to him.

"She went to Trades last I heard. You're the smith she talked about, aren't you?"

Gar could scarcely pull his wits together. The woman before him had the rounded Sumerian head and hooked nose, but a mouth that smiled easily and small ears tucked neatly behind raven hair. Every feature about her sang a lovely tune.

"Um, I suppose so," he stammered. "Been a while. How'd you…?"

The woman's eyes sparkled with mischief. "I guess you don't remember. I'm Milsah, *nigenna* sheaf counter. I saw you here in the market square. You were working the forge at the Solstice festival."

"You saw me?"

She flushed red. "What I mean is, I was at the pavilion in the square when you showed the crowd how you make a plowshare. I watched you shape it with a dozen blows. Really masterful work. We spoke for a bit, but the crowd was thick and you had other questions to answer."

Gar barely heard her words. The sound of her voice slid past his ears like a smooth river current. A lock of black hair had fallen loose and draped the side of her face, an attractive frame for snapping black eyes that gleamed with sharp intelligence. He felt if he gazed at her too long he might fall into those eyes…

"Kind of you to say so," he blurted, and abruptly regretted his stilted manner. She was being gracious, and all he could think about was the shape of her mouth, the small tuck in her chin, the rise and fall of her bosom…

"If you would like," she said, "I can take you there."

"Take me? Where do you mean?"

"Trades, Street of Trades, you know, where they took the girl. There's a smithy down there, fellow told me about you. That is, I mean, I told him about seeing you at fest—um, festival, because he works the forge too. But he's quite a bit smaller and nowhere near as strong. He might know where to look. Come, I'll take you."

"Take me where?"

"To find the girl."

"Oh, yes, Uruna. Trades, yes, I know where it is."

Her face clouded. "Of course, I should have known."

What was he doing? This vision of loveliness was offering to walk with him, talk to him.

Climb out of your stupor, man.

"But I often lose my way in the city," he managed. "If you're not too busy…"

She beamed up at him. "It would be my pleasure."

With a sudden gesture she reached for his arm. At the instant of contact he felt a thrill like none he had experienced before, a rapturous joy he hoped might never leave him.

What was happening to him?

She kept her arm looped through his all the way through the city. He imagined how they must appear to others, just another happy couple out for a daily jaunt.

As they came upon Trades, he realized he had no recollection of their path through the city. Milsah completely filled his senses. Her light chatter was a delight to his ears. Her graceful walk, her facial expression, the angle of her head as she laughed and talked and looked about, filled him with wonder. Her easy, long-legged gait matched his own, felt natural. And now that they had reached their destination, he was disappointed that their journey together must end.

A lout picking his nails in the shade of the smith's awning made a rude noise in answer to Milsah's inquiry.

"Girl beds down with the asses out back—when she gets back from whatever she's up to. Don't see her much."

Milsah frowned. "She doesn't have a room in the loft?"

"Them's for paying folk. No, she got herself a little space apart from the animals. Keeps it tidy, don't make no bother. I give it to her, you know. Had no other up top. No rent from the temple, so that's her lot."

Milsah must have sensed Gar's growing disgust with the man, for she laid a restraining hand on his shoulder while she continued to address the layabout. "May we see her quarters?"

"Quarters? Hah! Sure, help yourself but don't step in no manure."

Gar was still seething when they came upon the stall set aside for Uruna's bed. A tattered blanket was folded neatly upon a milking stool. She had appropriated two harness pegs of the five nailed to the back wall. A cook pot sat in one corner and a privy pot in the other. If she had a drinking mug she must have taken it with her.

Gar gnashed his teeth and kicked a loose pile of straw. "She's a queen!" he roared. "Someone lied. Said she went abroad with a priestess, when all along she was kept in this—this donkey barn! Damn their prissy Lukur hides! Oop—sorry, I don't mean you."

Milsah bent and straightened a corner of the sad little bed cover. "You might as well, Gar, for I'm one of them—but not for long. This is just another example of their growing disregard for commoners. I see it almost daily. The top few have made a sham of temple service. A stable corner is not how we care for the needy."

Gar took a long, deep breath to calm himself and Milsah gave him a startled look. She had probably never experienced the displacement of so much space by one man. But he was struck more by Milsah's words.

"You say not for long. Are you planning to leave the temple?"

"I gave notice to Niccaba last week. I'll continue to assist my friends through Spring seed counts, then—well, I don't know what I'll do."

Marry me and live a Nord life, he wanted to say. Instead, he followed Milsah back into the Street.

"There's but one person can make this right," he said, as they trudged back to the Aniginna. "And I won't find her at temple."

Milsah squinted up at him, her keen mind already following his. "She won't give audience to a Nord, much less heed his advice. That much we know for certain at temple."

Gar plodded ahead for a few paces. "She hasn't met this Nord."

He continued at a steady pace all the way back to Aniginna Gate, his eyes straight ahead, his jaw set granite hard. It was an expression Milsah would see often and grow to admire in years to come.

Nearly as much as she would love the man himself.

"Temple woman come looking for you while you was gone."

The nail-picker nodded at Uruna to lend importance to his news. He usually had nothing to say to her when she returned from a day of constant activity. In all likelihood, pitifully little occurred in his drab life.

Uruna didn't ask the name of her visitor because she didn't care. Her mind and soul were still wrapped up in the tragic scene she had left moments ago—an old man left to die alone, abandoned by his own family and the temple as well.

After nearly a year amongst the poor, her opinion of temple caretakers had diminished greatly. In that short time she had accumulated a score of affronts committed by the so-called holy order of Lukur. Before she'd left, there had been talk of cutbacks in welfare services—fewer beds for the infirmary, an oven shut down in the communal bakery, cancelled granary audits—while at the same time wharf merchants regaled pub patrons with tales of the "easy money" flowing from Ekur.

Picker, as she had dubbed her layabout landlord, still brimmed with the import of his day.

"Lady brung that big Nord with her. The red-haired one, big as a barn."

Gar? Could she have missed a visit by Gar? What was he doing away from his forge? What had brought him to Trades?

She almost asked Picker, but remembered doing so would encourage his mean temperament. He would attempt to nettle her with little privations—thefts from her meager trove of personal belongings, a donkey turd left in her stall, the hay swept out to leave bare boards for her bed. He was a miserable excuse for a human being, almost deserving pity, but her life would run more smoothly if she ignored him.

"They like to had a fit, coming out of your place. Didn't approve of it, you could say. Now, I seen worse over to Old Town—"

The man rattled on, but Uruna left for the stable, her thoughts elsewhere as she tried to imagine what could possibly cause Gar and a temple matron to inspect her shabby quarters. When nothing came to mind, she realized she was in desperate need of food, and so set about putting a fire under her cook pot. She boiled a cabbage given to her by one of the old man's relatives and ate it with a dried-out hunk of flatbread bequeathed by a kind-hearted street vendor.

She was licking her fingers clean when the Picker appeared at the stall's end.

"Woman here for you. Not the same as before."

Uruna grabbed her shawl and tote and went out front. The woman was a stranger to her and had a man with her—a man of means, by his fine raiment and trimmed beard.

They stood apart, he sweeping his eyes over the trade clutter with his mouth drawn down at the corners in disapproval. He glanced over at Uruna and rolled his eyes.

"But she's just a girl," he whined to the woman.

"You heard Rimi," she replied. "Go ahead, tell her."

The man cocked his head and sniffed. "Heard about you from my manservant," he said. "Has family in Na Purna. Seems to be a problem there with a cobra."

Uruna's pulse quickened. Memet was nearby! She felt him signaling to her. But from Na Purna?

"What sort of problem?" she asked, already getting a gist of the answer.

"Where to put him. Fellow says it's not working, whatever that means."

At that point the woman shifted her shoulder and unslung a basket and gently lowered it to the ground.

Memet's basket.

"How did you find him?" she asked.

"Brought to us this very morning by a fellow called himself Ashur. Said the cobra's restless, said you'd know what to do with him. We spent the day tracking you down. Everyone at temple seems to think you're off in the provinces, but Rimi said no, the traders know differently. Chased you all over the city, healing this and visiting that household. Seemed to just miss you at every stop. Now that we've found you, I can go home to my family."

The whole time the man was chattering, Uruna was getting signs of restless urges from Memet. She had to get him out of the square before something drastic happened.

She hauled the basket to her own shoulder and offered a smile. "I thank you, sir, for your kind trouble. He'll be fine now."

"Where you going to put him?" the woman asked. "Can't have a cobra loose in the city, for pity's sake."

Uruna gave her what she hoped was a reassuring smile.

"All taken care of."

"Then you'd be taking him to the snake lady in Tent Town?"

"Um, that's the idea." She probed, got a name, decided to ask anyway. "What is she called again?"

"Sittuma. Now, I know it's late, but you'd best get him outside the gate before last call."

"Thanks, I will. Inanna with you."

When they were gone, she went quickly to her stall and popped the lid. Memet rushed into her arms and she wept tears on his head. They spent several moments in silent reunion before he revealed his purpose.

Change comes soon. New faces, an end to your abuse, a new journey, hard work. Prophecy languishes. Resume with vigor.

They spent the night together, with the little jenny in the next stall completely unaware of her deadly neighbor. In the morning,

Uruna wasted no time with pleas for healing, but went straight for Uruk Gate.

Sittuma lived in the tent warren abutting Nippur's outer wall. Uruna had been there the previous day calling on a sick woman, hours before the abandoned elder. Ailments were common among the destitute. Would that pose any risk to Memet?

Uruna wound her way through the maze of tents, remarking to herself that few of the occupants lived as well as she in her soft corner of straw. In a strange twist of fate, she would now place her welfare in the hands of one of them.

She paused before a reed lean-to and rapped on the siding. The fenced garden out back enjoyed a mimosa's shade.

I will come visit soon, she promised the cobra.

A woman appeared at the open doorway and pointed at the basket. "That him? Sittuma said you was coming. She's back this way."

Chapter 22

Healing and Birth

Gar did gain Heganna's ear, and Heganna gained Niccaba's after hearing his tale. Still, winter came and passed without further recourse by the temple elite. None would say outright that Lubna herself had designated the orphan as unfit, but Uruna would have found no fault had she known anything about it. She was approaching age eleven, and already in her bones she felt the restless stirrings of womanhood. The change had come on with a rush, as if her body was eager to catch up with her mind's insatiable reach.

She took her leave of the Trades compound and marched quickly up the street, bearing her pain and needing to distance herself from the small crowd gathered to witness the miracle in her wake. She would drown in their cloying gratitude if she stayed another moment. It was always thus.

During the last six months, her role as pot-scrubber had given way to a more elevated renown among Nippur's common folk. To them she was established as both seer and healer, yet news of her new status had failed to reach the lofty realm of temple discourse, where she remained all but forgotten.

Her humble stall abode had proven adequate for her needs, but came far short of the enclosed dwellings she visited, where family and neighbors shared lives. Nights alone with an animal or two were not much different from her years on the Zab road, but as she watched others enjoy human company, she feared her turn might never come. Her brief taste of Gudamma's loving warmth was a memory fast fading beneath a ponderous accumulation of mental learning and physical toil.

The temple life she longed for continued to lie just beyond her reach. The ladies there busied themselves with duty and service, as rightly they should, but her attempts to find her own place in that life always met stone-walled defeat. She was too young, an outlier without proper lineage. As far as the Lukur were concerned, she had found her lot among the trading class and ought to be content with it. Indeed, she had found another way to serve—or rather it had found her, for certainly no will of her own was involved. She reasoned that her resulting personal strife was godly preparation for life's later burdens. Besides, the work did have its rewards.

She had left the stable hand's son staring after her, his ruined fingers restored, his parents blubbering gratitude to any god who might listen. As for her own hand, a withered claw she hid in the folds of her cloak, she could only trust that the same god who had healed the boy would remove her affliction in time to scrub pots in the Gipar scullery.

Two women accosted her at the first street crossing.

"You're the one, you are!" said the taller of the pair.

"I mustn't be late at temple," Uruna said, trying to deflect the attention that now followed her nearly everywhere in the city warrens.

"You had time for that scoundrel tends the cattle."

Her companion pointed away down the cross street. "There's a woman in labor just down there. Been in trouble since early last night. Even got the midwife wringing her hands."

Two lives at risk. Uruna could not refuse. "Show me where."

Family men and women ringed a small room. Uruna found the air stifling and foul with the scent of blood. The moment she stepped through the doorway, the babe's voice rang in her head. Words she could not understand nevertheless painted a clear enough picture: This child did not want to be born.

The mother lay spraddled on a dining table, a bloody straw mat spread beneath her buttocks, her head cradled in the lap of another woman.

The sister.

As she considered that woman, she got a further sensation there of great strength and abiding love. Then a name: Ahea.

An older woman squatted at the mother's feet, her face rimed with sweat, grim concern pinching a peasant drudge's features.

Midwife—Dara.

Uruna stepped to the exhausted mother's side and took her hand.

"Clear the room, please," she said to no one in particular.

The sister responded with a torn look.

"Except Ahea and Dara. You are both needed."

By now she was accustomed to astonished looks when she spoke names before they were given. Her youth was forgotten, as the authority in her voice convinced adults twice and thrice her age to obey.

As the last relative departed, Ahea heaved a great sigh and shifted her weight, releasing the tension Uruna felt emanating from her small body.

"The mother's name, please," she asked, noting how odd it was that she hadn't heard it like the others.

"Ningikuda," the sister replied. "We call her Ninki."

Uruna felt the need for two points of contact with the mother.

With her left thigh pressing Ninki's side, she rested her right hand on the woman's brow and immediately felt a resistance. Whether it came from child or mother she could not tell, so she probed further.

Who art thou?

The answer came forth without hesitation: *I am called Bau Antum.*

A girl's name…but not a girl's voice. A woman?

Uruna summoned the babe. *Thou must come forth. Thy mother awaits.*

No! She is still mine!

So! Not the babe's voice, but this Bau Antum. And from where? Beyond the grave? A spirit unwilling to relinquish her mortal past? Uruna had never experienced such mystery before. What must she do?

As if in answer, a shadow passed over her thoughts, immense and brooding, as another took command. Uruna felt part of herself back away in homage to a greater force, an all-powerful presence, yet all-loving.

How could this be happening?

At once the babe asserted herself upon Uruna's awareness, a soul now ripe with life and eager for birth, fully formed, focused, as she cast her love upon her intended new parent.

Not the mother, but the sister!

Before Uruna could utter her first question, the midwife stirred. "She comes now! Push, Ninki, push!"

Uruna drifted, her mind and spirit now disconnected from the birthing process. When the child emerged, the midwife caught her up by her tiny feet. The infant emitted a soft cry, but Uruna's attention was jerked away as a much louder cry rang through the room.

Not Ninki, the mother who had closed her eyes and succumbed

to utter exhaustion. Behind and above her, Ahea bent forward, her shoulders shaking with sobs of relief.

A voice spoke in Uruna's head: *To this one shalt the babe cleave in sickness and in health, even as they unite in Heaven. Selah.*

Uruna went to the door and bade the family return to Ninki's bedside. As the room filled with joyous wonder, she started to slip away when a man caught her arm and pressed a clay coin in her hand.

"I am Ninki's husband. Inanna's blessing on you, little queen, for your magic and your love."

She wanted to tell the man it was not she who had wrought the miracle, but he hastened back to his wife before she could speak.

The moment Uruna stepped into the street, she was met by a tall, dark-skinned man.

"I heard," he said. "Once again you bring a miracle to the wretched. I am Jebbut, if you recall."

"Yes, Lady Heganna's houseman. You look well."

"Thank you, but if you would, missy, please accompany me to Hanza House directly."

"I'm sorry, but I have chores."

"Madam herself requests your presence. I'd receive a tongue-lashing if I returned without you."

Heganna? The richest woman in all Sumer had asked for her? After complete silence for two years?

"Please give madam my respects, but I must refuse."

As she moved away down the dusty street, Uruna felt a strange new energy, and quickened her step for the journey to temple. It was only as she approached Aniginna gate that she understood the reason.

Her hand, the recipient of the stable boy's pain, and which she had placed on Ninki's brow without realizing its transformation, was whole again.

Jebbut splayed his hands in helpless apology as a woman emerged from the shadows between the birthing house and its neighbor. Her hooded cloak was tattered and she wore sandals borrowed from a house servant. She had drawn the folds of her cowl forward to hide her face, but when she spoke she could not disguise her high-born nature.

"You might have been a bit more insistent."

"She's strong of will and devoted to such duty as she's been given."

"So I've seen for myself. The rumors are true. First the stable boy, now the childbirth. She's a walking miracle! I should have stopped this foolery when the Nord first told me."

"She has done so much for the street folk, madam. I doubt it would be so if the temple ladies had not sent her down here."

"Augh! They squander her talents while they fairly parade their bigotry about the halls."

A second woman stirred at her side, similarly garbed as a worker but moving with grace in a street where most women her age were bent from years of toil.

"I can catch up with her," Kinar offered. "There's still time."

"No, we can't create a scene. But I will not have this failure repeated, do you hear me? Both of you."

A silent nod from Jebbut.

"Yes, of course," said Kinar.

"Then get busy and at least get that girl out of scrubs!"

"I'll see what I can do," Kinar said. "It may take some persuading before—"

"Tomorrow won't be soon enough! You have the power now, use it."

"Of course. Tonight."

A softer tone from Heganna. "Oh, my dear, they have me

railing at my best friend. Forgive me."

"That won't be necessary. I agree most emphatically. But this isn't just about the girl, is it?"

A hesitation before the Hanza matron answered. "No, much more is at stake."

She cast her eyes at the starry sky overhead, then hooked her arm through Jebbut's proffered elbow.

It's everything, she thought to herself, before the three of them struck off up Trades' narrow lane for home.

Chapter 23

Party Servant

The woman who came for Uruna the day after the childbirth in Trades was a Lukur she had never met before. Her showing up among the trades class took Uruna by surprise, but the events that followed nearly rattled her silly.

She caught a glimpse of what might be in store the moment she was ushered through the wide gate to Hanza House. She was further amazed by the houseman as he met her at the door.

"Madam cannot see you right away," said Jebbut. "Let's get you into something more fitting for the occasion."

Uruna had no idea what sort of occasion he referred to, but she was given no time to worry, for a different woman immediately hustled her off to a changing room.

The rest of the day passed without further such jolts until—as she was leaving the kitchen with her tea tray—she caught sight of Kinar at the far end of the house.

But hadn't Kinar moved out last year to the provinces? To spend years abroad? What was she doing back in Nippur so soon?

Uruna stood in place and stared in disbelief at the woman she considered her best friend. Before she could gather her senses,

Kinar disappeared into another distant room without noticing her.

The Hanza matron herself finally appeared in midafternoon, stern of visage and seemingly preoccupied with matters of great importance. Uruna kept to the kitchen, unsure what was expected of her in such grand surroundings. At length, Heganna called her out into the hallway. When Uruna hesitated, Heganna ducked her head back around the doorway.

"Where is that girl? Oh, there you are," she said. "Finding everything you need?"

"Yes, madam."

"I hope—"

Heganna stopped herself in midsentence and stared.

"But you're so..." She began, then turned and retreated back down the hall.

Uruna had no idea what she might have done wrong. Surely she must wait by the serving table for her punishment and hope she hadn't committed too grave an offense. She really liked it there, and felt a growing excitement, despite her misgivings about proper behavior in august company.

After lingering for what she considered to be an appropriate length of time, she figured her penalty would be meted out later.

Toward evening, a housekeeper appeared with flints and instructed her to go around the house lighting oil lamps. As the first guests arrived, Jebbut ducked through the door and paused to give last-minute instructions to the kitchen help. He opened his mouth to speak, stared at Uruna for several moments, then swallowed hard and cleared his throat.

"Um, are we all ready?" he said to the crew.

Everyone nodded and waited for his signal to start. Jebbut simply nodded back and sped away.

A serving girl approached Uruna with a frown. "You are quite a distraction, you know," she said, and proffered a black ribbon.

"Best tie back your hair and keep your eyes to the floor. These folk don't expect pretty amongst the help."

Uruna didn't know what to make of that until she remembered having made a similar impression years ago on her first meeting with the old queen. Was everyone here so taken with appearances?

No matter, she thought as she pulled her hair tight against her skull and bound it with the ribbon. She hoped she might escape further notice as the evening wore on.

Kinar looked about as more than one hundred persons of privilege filled sprawling Hanza House, gathering in comfortable groups to mix social obligation with abundant food and drink. Heganna had found an escort for her, a widowed planter of middle age draped in finery and possessed of impeccable manners, but not a trace of wit.

She was herself dressed in a full-length white gown with gold and lapis adorning her neck and arms. Several ladies had remarked on her high beauty, and her mood had risen to match their esteem. It was always pleasing to be admired, but she hoped tonight she might also enjoy a matching regard for her intellect.

She had returned two days ago from a no-name plantation below Adab, ending her "exile" as she put it to any who would listen. Her presence tonight had earned a frown from Lubna Seddua, until it became clear to the woman that Kinar was Heganna's house guest. On that score, none dared challenge the greatest landholder between the two rivers, least of all a temple bureaucrat who consistently lost to her in court disputes.

Kinar half-listened to her escort's banter with two equally vapid merchants, more interested to watch Uruna balance a loaded tea tray on her way through the crowd.

The girl gave little thought for hand or foot. Perfect grace allowed her eye to browse the room without a faulty step. A serving minion free to roam as she wished, she observed and chose, reconsidered, and chose again. Kinar could almost hear Uruna's thoughts as she approached a clutch of ladies in conversation.

There's a likely group, and needing drink.

Uruna glided to the elbow of the senior woman and waited with her tray, a quiet presence needing not to speak, a piece of backdrop, nothing more. Uruna had learned to mask her natural beauty with lowered gaze, shapeless smock, and hair pulled back in a severe bun. She bided her time, hovering nearby to heed the repartee.

The luminous gray eyes took it all in, followed each gesture, noted the slightest facial tic, while the ears listened, learned, absorbed each nuance of intonation. A human sponge, she would soak up thoughts spoken and implied. She would distinguish heartfelt affection from mere flattery, contrast mild deceit with subtle misdirection, catch an adroit deflection, a condescension, an accommodation, an outrageous lie. Her mouth might smirk at a joke well told, then quickly lapse into sobriety lest she be noticed. She would stash away in her prodigious mental storehouse every grain of value, would hold it there undiminished by time, for consumption in the winter of her purpose.

Kinar had already seen the process at work, had watched it unfold and had even experienced the outcome for herself. The prospect of that daunting capacity one day maturing in a woman of power inspired a measure of awe approaching reverence—and no little terror to lesser souls steeped in fear. The force being molded on tonight's occasion, accumulating, aggregating, weighing, gleaning significance from the mundane, had no equal now or in any lore told.

Lady Calla Sin appeared before Kinar just then, interrupting with her usual company of daughter and two matrons from Kissura. Calla operated a Sedduan stronghold midway between Nippur and Uruk, but seldom ventured outside Nippur's gates.

Several of her lands abutted Kinar's own, and her careless incursions had caused frequent boundary disputes. Kinar had won the lion's share of those contests largely through Heganna's subtle intercession.

Calla's daughter, Delondra, was twelve and showing signs of her mother's full figure. A plum ripe for temple picking, had she a brain to go with the body.

"How good to see you again," Calla gushed. "We've missed you at temple."

A thinly veiled reminder of her singular victory at Kinar's expense. Having squeezed Kinar out of Heganna's protective orbit, Calla esteemed herself to be firmly aligned with Lubna's power clique. She hadn't yet learned of last night's bout in this very room, an ad hoc Council meeting which tomorrow would reverse the tide set against Kinar.

"Thank you, Calla." She replied, and turned to the girl. "My, Delondra, how you've grown. That's a lovely gown."

"And yours," the girl rejoined with a bright smile. "Did you make it yourself? It must be difficult to find a good dressmaker in the provinces."

Kinar ignored the girl's maladroit slight. "It's one Heganna kept for me in my room here while I was gone. No use for pretty in road and field, as I'm sure you can attest. How are your verses coming along?"

Delondra's face clouded. The greatest hurdle in her path to priestesshood was a poor memory. Until she could recite the passages without prompting, the happy event would be held back. The girl's slow wit was a sore spot with Calla, and she rose quickly to her daughter's defense.

"She can recite the first and second Alla Manna without help. We'll have the rest down in plenty of time for Springfest."

"To be sure."

Good gods! Spring was half a year away. Uruna had mastered the entire song at one sitting when little more than a tot. Some at Council might one day see an advantage to putting a fool such as Delondra Seddua in charge of temple affairs. If such a disaster were to be averted, Uruna's ascent must be assured, and with all haste.

The younger of the two matrons in Calla's company felt obliged to heap scorn on Kinar's earlier backing for Uruna. "Looks like your little street waif will have to miss out. Saw her around here somewhere tonight, serving tea, of all things."

Calla chimed agreement. "What else can the poor child do? I mean, she's without kin, has no line, and you've certainly no family to give her."

Kinar's face grew hot. Her loss had happened nearly a decade ago, a painful private matter needing no reminders. This bumpkin's manners had failed to improve with elevated rank. None would blame Kinar for slapping the woman's face. In fact, now might be just the time to give the woman a lesson.

She felt a tug on her sleeve. Uruna stood at her side, the empty tea tray tucked under one arm, a sense of urgency about her.

"Madam, pardon, but Lady Heganna wishes to speak with you."

Kinar shook off her urge for battle and stared down at the young girl. "Really? Now?"

"Yes'm."

"Where is she?"

"The cooking chamber."

"Heavens, what is she doing there? Oh, nevermind, thank you."

She excused herself from Calla's smirking clutch and set off for the hallway, Uruna out front.

"I can find my way quite well, Uruna," she said.

The girl spoke not a word, but bulled ahead past clusters of guests, down the hallway, and through the cookery doorway. She stopped before the baking table and set her tray on the planks, then spun around with both hands on her hips and a stern frown.

"That woman!" she said.

Kinar stopped short. "You mean Heganna? I don't see her here."

"No, I'm talking about the snide one from Kissura. She behaved very badly. I'm surprised you stayed polite as long as you did."

"Just a minute. Where's Heganna?"

Uruna waved an arm. "I don't know, probably out in the garden talking to her poppies in the moonlight."

"She didn't call for me."

"I think that's pretty obvious."

"You cooked this up?"

"It was plain madam was goading you to a brawl. I could see no other way."

Kinar grabbed a nearby chair and quickly sat to consider the implications. Uruna had followed her nose for trouble and lurked nearby without discovery. Having overheard Calla Sin's wickedness at work, she'd concocted a scheme of her own, the same way a clever ally might—a perceptive adult ally at that. And she had rescued Kinar before the confrontation got ugly enough to spoil Kinar's homecoming.

You're barely ten years old! she wanted to scream at the girl. *How can you be so exasperatingly clever? Where did you acquire such artful subterfuge? You dissembled before the liar of all liars, you naughty little wonder!*

She said none of this, of course, but drew Uruna close and kissed the girl's forehead. Such profound devotion, such crafty invention, certainly deserved no rebuke. Uruna understood her place among adults and played the obedient servant to perfection. Kinar was almost persuaded to ask the girl's advice for her next move. Instead, she merely brushed a loose strand of hair from Uruna's face.

"Thank you, madam," she said.

A grin. "My pleasure—madam."

"We must forgive Calla Sin, of course."

"She can't help who she is. I think she's very fearful."

"M-mm, insightful of you. Her failures in life would shake most women to their roots."

"But we cannot trust her in the matter."

"No, that would be foolish. Now listen to me, Uruna." Kinar drew her astounding collaborator to her lap. "To an ordinary serving girl I would say at this point you've done well enough, now run along home and play with your friends. But to you, Uruna, I say: Fill up your tea tray again, and go back out there and glean more ripe kernels of wisdom. For that is the purpose for which you are fit. *Most* fit, indeed."

Uruna sobered and got to her feet. She crossed her ankles in an awkward pose and picked at her skirt and twisted her torso. "I think I love you most, Kikki. May I still call you Kikki?"

"Please do, always. After tonight's episode, I'll trust you to know when it's appropriate."

Uruna nodded that she understood. "Then we'd better not let Calla Sin catch us getting cozy."

Kinar smiled. "I've something to tell you." She waited for Uruna to retrieve her tray. "I had a discussion with Heganna earlier tonight. I'm coming back. She has plans for me at temple again."

"That's wonderful news! But what will Lubna have to say about it?"

So, the girl knew the schemer of all schemers for the ambitious demagogue she was—and why not? Uruna was fast becoming a formidable force in her own right. Kinar made a mental note to recall this night in years to come.

"Lubna might talk a good streak," she replied, "but that'll be the extent of it. She can rant all she wants, but in the end, Heganna has the upper hand with Council. A quiet hand, but unshakable now."

Uruna squinted. "One day I hope you'll be able to tell me the secret."

"Which secret is that?"

"How she does it."

"And why should I tell you, young lady?"

"Because I will need her wisdom and your loyalty when I am queen."

They left the cook room separately, Uruna with a fresh tea tray, Kinar in a daze as she rejoined her escort. She floundered through the rest of the evening, unable to stay with any conversation.

Queen!

Her mind rocked to and fro between fearful doubt and the thrilling conviction that Uruna's uncanny foresight was stubbornly intact. Soon enough, that perceptive declaration by Uruna-the-child would become fact for Uruna-the-woman. Kinar had realized it the instant the word was spoken.

But what the child did not know, and what Kinar could not bring herself to reveal to her so soon, was another truth as certain as the sunrise.

The road to that end would be painful and fraught with treachery. Death must be served before it was finished. The question was, whose?

Chapter 24

Garden Conspiracy

Contrary to Uruna's invented story, Heganna was not in her garden. But Niccaba was, for she valued its privacy as the opportune sanctuary for her purpose. While she waited for Lubna Seddua to break away from the crowd inside, she considered her options.

Temple Ekur could not go much longer without an Entu. Further delay would attract unwanted attention to political affairs best kept quiet But behind Lukur indecision lurked an opportunity. A narrow window of time that rewarded only the prudent. She must waste none of it.

When Lubna appeared at last, the two repaired to a clay bench at the garden's south wall. Bathed in brazier light diffused by fine-mesh netting, the two distant cousins spoke in hushed tones.

Niccaba laid out her plan, a concept as plain, simple, and direct as the woman herself. First, nominate for queen the most senior priestess available to serve. Sweep aside as ludicrous any objection that Council had previously rejected such a woman for valid reasons. Quash any suggestion she hadn't the wits to rule. Then set up a shadow throne from which to guide the old dear and act in her place when and where she could not function.

To that end Niccaba solicited and easily obtained Lubna Seddua's most willing consent.

"I have the perfect candidate," the latter replied almost before Niccaba finished. "Loyal, long-suffering, meek. She's ninety if she's a day."

"Who would that be?"

"My own grandmother."

"Great Goddess! You can't mean Semma Karkahn?"

"Couldn't be more serious."

"Forgive me, but the woman forgets to dress herself most days."

"An invention of gossip mongers. Semma belongs to a dying sect of ascetics who hold against adornment of any kind. It is true they convene in the raw for the sun-crossing rite, usually in the central park, but the affair is discreet and conducted in utmost reverence to their goddess."

"They shun dress in public?"

"Yes."

"As a religious conviction."

"Unconventional, but true."

"Not quite what I had in mind, Lubna. Can't we do better?"

"Before you reject her out of hand, there's more to sway opinion in her favor."

"Please tell me before you tarnish my faith in your good sense."

"Simple. She's a hoarder."

"And that benefits us in what manner?"

Lubna's eyes flashed with pleasure. "The manner of gold."

"Say more."

"She's kept it from every daughter spanning three generations. I discovered it quite by accident—after a little manipulation of my own. When she chokes her last, which won't be long, we'll parcel out the spoils."

"All well and good for Sedduan coffers, but where's the profit for Council? The Lukur must see some benefit to their interests. How will a secular legacy accrue to sacred assets? For that matter, what will induce the old biddy to part with her hoard in the first place?"

"As queen, she'll cede it over to Council by special edict, so sworn before her adjutant, you, and witnessed by her loyal chancellor, me. Any such inheritance withheld from the public good long past allowable time limits must be challenged."

"Your sisters and cousins will brook none of it."

"It will be a Council matter. They have no vote in chambers now, nor will they then."

"How might Semma reign? Is she able to convene a quorum? Contend with a crafty foe? Could she argue matters of policy?"

Lubna understood where that line of thought was going and had a ready answer.

"As every queen before her has done, she will consult others, determine the will of the majority, and abide by her Council's decisions, barring unforeseen extenuations. Nothing will change in that regard. Only the strength of the mind behind such direction as we put before her. It is a right and just thing we do to grant Semma her due."

"Nicely put, my dear," Niccaba said. "Although some will perceive a measure of subterfuge afoot and fight her nomination,"

"None present at Council will fail to see opportunity as well."

"And that keen sense of purpose is what drives the Lukur heart."

"I shall explain her nomination to her gently. We don't want the woman fainting dead of shock after so many years on the sidelines."

"Good point." Niccaba smiled to herself as her satisfaction grew. "Tell me as soon as you're ready. Meantime, I'll oil the skids with those in my clan. We mustn't dally."

"Agreed. Now, about the child. Did you see her hereabouts tonight?"

"Yes, properly serving tea when there's spirits aplenty. I'm not sure how she acquired Heganna's favor, but we'll make sure tonight is the end of it."

"Please do so. She's charmed enough Lukur heads already. And what about Kinar's presence? I thought she was to be kept occupied elsewhere."

Niccaba answered with an assuring nod. "Indeed she has been. Tonight's visitation being just that, she'll return to her provincial responsibilities."

Lubna got to her feet and straightened her skirt. "I must get back inside and go to work on the emissary from Uruk. Fellow calls himself a priest, considers himself a fit opponent."

"Enguda, you mean? What does the high priestess see in that cold fish?"

"I don't know, but he bears watching. Never underestimate that one. Lady Udea and her council seem to be infatuated with the rascal."

"Don't believe everything you hear from that quarter. The whole temple runs rife with rumor."

"And who else but Enguda do you think originates those stories?"

Lubna returned to the house and headed straight for the Uruk enclave.

Brave girl, Niccaba thought with a wry twist of her mouth. *Into the lion's den. Watch for claws. That lot hunt together.*

Chapter 25

Mentor Heganna

Uruna stayed the night at Hanza House in a cramped servant's room off the larder. Once a storeroom, the windowless space was stuffy and ill-suited for slumber. When a maid opened the door the next morning, Uruna felt she had only just gotten to sleep.

"Madam will see you in the garden," the maid announced.

"You mean Heganna?"

"Mind your manners, girl. She's 'Madam' to the help around here."

"What does she want with me?"

"Don't know and don't want to. Prob'ly a scolding for last night."

"What'd I do wrong?"

"Not for me to say. She'll tell you sure."

Uruna washed at the scullery and snatched a plum from the table. Cook caught her and chased her out with a playful sweep of broom.

She found Heganna bent over a stalk of hollyhocks as though examining each stem for pests. She looked up at Uruna's entry, her stern gaze filling Uruna with trepidation. Somehow, somewhere, she had caused offense to the richest woman in the land.

"Let's sit over here on this bench," said her employer.

Uruna had noticed the bench as a favorite spot for the great lady's guests to convene in private. As they sat, Heganna bent and plucked a fallen rose stem from the ground and twiddled it idly as she spoke.

"You are a remarkable young girl," she began.

But what? Uruna waited for the other foot to drop.

"If this bench could talk, it would speak volumes. Do you agree?"

Uruna faltered. Indeed, she had served several couples on this very spot last night, arriving in time to hear snatches of dialogue just before they were cut off. What they did not know, nor could suspect, was that she heard words spoken from the human heart as well.

"Uruna, you know and I know, there are demons at work in every corner of the world. The most ambitious Sumerians flock to my door because they seek power and they believe it reposes inside these walls. What does that tell you about them?"

"They seek it in the wrong place. Forgive me, I didn't mean to offend your home."

"No offense taken. You must always speak your mind with me, without fear."

Heganna plucked a thorn from the stem in her hand and flicked it away. Was there a symbolic meaning for Uruna in the gesture? She had much to learn about the enigma whose mere glance could command the empowered, but who showed only warmth toward her household servants.

Heganna continued, oblivious to her effect. "Now, you saw many a couple on this very bench as you served tea last night. I watched them from inside, but more important, I watched you watching them. You completely astound me. Your face and stature paint the picture of a child, but inside lurks the mind of a grown woman. I think you already know this much but are afraid to admit it. Or rather, too wise to say so."

Uruna could only stare at Heganna in dumbfounded wonder. When would the punishment rain down on her head? How much longer would Heganna torment her with such talk?

"I'm sorry if I—"

"Don't!" Heganna bellowed. "Never apologize for using your god-given talents." She grasped Uruna's hand and drew it to her bosom. "If you learn anything from me, Uruna dear, let it be this. The true sin is to deny your godly gifts. They are precious beyond measure! We're all endowed with some degree of divine favor, but yours must withstand mortal jealousy and hatred. There are venal spirits out in the world. Do you know what that word means?"

With her hand still clutched in the great lady's, Uruna struggled for an answer. "It means—it's like the black things that torment people."

"Yes, I imagine that's what you see with your incredible perception. Was that what you witnessed on this very bench?"

"I don't understand."

"Last night at the party. Lubna met with Niccaba. They talked, right here on this spot. I set Jebbut to watch the garden. From up top." Heganna released Uruna's hand to point upward at the roof.

Oh, gods! Did she mean Jebbut and household were spying on her?

In reassuring tones, Heganna went on. "It's all right, he and I have done so for years. But he dares not get within earshot. The rest of us mortals have to be close enough that we may be seen listening. You appear as a child, at the other edge of the garden, or on the terrace attending others—while you hear their thoughts, or whatever it is you do. What did they say, Uruna?"

Uruna discovered her hands fidgeting in her lap and stopped.

Heganna knew so much! Was she a serpent seer in disguise? But she was waiting for Uruna's answer.

"They spoke of the new queen."

"Ah, of course. Her choice is imminent. Did they utter her name?"

"A grandmother. Sam—Sem something."

Heganna leaned her back against the wall and closed her eyes.

"Semma Karkahn. A blithering old dear, sweet but enfeebled. Must be a hundred years old."

"She's ninety one years and four months. Her mother was Alittum of—"

"My gods, you can't be serious! But of course you are, what's the matter with me? You're a heaven-sent marvel! Anyway, I doubt the woman remembers so much herself. I mean, make her queen?"

"Do not be fooled. She makes herself look that way to foil plots by her own kin. She's packed away wealth, but trusts no one with it. She'd rather let it sit in a room—no, it's larger, I see a cave— she'd rather it were lost than her wasteful daughters find it."

"You're quite sure of this?"

"No more sure than any other story that unravels in my head."

"Have you ever been wrong?"

"Once or twice, but it was more like—" Uruna groped for words. "—like a story being told in my head, then fading away before I hear the end."

A tremor shook Heganna's head and her eyes bored into Uruna's with startling intensity. Uruna's hand was cramped once more in Heganna's feverish clutch. Heganna looked down and released her grip.

"Forgive me, dear! Oh, did I hurt you?"

"No, it's all right. But this passion that's overcome you. What does it mean?"

"Everything, Uruna. It means everything in the world."

The Hanza matron gathered herself with a shudder, as though shaking herself awake from a dream. "Now, let's go inside where it's cool and have tea. This matter bears the most careful attention."

"But that's all I heard. I don't know any more."

They climbed the step back into the house, Heganna lifting the hem of her embroidered linen dress.

"Don't you believe it, my dear," she said. "There's more, and we'll find it. This is just the beginning."

Lubna Seddua was less sanguine about Kinar's return from the provinces, since it would mean Kinar's return to influence in temple affairs after scarcely a year's absence. She would resume court service and continue to represent rival Hanza interests at large, one more voice—and a strong one—opposing Lubna's selection for Entu. Shua Kinar might even vie for the position herself.

Two days later, Kinar made her return official by rejoining the ladies at Council. In short order, Kinar shocked everyone with her own nomination for Entu.

"Semma Karkahn," she stated, causing every head to turn in her direction.

Lubna was hard-pressed to keep her face locked in an expression of stately reserve. Her own choice?

She glanced at her cousin. Niccaba's stunned reaction reflected her own.

Was their plot hatched before the egg was conceived?

They had little time to wonder, as the business of invoking a new queen took over, and settling the aged woman into office consumed every waking hour.

ASCENT

Chapter 26

May You Die

Nearing midnight, the Gipar's hallways lay stilled in slumber, except for the clamor of two voices ringing from the far end, where the ancient queen kept her chambers. Uruna bore her tea tray to the door and nearly stopped at the threshold. From deeper inside came sounds of a heated dispute. In the Entu's very bedchamber? The hour was late, the proper course would be to turn around and leave. But how would she then answer to the queen's demand for tea?

She set her mouth in firm resolve and boldly entered the vestibule. No nightly attendant stood at the bedchamber door, but the queen was not alone. Beyond the interior doorway, Lubna Seddua was doing most of the talking—at almost a shout.

"You've no right!" she yelled. "Mother Dellanna intended the trove to be used, not squirreled away out of sight for decades!"

Semma's reply came in a tone of sweet indulgence. "How could you possibly know what Dellanna intended? She died years before you were born."

"Doesn't matter, the point is—"

Semma cut her off. "Nor was your mother present! I, on the

other hand, was there! I committed her words to memory. Which I still have, by the way, despite your conniving lies to the contrary!"

"Spoken by a crone who forgets where she left her slippers most mornings."

"I do forget the inconsequential and trivial. But this decree I have lived with all my life and shall continue to obey from perfect recall until Inanna takes me."

Lubna softened her tone. "Grandmother, please. We are trying to be reasonable."

We? Was a third party in the room? More likely Lubna was making her usual attempt to conjure a consensus out of thin air.

Uruna could not decide what to do. They still didn't know she was there. She looked about for a place to leave the tea. There was none to be found unless she dropped it on the floor and fled. Perhaps if she cleared her throat, or rattled the cups to draw them from argument…

"Phah!" Semma spat. "Reasonable would be for you to get back to your scrubs and leave me alone!"

"I haven't done scrubs in twenty years, madam. I am the temple chancellor, not a child. My chief concern is the economy of this land, and you, Semma Karkahn, are standing smack in the path of progress!"

"Do not forget I am Entu! I have seen fifty seasons more than you! I am not blind to your ways. The trove shall not be yours while I yet live."

Time to leave. Uruna stooped and placed the tray on the floor, careful not to spill its contents. She straightened and backpedaled, got as far as the doorway again, when Lubna's shout rang out from the other room.

"Then may you soon die!"

Uruna's blood turned cold. Still at the door, she hesitated.

Semma shouted something else, and Uruna backed further into

the corridor. She had barely cleared the threshold when Lubna stormed out of Semma's room, a black look of utter hatred marring her features. She saw Uruna just a few steps away and called out to her.

"You, girl, stop!"

Uruna turned and took the hallway at a steady pace, hoping to appear as a minion simply wending the halls on an errand. Lubna caught up in several long strides and grasped Uruna's arm and spun her about.

"How much did you hear?" she demanded. A cheek muscle twitched, signaling a severe imbalance Uruna hadn't noticed before but now felt in her bones. The woman was dangerous, teetering at the edge of violence.

"Not a lot," Uruna replied, trying for a steady voice.

Lubna kept her hand fastened on Uruna's arm as her eyes flashed venom, her body fairly reeked with apprehension. A dot of spittle gathered at one corner of her mouth as she spoke.

"Listen to me, wench, you will forget anything you overheard in there. You can't possibly understand what's involved, so heed me well, lest your ignorance cause a presumption for which you would earn grave punishment. Is that clear?"

"Quite clear, madam. I only delivered tea and left."

"Good girl. Now run along back to your chores. Run!"

Never had Uruna beheld a more repulsive transformation in a human being. But in spite of the woman's vitriol, Uruna felt Enshiggu's caress wash over her own soul, imbuing her with godly abiding strength. She turned about slowly and ambled away as Lubna's hateful stare bored hot hatred into her back. She did not feel safe until she rounded the first corner.

Well, that was enough drama for one night. She didn't care what they thought, she was finished with kitchen duty for good. Indeed, had run her last errand for the haughty Lukur. Too many were flawed, and several couldn't hold a candle to a commoner. Tonight had demonstrated one in particular to be hopelessly craven. Ekur suffered enough iniquity to convince the most forgiving heart that the women responsible no longer deserved respect.

On wakening the next morning, she put the matter aside to focus on worship, and was just about to beseech the gods for heavenly grace when the previous night's impasse rose vividly to the surface once again.

Shua Kinar interrupted Uruna's prayer without apology, her overriding alarm plain to see. She had been called to Semma's chambers, she said, a highly irregular occurrence for her.

"You were there last night when Entu was threatened." She stated it as simple fact, although her eyes betrayed an underlying doubt.

"I delivered her evening tea, yes."

"The lady found her tea service on the floor. You had kitchen duty last night, so you were there."

"Yes, I was."

"Why didn't you serve Entu at her table as is custom?"

"She was busy, I had other matters to attend to."

"I see."

Kinar pondered Uruna's evasion, then bent to a new purpose.

"Remember what you heard last night, love, and what you were told. I know such things never truly leave your memory, but this case is especially vital to keep. Not necessarily to answer those who may enquire in times to come, but rather for you to use as you walk your path in life."

"You speak as if you were there."

Through half-closed eyes, Kinar mulled over Uruna's choice of words. After some consideration, she came to a decision and drew a deep breath before continuing.

"Some in our midst have fallen," she said, "lost their way. They stray far from the path chosen for Inanna's faithful. They embrace deceit and clever designs, seeing only the shorter view when those ploys succeed, not when they fall of their own ponderous weight.

"You love without question. That is your gift. Let no one distort your view of mankind, Uruna, for that is your power. Your steady strength, your steadfast belief in man's goodness, cannot be diminished by the faithless, the godless, the wicked. Though they cloak themselves in the trappings of might, they are weak as lambs, and will fall away before your light. You must endure this recent perfidy as you will others to come. From each trial springs a lesson telling you whom to trust and whom to forebear."

Uruna clasped Kinar's hands. "You have my trust right now, Kikki, for you've affirmed what I know in my heart. I can only feel sorrow for those so steeped in fear they cannot move rightly. It must be awful to be so cut off from the source of all good. I think such a soul is driven to convince others to feel the same, or else go mad with loneliness."

Kinar stared long into Uruna's eyes. "I see before me a queen at hand. She awaits only the appointed time for her anointing."

"Oh, Kikki, I'm only a girl of twelve."

"True, a point that will be raised more than once against you. But equally true, and undeniable, is that you offer the world the wisdom of a sage. The others see it. They relish it, for they are hungry for a leader with answers, a woman for our time and times to come. Be ready for that day and hour."

Chapter 27

Military Camp

The first outcome of her "talk" with Heganna, despite Lubna's strident objection, was Uruna's return to her former living accommodation inside the Aniginna compound. She would henceforth reside within the Gipar and continue her studies for induction into the temple role originally planned for her. No one knew exactly how Lubna Seddua was eventually persuaded to concur, although it was widely suspected that wealth had changed hands. The salient point was that the deed was done, Uruna's stable days were past and Memet was back in his Aniginna garden retreat.

As Uruna had guessed, the richest woman in Sumer had an ulterior motive besides her avowed devotion to Uruna's welfare. To that end, she arranged through intermediaries to have Uruna dispatched downriver to a nameless all-male camp.

According to temple gossip, the mysterious redoubt was a home away from home for adolescent males who aspired to a life of adventure. More particularly, according to Heganna's potter husband Sebbu, the young stalwarts were instructed how to hunt and slay wild animals. Heganna herself suspected a great deal more went on there, but as women were only allowed prearranged visitations, the more advanced lessons remained a mystery. Her son had gone there two years ago and had not returned.

"He's fourteen, still just a boy, really," Heganna had pined. "I want him home, but I know that's beyond even my doing. Perhaps you could..."

She had shrugged and said no more, causing Uruna to surmise that some inkling of her own healing work had seeped into the woman's awareness. Maybe Heganna believed Uruna possessed a mystic charm that might entice the lad from his protracted wilderness retreat. However wildly misplaced her reasoning might be, Uruna could scarcely refuse.

Two days later, on the twenty-first of Enten, Uruna embarked on what Heganna had assured her would be her own great adventure. Kinar had painted a scene of romantic action akin to a dance, although neither lady had even glimpsed the military camp to which they dispatched a girl of eleven. The disparity between their dream and her reality would shock Uruna to her roots.

Just an hour after dawn she stepped into a swifthull sent from the camp to fetch her. The two young oarsmen shoved off so abruptly she was jerked from her seat and thrown onto her back on the bottom of the boat. Neither oarsman offered help, as each bent to his paddle with fierce vigor, sending the craft sizzling over the river with powerful strokes from their hard-muscled bodies. The grim set to their jaws prevented conversation, as they raced their craft at breakneck speed, faster than any in her experience. After a short while she feared the hissing water might wear a hole in the sleek hull. Were they under some directive to get back at a certain hour? Or was this mad sprint the only way they'd' been taught to paddle a boat? Given no chance to ask, she contented herself with committing the scenery to memory for questions later.

Equally disconcerting were the opaque souls presented to her special senses—each essentially a blank, obdurate wall. It was as if the young men from that place had displaced all emotion with impenetrable resolve.

She really wanted to be elsewhere. Only last week, she'd learned of the birth of a girl child to Gar, her Nord benefactor from years ago. The big man now headed the forges at Na Purna. News of the new life had brightened Uruna's day, and she had set aside this particular day to visit the mother and her baby, Retha. She had even woven gifts for both on a borrowed loom. But Heganna's mission took priority, and thus she resolved to apply as much diligence to the task before her as she had to weaving the gifts.

No one at the camp came out to greet her as Heganna had promised. The two crewmen slammed the bow hard into a mud bank, jarring their passenger loose from her seat again. This time Uruna nearly banged her head on the upswept prow.

She turned to ask what she had done to anger the fellows so, but both hopped out into the shallows and left without a word. She watched their shadows recede into a forest of palm trunks, an adolescent display of disdain she did not find amusing. In fact, an undercurrent of muted hostility infected the whole place, making her feel like an enemy invading sacred soil.

Perhaps she was.

Not so many months had passed since she'd last fended for herself on a slippery riverbank. She got out of the swifthull and followed the oarsmen's course through the thick shade until she came out at a broad clearing.

In the open space before her, smoke from a half-dozen small cook fires drifted lazily upward. A long pole building with a thatch roof offered the only shelter from the elements. But the activity in that expanse sent her senses reeling.

At one end, a grown man barked a cadence at a dozen or so lads who crawled up a rope net suspended between two hewn palm trunks. Their descent ended in a mud puddle from which they attempted to sprint at top speed, spattering themselves and one another so completely that they emerged as unrecognizable brown blobs. In other circumstances such behavior might have been construed as a form of play, but there was no laughter involved. Not so much as a smirk lighted the young faces drawn in grim sobriety as they addressed the next instructor with a gritty resolve.

Closer by lay a flat rectangle marked off by felled palms. Inside, two boys flailed at each other with poles, each receiving a good many blows and successfully fending off far fewer. Teeth bared, heads and torsos battered and scratched, they appeared committed wholesale to beating each other until one or both dropped.

Another group of lads confronted an array of straw bales marked with charcoal to resemble the faces of foes. On a shouted command from another male adult, they heaved short spears at the targets with varying degrees of success. Another bunch did likewise, but using bow and arrow.

A sharp-featured bald man with no beard and no shirt got up from a mat a few yards away and approached her.

"I'm Targa. You must be the Hanza girl."

"My name is Uruna. I came seeking a boy—"

"I know about that, but he's not here. The advanced team are all downriver, left last night for the hunt."

"How do you know whom I seek?"

"She sends someone down from the city at least once a month, the rich lady does. Usually a manservant. In fact, you're the first female she's tried it with."

"Tried what?"

"To take him back. That's what you're here for. Don't deny it."

"I came to speak with him and convey his mother's good will."

"Ox dung! Heganna's been trying that trick for two years. The lad's plenty happy to live here. One of our best, in fact. The master takes special interest in him. Your mistress should be proud instead of trying to drag him back to that temple dreck."

"Well, I had hoped to learn as much from Anu himself, but I guess that won't happen today."

"We don't call him that. He's Teguzzu, *hunts-with-no-fear* to the Old Ones. Already took his first boar alone."

"But he's only eleven."

"Twelve, but makes no difference, not with him. That one's a man already, by all reckoning. Almost man-sized, too. Now, you'll have to keep your own self busy till nightfall, when the others come back. We'll put you up as best we can, but the lads and the men all sleep under the stars. Got no soft bed cushion for the likes of you."

"I slept on the stable floor at Trades. I don't expect special treatment."

"Good, 'cause you won't get it."

"Maybe I should talk to someone else."

Targa pointed across the compound to a pair of knees propped up in the palm shade. "Over there's Suba, cut his throwing hand good, so he won't be doing anything like you see here for a while. Maybe the slacker would appreciate female chatter, I don't know."

"Thank you, I'll just tend to my weaving like a good little female."

"What weaving? You didn't bring a tote."

"Left it in the boat. I had a feeling this might be a short trip."

"What'd you bring with you?"

"Something for Anu—I mean, Teguzzu."

"Well, go fetch it and I'll make sure he gets it when he comes back."

"Doesn't work that way. I'll take it back with me tonight."

"We don't travel the river at night, girl. Unless on a test."

"I'll take myself."

"Little thing like you? Alone? Where you been, missy? There's trouble on that river. Snakes swallow you up, eat you whole."

"I sleep with a cobra, I've taken my own boar with my uncle, and I go where I please. Your experience with 'females' appears quite limited. I imagine you don't see many out here."

"Hunting is man's work, done best by a man knows animal ways."

"I think I'll go over and say hello to Suba."

"Good idea. Wake him up. That soft one'd rather sleep than pull his weight."

Uruna had had enough of Targa's blunt disregard and hoped for a better chance with the boy in the palms. With nothing to thank Targa for, she gave him her back and crossed the compound, determined not to let either of them spoil her day.

Fifteen paces from the supine form she heard Suba's snore. He was big for his age. Almost Nord big.

He lay on his back with his knees pulled high and both arms spread wide like a soaring gull. She prodded one foot, and got a frown for her effort. Stepped on his big toe, but Suba only shifted his foot and grunted.

"S00-00-ba!" she crooned, as she imagined his mother might have done when he was little. Then she stepped hard on his other toe. "Suba, Suba, time for supper!"

Suba jerked his feet away and tossed his head from side to side, mumbled a curse, blinked his eyes, snapped fully awake.

"That damn Nabi!" he cursed, still shaking his head. "Sent me back to the city. What am I doing at Temple?"

Uruna laughed. "Temple came to you today. I'm Uruna, sent down from Nippur this morning."

Suba knifed up onto his buttocks and wrapped two brawny arms about his knees. "Well, if this is Nabi's idea of punishment, I'm in for more. Gods, but you're a lovely sight!"

Uruna felt her cheeks color. No boy had ever spoken to her like that. In fact, most of the Trades boys were more likely to plant a foot on her backside and shoo her back to her scrubs. But this one was not only forward, he was truly handsome.

"You sleep rather soundly," she said. "Isn't that a hunter's folly?"

Suba's grin exposed a perfect set of white teeth. His eyes were darkest blue, and his shoulders were nearly as broad as a door. A hint of humor lighted his gaze.

"A bigger folly," he said, "is roaming around here without a woman in sight for months on end. But that's how Nabi wants it, so that's what we get."

"Do you have to do everything he says?"

"Yes, unless we want to go running back to our mother, those of us that have one."

"Who is Nabi, anyway?"

"You mean you weren't told before they sent you?"

"Enlighten me."

"Nabi Gahn is the master of all masters. Not just for hunting game. He shows us how to win at—ah, you almost caught me. He warned us about a woman's wiles."

"What are wiles?"

"Don't look at me with those big, gray eyes like you don't know. That witch Sarni sent you down to woo me away, didn't she?"

"I don't know any Sarni. I'm just a scrubbing girl from the Trades."

"Prettiest scrubbing girl I ever saw, just standing there looking gorgeous because you can't help it."

"Please, I only came—"

"Come sit." Suba patted the reed mat next to him.

"I'm not sure that's such a good idea."

Actually, she thought it sounded wonderful.

"Always a good idea," Suba crowed. "Man-woman, boy-girl, meant to sit together. It's the way of the world. Sit and sit. Or sleep."

He's just the camp tender. Can't hunt worth a

"Well, if you promise not to tell Targa."

"That old fool? He's just the camp tender. Can't hunt worth a shekel."

Uruna sat down and folded her legs to one side. She'd never been so close to an older boy. At least, not alone...

"I don't suppose you know when they'll be back?"

"Who, the little archers? Probably by mid-afternoon in time for their naps. Is that what you came down for?"

"No, someone older."

"Oh, so you're being attended now."

"No, silly, I'm not old enough for that. I'm not even *kadishtu* yet."

"I find that hard to believe." He placed a finger on her cheek and drew it down to her jaw in a soft arc. She shivered and gasped.

Suba jerked his hand back. "Sorry, I thought—see, being out here in the field so long, all you see is a bunch of blokes and four hard-nosed trainers who yell at you when they aren't giving you a sound beating. Oh, don't look so shocked, it's part of the toughening process. We learn how to balance pain—wup, see, there I go again, telling secrets."

Uruna feared she might swoon at any moment. She could listen to Suba's smooth voice for hours. Physical power simply oozed from him, yet she detected a gentle spirit behind all that strength.

"You're Nord, aren't you?" she blurted, and instantly regretted the impulsive outburst. Gods, how childish! Where was her self-control?

Suba didn't seem to notice. "Good guess, but only on my father's line. At least, that's what I'm told. How'd you figure it? My size? Everybody always goes 'oo' and points."

"I lived at Na Purna for a while."

He leaned in to look more closely. "You're the snake girl."

She shrank back, put off by the familiar dismissive slur. But

Suba's disarming smile seemed genuine.

"I've always wondered what the cobra thinks about us," he said.

"Well, that's a new one," she replied. "Most reactions are to run for a shovel or a stick. What *do* you suppose he thinks?"

"Probably that we're far too large for our own good and would best be avoided."

"Hah! You're close to the mark, at least with the king, so I'm told. My own experience is limited to the Naja variety."

"The fellow with two eyes on his back."

"Yes, but hardly safe to keep around the house."

"Is it true what they say? I mean no offense, but do you actually sleep with one?"

His curiosity seemed genuine enough.

"I used to when I was little, but not so much anymore. Memet's content to stay in his basket or in the garden."

"Would he warm to a stranger?"

"Why do you ask?"

Suba appeared to consider his answer. "I had a snake myself once, for about six weeks. Then he ran off. Not a cobra, mind you, nor an asp. Just an old ratter. He was good for keeping mice out of the barn and he'd come when I snapped my fingers. I think he felt the sound and found it pleasing. I once found him coiled against my back on a cold night. He wouldn't do it again, and left shortly after. I think he went off to sleep the winter."

"You weren't afraid?"

"No, he was afraid of *me* mostly. Or more like respectful. You know, just a little rat snake, the length of my arm. I mean, think of the difference in size between us. We must seem immense to them."

Uruna sat entranced. Never in her life had she talked snakes with anyone at such length. She felt at ease with Suba, too, almost like they had known each other for a very long time.

"Where do you live, when you're not here in camp?"

"Oh, here and there. We're all supposed to go home for winter break, but I usually stick around. You know, the place needs looking after."

She wanted to ask about his family, but he didn't seem to want to talk about them. Maybe the camp was as much of a home to him as a stable was to her. She scanned the grounds from one end to the other.

"I don't see much that needs attending except some logs and ropes. Do you sleep in that thatch building over there?"

"What, that? No, we burn it."

"Why would you set fire to a perfectly good building?"

"Because it's not perfect and it's not good and we use it to test ourselves with fire. Just before home break we set it ablaze. The bigger lads have to climb inside and run through it. Then we all stand around and watch it burn down. When we come back from break, first thing we do is build a new one."

"What a strange idea! And dangerous!"

"Oh, not as dangerous as the lion pit."

Uruna looked more closely at Suba to be sure he wasn't toying with her. He pointed across the compound toward the other end where a mat of sticks lay on sunbaked sand.

"Let me take you over there where you can see up close."

They walked across the compound, avoiding sparring groups and ducking around targets. Once in a while one boy or another would pause for a long look at Uruna and get his head slapped for the lapse in attention. Suba found her effect humorous.

"You're setting these boys back a week, ten days in their discipline."

"How awful! I'm so sorry, maybe I should leave now."

"Don't you dare. This is too much fun."

Suba stopped before a haphazard pile of dried reed stalks and drew Uruna to the edge.

"What am I looking at?" she asked.

"The mat covers a pit trap. We learn how to set it up for an enemy in pursuit."

"You put a lion in there?"

He laughed and pulled back a corner of woven reed matting. Uruna peered down at five ranks of four sharpened poles sticking straight up.

"They're braced to keep them stout enough to bear his weight," Suba said. "We chase the lion to the pit, he falls in, dies."

Uruna shrank away. "How horrible!"

"Yes, but think what he'd do to us."

"I'd rather not."

"The more honorable method is what Teguzzu is learning."

"More honorable?"

"Yes, you face the lion on his ground, armed only with a spear. When he charges, you aim for the chest and throw."

"What if you miss?"

"You don't."

"I think I'd like a drink from the urn."

"Sure, me too."

They returned to the shady spot where they'd first met and spent several quiet hours napping or doing nothing. The sun was dropping behind the tree tops when a troop of boys trudged back into camp. Uruna watched them assemble in two rows facing an older man. Some of the boys showed signs of cuts and crude bindings covering wounds of one sort or another.

Suba caught her watching. "That's how you learn. Some of that's from rush blades, some from another bloke's knife in mock combat. You learn to live with pain and salve. After a while, it's just a part of life."

"Is that how you hurt your hand?"

"No, I grabbed an opponent's sword the wrong way. Embarrassing, really."

"How long before you can go back out?"

"It'll mend pretty quick."

She turned her thoughts to the reason for her trip.

"Which one's Anu—I mean Teguzzu?"

"He isn't there."

"Did something happen to him?"

"Teguzzu? Nothing happens to that animal. No, he'll probably set his own camp tonight."

"With Nabi?"

"No, that's Nabi, the one making the boys stand a bit longer."

"That's cruel. I think he's mean to do that."

"Yep, mean and nasty and unforgiving, and we all hate him because we can't suffer enough to suit him. But on the other hand, we respect him for what he teaches us. We can survive anything the bush gives us. Anything."

"Does anyone quit?"

"You said the wrong word. Don't let Master hear you say it again. Around here, you keep going no matter what. Which, by the way, I've got to do."

He pushed off with a limp she hadn't noticed before. Had she stepped too hard on his foot? Or was a lingering pain from an earlier wound another token of combat these boys admired?

Uruna spent the first half of the night near the cook fire, chewing dried meat from her tote. She received no offers of food. Every person in camp was expected to catch, preserve, and prepare his own meals. Even the wounded. If you failed, you went hungry.

She was glad she would return in the morning.

Just as she felt herself nodding off, the hunt master himself appeared out of nowhere and crouched on the other side of the fire. His dark eyes bored into her with feverish intensity.

"You can tell your mistress we won't abide another visit."

"And a good evening to you, sir."

"Nothing good or bad about it. Just dark and dangerous."

"Are there lions about?"

"Not that we've seen, but one of the lads wounded an old boar the other day. He'll be out for revenge, and fire doesn't scare him."

"Know what you mean. Killed my first boar last summer."

"Arrow or spear?"

"Arrow. He was small."

Gods, he had her talking like him. But that was how campfire talk went, the same as on her hunts with Ashur.

"Alone?" he asked.

"No, my uncle was nearby. And a couple of Nords. But I bagged and skinned it myself."

"Who's your uncle?"

"Fellow you wouldn't know."

"I might. I get around."

"He doesn't. Sticks mostly to the north, comes from Elam."

Nabi's eyebrows shot up. "Elam fellows are good hunters. You're in prime company."

"I know. Where's the Hanza lad?"

Nabi lifted his chin. "Out there."

"Sticks to himself, huh?"

"Yep. Been that way from the start. One in a hundred. You wasted a trip."

Uruna stared into the fire a couple of moments before she answered.

"I don't think so."

The master hunter stood up, straightened. "Too bad you don't have a pair of balls. You'd do well here."

And that, Uruna would learn one day, was as good as anyone got from Nabi Gahn.

Chapter 28

Report From Duda

Less than a mile below Gula Gate, where river gloss made a black mirror for the star-studded night sky, a lone traveler approached from the south and paused on the roadside. A robed figure emerged from a crumbling chapel relic and gestured for the traveler to stop.

"Come no closer."

"That's fine, I do not care to."

"You have news of the token," said the voice from inside the cowl. "You found its meaning?"

"Better than that," answered the master of a dozen ways to kill. "The runes describe a trail to the treasure alright, but closer than you thought. Practically in your lap."

"Tell me something I don't know. It's near Adab."

"Wrong. An older place. A city lost to the lore your foolish lines attempt to keep alive. I speak of Duda."

"Not a place, but a god—an old one who left us long ago. You heed the talk of old women who mutter incantations in the wind."

The hireling bristled. "I do what you cannot! When will you listen to aught but yourself? It is the desert Duda of which I speak, not a forgotten deity. A city now buried in the sands, but once as great as Nippur."

"Let's say you're right. How did she find it, eh? How did a dotty old crone who can barely walk discover a lost city?"

"That's not the point. The token speaks clearly of this Duda and a great hall inside it. Says, 'Therein lies a secret of utmost value.'"

"You get all this from a token the size of my thumb?"

"No, from the fire-talker who held it."

"She caught you napping, that one did."

"She spoke of a staircase of stone descending into the bowels of the earth, where once a thousand souls trod in daily life. To find it one must lift the shade of one's mind, she said."

"A fool's mutterings—to another fool. Tell me something I can act upon!"

"Such impatience does not become you. Try this one, then. She says the time is near when all will be swallowed by a tempest and lost beyond recovery. Says, Look to the east, whence one arrives with wisdom and might but a soft voice. Then she says, Look south to the star of Egypt, whose blood was spilled in sacrilege, whose sons will avenge from everlasting to everlasting. And last she says, Unto these are given the keys to Heaven and Eternity."

"More rubbish. These old soothsayers are all talk and no show."

"Speaking of no show, I've awaited payment too long. Much longer, and my door will be closed to you."

"Perhaps the best possible outcome. Very well, here, take your money."

"This is but half."

"For which you have earned less than half by giving me nothing but pap. I leave you. Do not come again this way."

"Perhaps, I should seek Duda myself. I might then profit whole from my own discovery."

"First develop an appetite for sand before you dine on it."

Chapter 29

Kadishtu Consort

One morning a few weeks after her futile trek to the military camp, Uruna woke before dawn to discover she had become a woman in the night.

She bathed and took care of herself, then wadded up the bedclothes and dropped them in the communal laundry bin. She reported to her ward monitor according to Gipar protocol and received a taciturn response.

"Nothing special, happens every day in this place. Now get started on your chores."

She explained that she no longer had chores but attended temple instruction instead.

The girl frowned and gave Uruna her back. Nothing further was said.

At day's end she was called to the adjutant's chamber to receive the temple blessing. Lady Tenith was there, at age twenty a minor figure in Niccaba's administrative section. She handed Uruna a small palmwood figurine of Goddess Lu-bhag carved in full-bosomed pulchritude.

For her bedside table.

To prove her new status.

Tenith apparently expected a response showing awe-inspired gratitude and wonder. Uruna feigned compliance and took the sacred thing to her room, chucked it unceremoniously in her clothes box, and left for temple, glad to have so little attention given to the event.

Such anonymity would not prevail, however, once word reached higher echelons. Years ago, the good Mothers had settled on a fictitious birth date for her, there being no oral record of her line. The Seventy-Third of Enten would arrive eight days hence, when she officially became twelve.

How propitious, they all agreed, for her flow to coincide with her coming of age. The happy omen merited celebration. Kinar took note of Uruna's casual disregard for the situation and took her aside for instruction in proper comportment.

"Do not take this moment lightly, Uruna," she said. "By such you become eligible for induction in the priestesshood."

"You mean as a *kadishtu* novice it will be my turn to tease and harass the younger girls?"

"Is that your belief of what it is, or were you so taught?"

"Neither. It's been my own experience."

"Ai! You should have told one of the Mothers."

"I chose not to."

She intended no impudence, no rancor. She was already well-known for speaking her mind with unmitigated candor.

Kinar changed her approach in like manner.

"You have to become *kadishtu* before you can make *naditu* priestess, and priestess before high priestess, and that before *entu* queen. That is how it's done. Each step leads to the next higher, and right now you are poised to ascend to the first rung of that ladder. Also," she added before Uruna's impetuous mind could jump ahead, "as you have discovered from your own experience at worship, there is the beauty of the ceremony to be enjoyed, cherished. As you will see, along with the pomp comes that rush of Heavenly favor, when your very soul is touched by divine love, and you partake of Great Mother's limitless bounty. Just as you experience when you prepare to become Her prophet."

Uruna stared back, speechless, her luminous gaze widened as she consumed every word.

"Do not deny yourself this birthright," Kinar finished.

The idea took root and flourished. With new eyes Uruna comprehended the vast scope of her future, accepted her role in it, marshalled intent, and set her goal squarely on her life's ultimate purpose.

Giving her full attention to Kinar, and resolved to resume her childhood mission against all opposition, she answered.

"Then we must begin at once," she said. "I shall be pleased to have your counsel throughout."

Kinar smiled, for hadn't she pledged her heart to Uruna years ago? That fidelity should hardly stop now that her ward was at last a woman.

The question paramount among the Serpenthood faithful immediately followed: Who should become Uruna's first consort? One of the lads who "attended" the bowers of Sumer's young lovelies?

Likely not, since the objective was to produce a prophet, rather than a well-endowed offspring. Ordinarily, for most temple maidens, her choice of consort was guided by a young adult priestess trained in the matchmaking process. In Uruna's case, however, ladies from society's most senior caste weighed in on the matter, persuaded by their own self-importance to admit that if the girl were indeed to become Ekur's chief seer one day, she must mate only with the best consort.

Of course, each woman promoted her own choice of candidate,

whether from her own offspring or that of a relative or a political ally. To ensure fairness, a committee was formed and votes were cast after considerable caucus and arm-twisting. Inevitably, the process bogged down, as reasonable discourse degenerated into bitter dispute and hostile accusations.

Kinar took steps to shield her ward from the fray, but Uruna learned of it anyway. As days of indecision dragged into weeks, Uruna concluded that any candidate thus proposed would only be a mindless dullard stripped of self-regard. And so she called on Kinar, who called on Heganna, who naturally proposed her own son, Nabi Gahn's elusive hunting apprentice.

Another of Heganna's close circle of friends, diminutive chief counter Ku Aya, brought the matter before Niccaba and took Uruna with her.

"I don't know him," Uruna pointed out when Ku Aya presented the choice.

Niccaba's smile showed condescension, the sage indulging the impressionable youth.

"Uruna, of course you don't know any of the candidates yet. How could you? That's why the choice is made by those who do."

"The Hanza boy doesn't care for girls," she countered. "He prefers the company of wild animals in forest and swamp."

Ku Aya hastened to allay that objection. "We'll tame him for you."

"I'd rather you didn't try."

"That decision is not yours to make."

Niccaba pondered the matter further. "It would appear it won't be ours either," she said to Ku Aya, "unless we drag the lad from the hinterland against his will. How can we be sure he'll perform? Has he any experience with the act at all?"

Ku Aya was insistent. "These questions have been answered to the satisfaction of the wisest women in the land. Their chief concern is for Uruna's success."

Niccaba bowed her head. "Indeed, as well as for their own. How well do they know the boy they propose?"

"Anu comes from the finest family in Sumer."

Uruna broke in. "Which, of course, assures his qualification without further question."

Ku Aya rounded on her. "Uruna, you're being insolent!"

Niccaba spread her hands in appeasement. "Madam, the lad refused to speak to Uruna at the training camp. Would not come out of the forest even to join his own fellows. And he is reportedly disdainful of his own master when the man calls him forth. You must understand how intractable he has become. His own mother doesn't know him."

"He can be trained."

"Indeed, we could send a few *galla* soldiers down there to force him home in fetters, where the stoutest matrons will bring him to heel. Is that the sort of husband we desire for the prophet's mate?"

They were getting nowhere. Uruna arched an eyebrow. "There was a fellow at the camp. Suba, by name. We had a most agreeable discourse while waiting for the renegade to show up."

Ku Aya bridled. "I know of him. He's Nord."

"And I'm Perzan," Uruna countered. "And Lady Niccaba's half Mede and pleased to point it out. What is wrong with people? They're so proud to count their lines going back generations, but at some point we all came from somewhere else. To be Sumerian is to rejoice in that diversity."

Ku Aya wasn't having any of it. "Nords are different. They tried to kill us, as Niccaba will attest."

Uruna didn't know why, but she felt a growing frustration with Ku Aya's unreasonable objections. "Well, their grandsires two hundred years ago tried to kill us—and failed, by the way. Today they're quite another story."

"How do you know these things? From a few weeks in one village?"

"I learned from Mena Ramush before she died. Also in class, from the ladies here. Do they think I haven't a mind of my own, because I'm young? I've seen more of the world out there than most women in their dotage."

"That's quite enough. I know you mean well, but the conclave has spoken. Anu will be your consort."

Niccaba drew herself up with a great sigh. "They won't find him, Aya-tum," she said. "Heganna's son has spurned us all. She hasn't seen him for two years. None of us have. We wouldn't know where to start looking for him. And Nabi Gahn will certainly be no help in the matter."

"But I *did* see Suba," Uruna piped up, "and I talked with him. The girls swoon over him. I found him delightful to spend time with. And one more thing you might carry back to this 'conclave of wisdom.'"

Ku Aya raised her eyes to the ceiling. "Tell us please, so that I may dissuade them with something besides a twelve-year-old girl's opinion."

"He likes snakes."

Ku Aya pulled back, eyes wide in startled surprise. "I don't see how—"

"Everyone expects me to attain Sight. The Sleep of Serpents requires a mate compatible with serpents. I will need such a mate for the purpose to which I have devoted my life: Prophecy. The Lukur will have their prophet in me, by me, with such a man. Since it takes years to master the potions, the rituals, the carefully-timed arousal, the mood of the guardian serpents, and since Suba is imminently qualified in the latter, we ought to begin the process at once. Besides, I like him and he likes me. Is that not a happy start?"

Ku Aya sat dumb for several moments. "They'll say you didn't try hard enough to find Anu, that you became infatuated with Suba instead. They'll want some proof that erases any doubt."

Niccaba bent forward in her chair. "Who would demand this proof?"

"The conclave."

"The Uzba are not temple women! Since when do the secular dictate to the sacred?"

"Since about a thousand years ago. You can't tell them apart any longer."

"Well, I can, and I shall." Niccaba turned toward Uruna. "I'll bring the Nord's name before Council myself, and—" she aimed a glare at Ku Aya, "Council will have the final word."

There followed an argument between the two priestesses: How might Suba be persuaded to leave Nabi's tutelage? Who were his parents and did they aspire to profit by the process? Who besides the conclave might oppose his induction, and how might that opposition be removed?

Forgotten in the dialogue were preparations for Uruna's forthcoming *kadishtu* induction, a lapse Uruna cared not to point out.

Given that foretaste of Lukur politics at work, she was at once both repelled and encouraged. Here was an example of the tedious deliberation that thwarted most temple affairs. By the same token, Niccaba hadn't questioned Uruna's own participation in the discussion. Did she now consider Uruna to be her peer?

More likely, her choice of Suba fit some other scheme in play. The question was whose ploy did it suit? And more importantly, why?

Chapter 30

Birth and Induction

Her last trip to Na Purna had been the previous year to count barley sheaves for the Nord *nigenna* allotment. Uruna had been too busy then for any visiting. Today, with her usual temple duties discharged early, she was looking forward to a relaxing interlude in company she enjoyed and trusted.

As she reached Gar's house, she was surprised to see the big man open the door himself.

"Saw you coming up the path," he said. "Good to see you again, Uruna."

He embraced her in a bear hug and waved a hand for her to enter ahead of him.

"Sorry, we don't have sheaves for you to count this time," he joked.

"I'm not here for sheaves, as you well know. Where's that baby?"

"Probably at the forge teaching Telgen how to hammer correctly."

At that point, Gar's wife, Milsah, appeared in the doorway to another room. "You're just in time. She's up from her nap."

Gar rolled his eyes. "She's always up."

Milsah led Uruna into the room where the infant sat in her crib, a halo of carrot-red hair about her crown. She cooed happily as she fondled a small gourd rattle, then stopped as she caught Uruna's presence. Two bright blue orbs tracked Uruna's progress across the room, incredibly sharp at such an early stage.

What happened next astounded Uruna and the baby's parents beyond words. Little Retha stretched both arms upward and reached for Uruna.

"Oona."

Milsah's eyes went wide with shock, while Gar made choking noises behind her. As for herself, Uruna did not hesitate to pick up the child. As she gathered Retha closer, the baby continued cooing her name.

"Oona, oona."

By now Milsah's eyes were bright with tears. "She's only four months, never said a word before."

Uruna bounced the baby in her arms, a rapturous joy flooding her own being. "She knows her Auntie Uruna, doesn't she? Yes, she does."

She then turned to Milsah. "She's beautiful. Just as precious as can be."

"But how—?" Gar spluttered.

"She's a special gift," Uruna answered, then took closer notice of the rattle clutched in the baby's small fist. "Where did you get this?"

The gourd had two lobes, each etched with figures. Head and body. On one end, someone had attached a knotted shred of dried palm frond—the tail. The whole effect struck Uruna.

"Gar?" she asked.

"It was a gift—among many that day. I don't know who—"

Milsah interrupted him. "The old woman, the one with all the bracelets."

"What old woman?"

"You probably missed her. She left just as quickly as she appeared. What does it mean, Uruna?"

The memories came crashing in on her mind, bright, clear visions of the same gourd shape, flashes of faces ringed about a room in which she lay as a babe, faces peering at her in wonder. Then sounds of voices raised in a clamor, a rush of wind, a blur of motion...a shoulder bearing her away, out of the room, past doors and windows, then upward, scaling a wall, leaping rooftops, diving, plunging...then another room, sanctuary...warm and soft and dark.

And tucked in her blanket, the gourd rattle. Speaking to her of comfort, love. Protecting...

"It's a serpent," she said. "The first sign of Enshiggu. I had one like it, the same figures..."

Her throat caught and she could not go on.

Gar and Milsah could only stare in mute shock. Retha's bright little face now attended the rattle again, held tight in an infant fist that shouldn't clench so soon, by a will that shouldn't emerge until months later.

By a soul whose form and presence were already in place. As firm as the forge iron, and serene as the river.

Uruna's *kadishtu* induction ceremony the next day went as she had expected—dull oratory accompanied by ornate finery calculated to attract godly attention, but a ritual common enough to induce a yawn or two in the back row.

Niccaba carried on in her customary drone, while Kinar served as Uruna's sponsor, although everyone suspected Heganna's considerable influence at work. For that reason alone Uruna would enjoy the first fruits of Lukur privilege in the form of tacit respect, an advantage she felt was unmerited. She retired from the elaborate ordeal anticipating the resumption of serpently pursuits with Enshiggu.

Not right away, apparently. Her intentions suffered a mild setback two days later when Niccaba stopped her on her way to temple instruction.

"We are blessed with a visitor you should meet. A most fitting young man from far off Egypt, a genuine prince from the house of Mahut. But also a serpently soul. At least, so we are told."

"But I thought you agreed on Suba—"

"Perhaps we should take a bird in the hand, hm-mm?"

"I still don't understand."

"You'll meet the prince tomorrow. It's all arranged."

"What's become of Suba? You said he was coming to Nippur."

"He's still down there in that camp with Nabi's boys. There'll be time for him. If the prince doesn't work out, you'll have your choice of suitors. This is only the beginning."

Uruna had scarcely absorbed Niccaba's blunt delivery of the latest twist in the proceedings when a second followed that evening. As she sat *semtu* in her chapel. Nashi ducked through the doorway and without preamble or greeting declared Uruna's new status to be both farce and milestone.

"*Kadishtu* honor of old is gone from these halls," she declared before seating herself cross-legged beside her pupil. "Lately the initiation has become a political commonplace, but it used to mark a girl as especially fit for godly ministrations. In your case, that much remains true, for your heart roves with the gods. But let's also realize that so much attention from the Lukur means you are elevated in their eyes."

"You mean my badge of rank?" Uruna opened her palm to reveal the copper shoulder clasp bestowed upon her at the close of the initiation. "They implied that if I'm a good girl I might get a gold one someday."

Nashi remained unmoved by Uruna's disdain. "I know, you're still a minion in many respects, but no longer a secular drudge. This means a great deal, Uruna, for you have become one of the elect bound to serve Great Mother."

"Yes, Nashi, I heard those words said, but I feel more of Her love here in this humble chamber than I did in that august hall."

"Of course you do. Find it in your heart to forgive those who have forgotten simple ways. Remind them how to love by serving mankind."

"And how much of this shall I reveal to my consort?"

"The Siamun Mahut? Love him too, and watch his heart grow. He is— well, he's good for you at this point."

"*Good* for me? I haven't even met the man. Tomorrow night I'm supposed to sleep with him."

"Uruna, I wish you could see the lad this moment, quaking in his robes, seated at his window a thousand miles from his home, still a boy in many ways."

"He's not full grown?"

"I believe he is fourteen. He's never ventured beyond the walls of his father's castle. He journeyed by river and sea for three months to get here. He's surrounded by strangers. Our ways are not his ways."

"Who arranged such a torment?"

"An unthinking parent or advisor. It doesn't matter. The important thing is for you to give the Siamun comfort and become his friend. Let the rest unfold at its own pace."

"But they expect me to take him—take him for a lover—the first night."

"Nonsense. First, you must like each other, then comes trust, and after that, tender entreaty. Then—who knows?"

Uruna frowned, her mind a turmoil. First she had been paddling Lukur waters in frantic haste, now Nashi had thrust an oar into the stream and made a hard turn toward shore.

"How do you know all these things?" she asked the venerable planter- sage.

Nashi stared into the brazier light for a moment before tapping her head with a finger.

"These eyes see what you will see for yourself one day. These ears hear words thought before they are spoken. You above all should know whence these gifts come. It is the divine at work in us."

"I suspect Niccaba arranged the whole Mahut thing months ago."

"Perhaps she did. I don't know. Does it matter?"

"It might matter very much, but I won't find out by asking her."

"Oh? Do I detect a bit of mistrust there?"

"She used to oppose my acceptance by the Mothers. Her cousin Lubna worked to have me banished, but then I think Niccaba prevailed to bring me back. None of that makes sense unless you see a design to it. I think Niccaba wants a prophet in her time, wants that very much. But her path to it is not the straightest."

She looked to see if those ideas fit with Nashi's perception. The intensity of the returning gaze fell upon her like a blow.

Before she could inquire, Nashi bent forward.

"All this was supposed to happen later. I don't understand how—you perceive intrigue at a most tender age. You perceive the lie, but you tread lightly in your pursuit of the truth it tries to cover."

Nashi paused to glance aside, her eyes searching the corners of the room.

"Here is the root of the matter, my dear young lady. Grave danger walks these sacred halls in the guise of sacred service. The few who once pursued wealth for its own rewards have now discovered a greater treasure abiding in their very midst. A budding prophet whose predictive power will one day surpass all other powers in value.

"As you and I sit here today, they aren't sure what to do with you. They only know they must nurture your innate gifts until they are made manifest. To that end, they will do anything—commit any deed no matter how foul or treacherous. In the broadest sense, you are the beneficiary of limitless Lukur ambition. In years to come, your every need will be fulfilled. You'll be given anything you ask for, right or wrong. But they'll subject you to intense scrutiny. Each will watch for the slightest chance to make you her personal tool for control. In light of that fact, you must be prepared to question every favor until you know from which quarter it originates and whose ends it serves."

Uruna's mind reeled from Nashi's portrayal of duplicity. She had expected an abundance of kindness among those in sacred service, a sisterhood devoted to the holy purpose they themselves sang and chanted at worship. Was it all smothered by human greed? Were the "good ladies" of Ekur so steeped in avarice that they would commit the very sins they were sworn to prevent?

Nashi had more to say. "Do not cloud your mind with doubt and worry. Do not so harden your heart that you overlook the love and kindness and truth that comes your way. The wicked shall come into your life only to pass out of it, leaving you wiser, happier, and above all, fulfilled. In that respect you are not so different from other women, for such suffering will reveal your humanity to others. In your pain lies the mortal nature which binds you to the people."

As for Uruna's prospects with the Siamun Mahut, Nashi had surprisingly little to say. "His life goes beyond my sight. Go to your young man and give him the kindness of your heart, the depth of your soul. The rest will follow."

Uruna suppressed a shiver. The rest would follow? Was that what was meant by mystery being the spice of life? Why had Nashi dropped her usual air of solid assurance the moment the consort became the topic of discussion?

As in so many matters, in the end Uruna must decide for herself whether Niccaba and the ladies, in their collective dignity and wisdom, knew a snake-charming rascal when they saw one.

Chapter 31

A Tryst of Sorts

Parchment lanterns splashed a mellow glow over the walkways and streams lining Nippur's huge central park. A river raft plied the widest course as it carried twelve passengers engaged in subdued celebration. Five adult couples stood on the open middeck, ranking Lukur and their spouses on hand to chaperone the two adolescents seated forward in a screened box. At the rails to either side, three ranks of polers guided the craft over the water's gentle meander.

Uruna kept her gaze straight ahead, unsure of anyone's expectations, least of all those of Siamun Mahut. She was in complete awe of his self-possessed bearing and his command of the evening's proceedings.

Hardly the quaking adolescent Nashi had portrayed, the Mahut scion showed the poise and aplomb of a genuine royal. Manly in every respect, he was practiced in how to treat a lady of equally high station, which he presumed Uruna to be.

His large black eyes with long, dark lashes set in a square-jawed face gazed about with serene composure, suggesting a quiet intelligence touched with a hint of arrogance. Sculpted lips bespoke a sensitive character and latent good humor, while his erect posture enhanced a tall frame commanding adult respect. He seemed to regard his hosts as equally royal in rank. A perfect set of teeth flashed as he finished answering Uruna's latest question.

"Nippur? Never saw anything like it. We have our own city, of course, but nothing approaching your jewel in size or grandeur."

"Did you pass Eanna on your way upriver?"

"What's that, another city?"

"The city is Uruk, the temple is Eanna. Quite a grand spectacle."

"Must have been nighttime. I fell asleep as we entered the river mouth."

"Well, Uruk is larger yet, but not much to look at. I saw it once, on a hunting trip."

"Ah, so you join the royal hunt for game?"

Uruna decided on a demure response to fit his expectations. "Er, a bit, yes, with my uncle. Just birds so far, but we're going after boar again next summer."

Ashur had told her she was ready for tuskers, but she kept his compliments to herself, lest she seem too forward. Siamun Mahut quickly assumed the role of master hunter.

"Be careful when you do. That one darts about like a loon in a mud mire, doesn't know its own mind. Just as soon run onto your pike as bolt for freedom."

"I'll remember that. Where do you hunt?"

"On the royal estate grounds. I don't like it much."

"Oh? What's wrong?"

"The animals are fenced in. You never really face your quarry on equal terms. Sabaf Mahut forbids the real thing, says we can't afford to lose a royal to such a whim."

"Well, certainly that would be tragic."

Khufu grew pensive for a moment. "Madam, I must ask a rather delicate question."

"Siamun, please call me Uruna."

"And I'd be pleased if you call me by my given name, Khufu. Siamun is my title."

"Oh, I see. Certainly, Khufu."

"As to my question…"

"Yes? I'll answer if I can."

"Have you done this thing with the serpents before? I mean to say, with a man? What I'm trying to get at is—"

"No, I haven't had intercourse."

Suddenly the royal aplomb vanished with boyish uncertainty. "Erm, not even with the cobra?"

"For Heaven's sake! My good sir, that is preposterous!"

In a remarkable feat of recovery, Siamun Khufu Mahut shrugged off her scorn. "The women in the *pra fura* do it, or something like it. At least, that's what's said."

"What's a *pra fura*?"

"A place men where a man goes to have a woman."

"Oh, like a brothel. Do the women there have—they sleep with cobras?"

"I'm not sure. I haven't—been, myself, you see. It's forbidden to royals, and all you can learn about it is through house slaves. If my father found out I'd even talked to that lot he'd have my hide."

"Well, I hardly think the bower is a fitting place for a serpent of any kind. Least of all the cobra, and certainly not the *naja*. But I'm told—have you beheld the king cobra before?"

"*Ankh-yaret* we call him. Yes, I've seen just one—a visitor brought him from Meluhha."

"And what did you think of him?"

"As he had just killed my amah, I thought I might like to chop off his head."

"Oh, goodness! I'm so sorry!"

"No need to be. I was just five at the time, and my mother found another."

"Another cobra?"

"No, silly, another amah."

"Oh. Is she like an aunt or a *naditu*?"

"What's a *naditu*?"

"She's a type of priestess. Actually, there are all kinds of *naditu*, but certain ones train for child rearing in place of the birth mother. Particularly when the mother has temple responsibilities."

"I see. Yes, close to the same. How long did your *naditu* live in your home?"

"I never had one." She'd never had a home, either, a truth probably best kept to herself.

"Really?" the boy remarked. "No amah, no *naditu*, so how were you raised?"

Uruna turned her wide gaze upon the royal prince from Egypt and answered with customary candor.

"By a cobra."

Khufu stared long and hard at her, apparently trying to decide if she was teasing him. At length, a wide grin split his face and he grasped her hand and leaned close.

"Then the stories are true!"

"I'm afraid to think what kind of stories you've heard."

Still holding her hand, he leaned back against the cushions and slumped in a most un-royal fashion, stuck out his tongue, covered his eyes with his other hand, and laughed aloud.

"I was hoping," he began, then peeked at her from under the hand. "You lovely rascal! Do you know how much this means to me?"

"I've no idea what you're talking about."

"Then let me tell you."

He turned to face her and held both her hands.

"I've been putting on a face. Do you know what that means?"

"You haven't been completely truthful?"

"Ah, no, not completely. Maybe not at all. You see, when your Lukur lady came to my father's house, do you know what his first thought was?"

"I can't imagine."

"He said to my mother, 'What are we going to feed her?'"

"Why would he say that? We regard your food as a delicacy."

"No, no, he meant we had no food in the house."

"What?"

"Uruna, my father was ready to beg alms from the fine lady from your temple. Duanna saved us from starvation. We had suffered a terrible drought. The fields were empty, the river was low, we had to sell all the cattle. Father sold our possessions to buy the last of our meals. Lady Duanna was a godsend. Her stipend to send me here—I-I'm not the rich prince everyone thinks. I'm the poor beggar son of a sheaf counter. I'm nothing!"

He dropped Uruna's hands and faced forward again, caught up in misery and heedless of the surrounding evening charm.

"We took your money so that my family might live another year. This suit of clothes I wear? See here, inside, the seam so crudely stitched? It's the last of a hundred from my dressing room, all sold to buy food. The jewel at my belt? Paste, a gift, if you will, from my own amah! To make me appear princely!"

"Khufu, you don't have to tell me these things."

"I want you to know the truth. You *must* know, before you carry this sham any further than you have to. You are the serpent queen. I am just a beggar at your door."

A lantern ashore glided slowly toward them and passed behind. The magic of the night was lost on Khufu. His mouth drooped at the corners, the handsome arrogance was replaced by a haunted look.

Was the same to be said for his serpent skills? Could he learn the rites of the first Steps to prophecy?

Khufu answered for himself.

"When one enters *semtu* for the first time, one must be pure in heart, clear of mind. I'm not sure—"

"*Semtu*?" Uruna rocked back, stunned. "You've done *semtu*?"

"Yes, but that was before everything fell apart. For some reason my father's house lost worthiness. Now I can no longer appeal to the god."

Uruna was about to refute that wasteful notion when Niccaba stepped forward.

"We're approaching Shutu Gate. Looks like you two have been getting on well together, it seems?"

Uruna realized she had entwined her arm with Khufu's as a comforting gesture. She released him with a furtive jerk and folded her hands in her lap, averting her gaze from Niccaba's piercing scrutiny.

"Yes," she agreed. "Siamun Mahut and I have found common interests."

"Marvelous news," Niccaba purred. "Now, if you, Uruna, would lead the party ashore? We have a little ceremony to finish this delightful evening."

Niccaba was all about rituals and appearances. The ceremony was mainly an excuse for her to present Ekur's Egyptian guest with a memento of his introduction to Sumerian culture, an effigy of Inanna carved in rare stone.

Khufu accepted the gift with a grave reserve which he maintained for the walk back through the city to the Aniginna gate. He thanked Uruna with a stiff nod and left for his quarters without promise of further acquaintance.

She resolved not to let his dour demeanor dampen her spirits, which still soared as she prepared for bed.

Semtu!

Just the fact that he'd mentioned the word was enough, but for him to have experienced that elevated state of being, to have shared the elixir she had shared with no other, brought her to her knees in prayer. She vowed to pursue her fate with this young man at her side, a kindred soul, equally humble and equally at odds with Ekur's abundance of material wealth.

Enshiggu-god, she prayed. *Open your heart to my new Egyptian friend. Bring us to your altar together, that as earthly mates we may chase the divine task you have set before me, and win sacred Sight for your beloved people.*

LEGACY

Chapter 32

Hunting with Ashur

The locust song clamped shut and a heron leapt up from the reeds and fled into the fading light. Uruna followed its track across the sky, wishing for wings of her own to escape her misery. Twilight's drab uniformity dulled the eye and worsened the already difficult human task of detecting contrast and movement. They would never find the wounded deer.

She was thirteen now, and this was her sixth hunting foray in two years with Ashur and the Nords from Na Purna. He had taught her well, and she had responded in kind, earning a grudging respect from the men.

Until today's fiasco.

She had sent her arrow into the flank of a young male antelope. The animal had bolted into the reed brake before she could draw her second shot. The entire hunting party had chased after it for what seemed hours before the Nord Ergon's shout sounded from ahead. Uruna bit her lip as she followed Ashur over reeds crushed in the animal's flight. Its prolonged agony tore at her heart.

When she closed upon the scene, she saw the beast was down and panting its last. It was her job to dispatch it, but Kumir stepped forward before she could move and ended the poor thing's suffering with a quick swipe of his blade.

His black look afterward betrayed his silent disapproval of his father's decision to include her. Hunting was a man's work, in Kumir's view, and here was one reason why. Her efforts today hadn't done much to persuade him otherwise, she thought as she waited to one side while Kumir field-dressed the carcass. When he was done, Ergon stepped in and hoisted the trussed package to his broad shoulder for the trek back.

No one spoke. The honor of the hunt was missing and all felt its absence, especially Uruna.

By the time they reached the boats, night was falling. She took a rag from her tote bag and went down to the river, doused the cloth, and scrubbed the red grease mark until it was gone from her left cheek. She no longer deserved the stalker's emblem.

When she got back no one seemed to notice its removal, or else they tacitly agreed with her decision.

The Nords took the kill and headed upstream to Na Purna with it, while Uruna rode the river seated in the prow of Ashur's swifthull, watching the lights of Nippur draw closer in the rosy light. Kumir and the two bush beaters kept to themselves in the other two boats. Worse than returning empty-handed, the botched hunt left everyone in a dour mood.

Ashur steadfastly refused to blame her, but Uruna knew it was her fault. As they stepped onto Nippur's muddy quay in the twilight, she turned to Ashur to speak, but he cut her off.

"We'll talk about it later," he said.

"I was going to say this will be my last hunt."

"No need for that."

"It's a matter of commitment. You said yourself stalking takes one's full attention. Mine is divided."

"Uruna, you don't need to just drop the hunt altogether."

"My mind is made up. I was going to tell you anyway. I'll be forever grateful to you and the men for taking me along."

"We didn't just take you along. You're a good huntress."

"Maybe, as far as my casual approach to it goes, but that's not good enough. Besides, other matters go untended while I'm out in the fen. Anyway, I want you to know how much the experience has taught me about hunting and the men who risk their lives to feed others. I won't forget any of you, Ashur."

He nodded. "Well, I can believe that much. You remember everything else that passes before your nose. That very trait made you easy to train. I'd have you by my side on any hunt."

"Even the boar?"

Her biggest triumph in all the outings had been taking her second boar last year without help.

Ashur smiled in the gathering darkness. "Even him," he said. "You've done well. Today was—could have happened to anyone."

"That's not my reason for stopping."

"Oh? But then we'll see you in dove season, won't we?"

"I think not. Spring is my busiest, with the planters breaking ground and opening the river and all. Please give my deepest thanks to Kumir and the others. Everyone treated me with respect as a fellow hunter. I shall treasure our time together."

Ashur swallowed hard and looked away toward the ruddy western glow.

"We've come a long way."

"Ashur, please..."

"I remember that day above the Zab like it was yesterday. You were just a little thing, so high, but you knew things. Oh yes, you knew. And now you're full-grown, and a marvel of a woman, but I still think of you as my daughter. Have done so from the start."

"Oh, Ashur, you're going to make me cry. It's not that we won't see each other again."

"I know, but now I understand what real fathers have talked about, the happy-sad moment when they watch their little girl change and go on with her own life."

She threw her arms around his neck and drew him close, just as she had a thousand times. "Around you, I have always felt safe, protected, cared for. Still do."

"If there's ever anything I can do, come to me, or send for me."

"I shall, I promise."

"Look, I have to tend the boat, stow a few things—"

"Don't worry about me. I know my way from here."

They embraced again, and Uruna realized how many of her fortunes she owed to the hunter who had devoted his life to her welfare, who had really started her on her path.

As she pulled away, she whispered to him, "Light a candle."

He nodded. "I do, every night."

It was an expression from the Zab mountain people, Ashur's people, a vow to turn one's thoughts to a loved one just before slumber.

Moments later on the footpath to the road, she nearly stumbled, blinded by tears.

On awakening the following morning, Uruna discovered further cause for regret, but it had nothing to do with giving up the hunt or shifting away from loved ones. In reflecting back, she could not account for when the transformation might have begun, but realized she had missed it completely on several occasions—as she slew the boar, on her victory march from a pheasant kill, and now just yesterday with the stag.

She had not felt their pain.

After Morning Call, she slung a tote over her shoulder and hiked across town to Khufu's apartment. As usual, the young man sensed her trouble in advance and greeted her with a steady gaze bereft of emotion.

"Your spirit is troubled," he said at once. "I take it the hunt did not go well."

"How did you even know I went hunting?"

"My limited version of Sight. Extremely limited. Comes and goes with the full moon." He opened his door. "Come tell me your woes."

The past year had tightened the bond between them. Khufu's tales of exotic Egyptian life thrilled her. He was an ardent companion, a pleasant conversationalist. But he refused to join the hunt, as the taking of animal life gave him grievous pain.

"Which one's wound disturbs you so?" he asked, beckoning her to a small cushioned bench.

"The stag's was bad enough, but my own is harder to deal with."

"I see no mark on you."

Uruna threw down her tote and squatted on the settee.

"I couldn't find the animal as I usually do—as I should have. I don't know when it began, but Khufu, I'm losing the part of me that feels what others feel."

"Come now, you're upset by the animal's death. It's part of the hunt, Uruna, you know that."

"It was suffering for hours!"

"That is sad, indeed."

"I couldn't find it because I couldn't feel its agony. We searched in all directions, but even when we found it, I felt more sorrow for myself than for the stag."

"Ah, my dove, to be sure, there's sorrow aplenty for taking a life. And remorse, and regret, and self-abasement. All right and proper feelings every hunter expects of himself. You prepared beforehand, of course?"

Indeed she had. To keep yourself honorable, you asked Shumu-gan for permission to take the animal's life. You prayed for its death to be swift, peaceful. You sought forgiveness for the wrong you must do to one of his creations. None of it seemed to be working.

"But Khufu, I'm changing. I'm losing the things I cherish!"

"Uruna, you're becoming a woman. It's a difficult time, especially for a sensitive such as you. Now look inside and tell me. What do you feel?"

"I don't feel others anymore! Oh, Khufu, what's wrong with me?"

She knew, of course. Other signs had crept into her awareness, only to be pushed away by adulthood's advance and a diminished sense of childish wonder. The sick and the wounded no longer called for her healing hands. Strangers remained nameless until introduced. She would go days without attending the serpent god at prayer. If she heard at all the sounds of serpent talk, they made less and less sense.

Khufu looked out the window at the horizon, as if the answer lay in some distant land. "We can only conclude the obvious."

"Please, don't say it."

"Your feelings, what you called 'touches' in your youth. They're fading."

"Fading? Khufu, they're *gone!*"

"Is that your greatest fear? That you can no longer feel the sick to heal them, or warn people from trouble?"

"Yes, that's my purpose!"

"Maybe it used to be, but it's time you focused on the real reason you were put on this earth. Prophecy! Uruna, you will become the prophet to lead Sumer through the times ahead. It is ordained. Enshiggu has told you so, has even told me. And nothing will change it."

Uruna felt the truth of his words, but somehow, somewhere along the path, she had lost sight of her goal. With her mind wrapped in a confused adolescent muddle, she had felt compelled to immerse herself in the arcane workings of the new Lukur culture. To contend with their beliefs and their doctrine, to partake in their daily life, she had felt obliged to engage in a dialectic that challenged her very sanity. But rather than seek solace in prayer at day's end, she had formed the habit of further attending to ritual. Thus depleted of physical energy, she'd allowed her spirit to wither. The insane downward spiral must be stopped if she were ever to recover her path, or open prophecy's door.

"Uruna, would you care for bread and honey?"

Khufu reached for himself without waiting for Uruna's reply.

Where had the noon meal come from...?

Noon? Good gods, where had her mind flown this time? She was crouched on the end of Khufu's bed like a toad, blinking vacantly ahead with half the morning gone!

Khufu continued: "Pondering the weight of the world again, are we?"

Uruna shook herself out of the reverie. What was this on her tray? A pomegranate?

She stared at its rotund ripeness, then plucked it from the tray and flipped it at Khufu.

Her consort looked up from his tea mug and easily caught the sphere in mid-air. "What is this thing?"

"The world," she said. "I was pondering the weight of it."

She listened to Khufu's laughter fade and felt her concerns fade with it. In a flash, she snatched the last biscuit from Khufu's groping hand.

"Greedy little piggy," he said.

"I've saved you from yourself," she replied. "Lest you begin to look the pig as well as eat like one."

Chapter 33

Khufu Hunts

Everyone was shocked the next day when it was learned that Khufu had stolen away with a pair of Temple hunters. Uruna could not believe what she heard when Kinar explained.

"He told the gateman it was a matter of honor," she said. "I don't understand myself, but it seems he felt unworthy for some reason."

Uruna went in search of Ashur and found him at the hunters' station near Gula Gate.

"I only heard about it myself a bit ago," he told her. "I might have tried to dissuade him, but it was too late. Don't worry he's in good hands."

"But where would they take him?" Uruna asked.

Ashur waved a hand toward a pair of hunters idled by bound-up wounds. "This lot couldn't say. He just wanted to find good boar grounds. That could be anywhere."

"Boar? He's going after boar? He'll be killed, Ashur! He doesn't know anything about boar hunting. He's just a boy, a very sweet boy. This is terrible! We've got to do something!"

It turned out the hunters Khufu had chosen were the least

experienced. The best were already out in the hinterland at work.

Uruna turned a scornful eye on Ashur. "Where would you take him if you had done it?"

Ashur scratched his chin. "Well, him being the consort and all, I'd try to keep him as safe as I could. Probably up along the river by Kish. Place up there is pretty well hunted out, so he wouldn't come across much boar. Sure wouldn't take him where temple hunters are stalking."

Her frustration mounting, Uruna clenched her fists at her sides. "I wish he'd approached you instead."

"What about the Nords? Could we maybe ask them for help?"

An hour later, three swifthulls set out about half a day from Kish, Gar in the lead with Engur, while Ashur with Uruna took the second boat. Two off-duty hunters in the third craft had volunteered after disqualifying any temple guards as being useless liabilities. The odds of their finding Khufu were slim at best, but Uruna held out a strong hope.

At nightfall they set up camp near the river road above Babyla.

"We'll never find his party after dark," said Ashur, stating the obvious. "It's best if we get a fresh start at dawn."

Uruna said nothing. She was too tired to argue and quickly fell asleep before the cook fire was set. Oppressive dread filled her heart, for she sensed the future did not bode well. Did that mean her touches were returning? Was she truly in touch with Khufu's peril? Or was her own sense of loss reflecting back upon itself? Neither possibility would save him.

Their first morning in the bush passed with no results other than a mounting sense of futility. Not one sign of man or boar did they find. It seemed wild game had abandoned those grounds and moved on. At midday Gar took Ashur aside and the two men discussed the situation. When they returned, they told Uruna Khufu's hunters likely had chosen another place altogether. Ashur was persuaded that they might have set out for Ninburdu Sector, north of the canal.

"But that's mostly Akkad wilderness," Uruna pointed out.

"Not all of it," Ashur replied. "Last year we found patches of wetland up there, some evidence of boar rooting. Game might've headed for other parts since then, but it's worth a look. I'm sure the other hunters know about it."

The trek took most of that day and the next, so that by the time they reached the hunting grounds, night was again falling. Later, just before turning in, Ashur told Uruna the truth she had dreaded.

"It's a small area, won't take half a day to cover as long as we spread out. If they're not there, we'll have to let these fellows go back to their homes, then wait in Nippur until word comes one way or the other."

Uruna could only nod her head in agreement. Ashur was too kind to say what she already knew in her heart to be true by now. Yet she told herself to hold out against despair. It was not hopeless, not yet. Hers might be the only hope to come to Khufu's aid.

"One more thing," Ashur added. "Bring your boar lance. I don't want you out there without it."

As expected, the morning brought no news of Khufu or his hunting party. Clinging to the last shred of hope, Ashur instructed Uruna to stay in sight, a tricky task owing to the mounded hillocks they encountered.

"Keep to my left," he told her. "We'll be dropping below each other's sight line. If we get separated, stay in place and don't rove around or we'll never find you."

They had been on the hunt for about an hour when one of the men gave a shout. It was Engur. He had found tracks in the hardened mud of a dry wash.

"That's a man's heel print," said Gar.

"Yes, but it's old," said Ashur. "Could be last year's."

"Still bears a look."

Ashur instructed the men to fan out and look for more tracks. Then he turned to Uruna. "You have a good eye, see if you can find anything newer."

"Is there a chance?" she asked.

Ashur merely shrugged. "We'll see."

She struck off to the left in a north-by-west direction and almost immediately found more tracks. The ground was as hard as before, but this time they were mixed with boar hoof prints. She followed the trail between two hummocks of heaped clay and kept going, careful not to get her hopes up. Here, the clay mounds grew higher and the arroyo narrowed. In ages past, river churn had molded these hills as if by a giant potter's hands. Now their twists and turns served as both predator's trap and prey's hideout.

She was so focused on the track that she almost missed the sound.

A harsh scrape, the sound of an animal on the prowl.

She looked up and her limbs locked as still as a statue.

Two lions descended the narrow defile, one behind the other. Of good size but young, maybe in their second year. An adult female would not be far away.

She lifted her boar lance and shook it, hoping these youngsters understood the weapon's threat. If they did not, and charged, even though she might take one she would never survive the mother cat's fury.

Was there any path to higher ground? Or was she doomed where she stood?

Fj-ff-fht!

An arrow caught the lead animal just behind the shoulder. As the lion toppled onto one side, its surviving brother cast about for the enemy. The next arrow struck it broadside, and in the blink of an eye both cats lay dead.

A hush came over the ravine. Uruna stood immobilized by fear, only the faint buzz of insects breaking the stillness. When would the mother cat appear? Or was she already slain?

She listened, not moving. A loose pebble tumbled down the slope from a crest some thirty feet above her head. She glanced up and caught a flash of naked human flesh, a sandaled toe, before the figure spun away and vanished behind the ridge.

Was it man or boy? With only a glimpse she couldn't be sure. A skilled hunter would never take cubs if he knew the mother still lived, or so she reasoned. If she was wrong, she would die down here in the jaws of an outraged killer.

She hollered after her rescuer and drove her feet in a hard climb toward higher ground. Halfway up the crumbling slope, the clay came loose beneath her weight and she slipped, lost her footing, and slid back to the bottom.

Cursing to herself, she managed another try on firmer ground, and scrabbled hand over foot, gaining and losing but mostly gaining. By the time she reached the top she was nearly out of breath. Before her lay an endless expanse of empty desert.

The other hunter was gone.

Well, she thought to herself, who was lost now? She or Khufu?

She heard Gar's bellow from afar and wheeled around. He was standing on a similar high point, his huge frame diminished by a distance of several hundred yards. She waved at him and he hooked an arm for her to head back his direction. The trek through the labyrinth of molded clay took longer than she expected. By the time she closed with Ashur, the others had joined him.

She reported her findings, including the lion encounter and her mystery rescuer.

"You can thank Shumu-gan he was a good shot," said Ashur.

Engur wondered aloud if the lion presence meant there was indeed game to be found in these reaches, but Ashur shook his head.

"Not necessarily. Only thing up here for lions to feed on is pigs. These could've missed the last move south. They were probably scrounging for small game before moving on themselves. Uruna's rescuer might have killed that she-lion before he knew she had young."

Engur spat in the dirt. "Cubs were doomed anyway."

That ended their discussion of Uruna's close call. Further exploration would bring them no closer to Khufu. They set out immediately for Nippur without a noon meal. No one spoke as they settled into an easy flatland pace, the last of their hope spent. Uruna could only pray that no harm had come to Khufu, and clung to Ashur's suggestion that the boy might have returned already to Nippur with a trophy kill.

The same listless pair of wounded hunters met them at the temple station: no word of Khufu's huntsmen.

Niccaba tried for a more positive note. "It's only been three days. These things usually take a week."

Yes, but the present situation was far from usual.

The Nords returned to Na Purna, and Uruna sent Ashur with them, adding her thanks for his efforts. She then returned to her room in the Gipar, fetched Memet from his lair, and sat before her small shrine, immersed in fervent prayer.

Kinar came for her shortly before midnight. "You must get food and rest," said her best friend.

Uruna could not answer. If she said anything at all it might ruin Khufu's chances. She must be his stalwart sentinel until word reached them.

She awoke to bright daylight sprawled on Khufu's bed, no idea how she'd got there, her empty belly reminding her of her sacrificial fast. A clamor in the hall outside had wakened her. As she reached the door, she realized she was still in her hunting togs.

When she poked her head outside the room, Kinar called to her.

"They found him! He's back!"

Uruna ran to her. "Thank the gods! Where is he now?"

As she got closer, she noticed a frown wrinkling Kinar's normally placid brow. Kinar shook her head, could not speak as a tear spilled down her cheek.

Uruna covered her mouth with her hand to suppress the sob that threatened to break her heart.

Niccaba pushed her way through the milling crowd to stand beside Kinar.

"He's been hurt," she said, "A boar got him, just as I said."

As usual, Niccaba's taciturn account did little to assuage anyone's feelings, least of all Uruna's. She turned to Kinar, praying for words of encouragement—anything but Niccaba's blunt delivery of lost hope.

Kinar put on a brave smile. "Let's get you down to the infirmary. We won't know how badly he was injured until the physicians have had a chance to tend his wounds."

"I'm not sure that's a good idea," said Niccaba.

"Well, good or bad, that's where we're going," Uruna rejoined, and brushed past the matron's dour look without another word.

The physicians were another obstacle entirely. They steadfastly refused to allow Uruna into his room, nor would they reveal the extent of Khufu's injuries. She caught sight of one of the hunters seated in the hallway outside, but as she headed toward him, a muscular female orderly stepped in her path.

"No one questions the hunters before trial."

Uruna stared at the woman in confusion until the truth dawned on her. The two huntsmen were being held accountable for whatever had happened.

"Did they commit a crime out there?" she asked.

"Not for me to say. Court will determine that."

"But did Khufu have anything to do with it?"

Kinar took her arm and led her to one side. "Uruna, if there was any crime committed it was in taking the boy in the first place. Whatever happens to him is on their heads, as it should be."

"I want to be with him," Uruna said. "I should be the first thing he sees when he wakes up."

"We've no idea how long that might be. Come with me, we can't be of any help to him here."

"Kikki, please!"

"No, now come along with me. Do as I say, there's a good girl."

Uruna let herself be led away in a daze, unsure where she was being taken. The news was bad enough, but worse was the realization she could not feel Khufu's pain. Couldn't find the blackness that needed healing. It was as if she had lost those senses entirely now, and the prospect frightened her almost as much as the prospect of losing Khufu. Her healing touch had been available to so many strangers, but why not to him?

What was left for her to do now? Was prayer her only recourse? If only she knew what to ask for. The ladies in charge would tell her nothing, which meant poor Khufu must lie suffering a pain she could not spare him. Why would they do this?

Kinar lifted a cup to her lips. "Here, drink this."

She was on her back in her bed again. How much time had she lost? Hours? Days? A single oil lamp glowed full in one corner, the window revealing that it was dark outside.

She struggled under her elbows. "What happened? How did I get here? Any word about Khufu?"

Kinar urged her back onto her mat. "Go ahead, drink."

She swallowed, tasted the bitter brew, winced as it burned the back of her throat. Something strong, not tea. The ceiling overhead started to spin slowly. An oddly dull presence penetrated her thoughts as the room darkened except for the oil lamp. She watched the lamp dim down and shrink away to the corner until it became just a small dot.

Then nothing.

The old one hunkered at the edge of the fire circle, her black eyes gleaming in the firelight as she watched the reflected stares from three jackals crouched nearby. They would keep watch the night through, ready to pounce at the slightest sign of sleep. But they would be disappointed.

The girl had not flinched before the lions. She had accepted her fate with a steady heart and a sure hand on her weapon. She might have taken the first cat herself, and in so doing distracted the other long enough to make her escape. She couldn't have known about the mother's demise two days before, so had to believe the greater threat might lurk nearby.

A moot point. Mights and maybes did not move the world. She had needed saving, clear enough.

A priestess now, she remained true to her character—strong, fearless, grounded in purpose. Not like the biddies clucking at her heels. She might be the one, but then again she might not. The signs were right. She was fast becoming a woman. Full of promise, but was there enough time?

Perhaps. Only the gods knew...

That dog on the left, the big one. Still as a rock. Hungry. Needs watching.

Chapter 34

Setback and Resolve

Tragedy reached Uruna next day at *disikku* the moment she stepped down from the offering table. She had wondered why Shua Kinar failed to appear at the midday rite. When she saw her friend's stricken look at the other end of the hall, her heart lurched in her chest.

"Come with me," was all Kinar said as she led Uruna quickly past the flower bearers, carelessly tossed both their holy vestments into the changing room, and skipped down the stairs in a rapid descent to the street.

"What's happened? Tell me, Kikki," Uruna tried, but Kinar only set her jaw more firmly

"Not here."

She led Uruna through the street throng and around the first corner into the temple counting house adjacent to Ekur.

Once inside, Kinar pulled Uruna into the shadowed anteroom and hugged her close.

"He's gone," she whispered.

A cry of anguish escaped Uruna's throat.

Kinar laid a comforting hand on Uruna's arm. "Khufu Mahut passed in the night."

"No!" she screamed. "Not him! Oh, please, not Khufu!"

Blinding tears welled up and spilled in a torrent down Uruna's face.

They wept together, Kinar feeling the loss nearly as much as Uruna, for she understood the depth of that despair, the unrelenting onslaught of Uruna's losses, every love—one after another—snatched away. And now the most bitter defeat of all. Could the gods have devised a more vicious injury?

Uruna willed herself to stop sobbing and pulled back from Kinar's grasp, twisting her mouth in an effort to thwart grief. When she had composed herself, she blinked back tears and drew a single long breath.

"Take me to him," she said.

For a while she was too locked in grief to notice their direction. Only as they neared the Nubian quarter and Jebbut's lanky, dark figure emerged from a doorway did she comprehend that Nippur's miniscule Nubian community had gathered to mourn one of their own.

Jebbut introduced a tall, elegant lady as his wife, Nayith, and explained that the local priest would see to the proper disposition of the dead. Nayith then led Uruna through a doorway into a small room where Khufu's inert body lay supine on a raised platform. Large urns stood in a row against the far wall. Otherwise, the room was empty.

Uruna moved closer for a last look at Khufu's face, but what she saw made her draw back in shock.

He didn't look dead at all!

Khufu's dark eyes gazed upward in open wonder, his face serene with pleasure, his finely drawn mouth stretched slightly in a bemused smile.

Her first thought was that this must be the work of a master embalmer. She'd learned of the practice from Khufu himself.

"We found him thus," said a voice behind her.

She turned, and received another shock.

Tula! The cleaning woman who years ago had dragged her to her exile behind the smithy in Trades.

Uruna turned to Jebbut for an explanation, but Heganna's wiry houseman merely shrugged.

"None here have seen the like of it."

"He looks like he's found the garden of the gods," Uruna said.

"Maybe so."

An idea struck her just then, and she asked the others if she might be alone with Khufu for a few moments.

"You were to be his wife," said Nayith. "It is most fitting."

Once the curtain was drawn across the doorway, she went straight to Khufu's body and pulled back the sleeve from his right arm.

Nothing.

She moved around to his other side and repeated with the left sleeve.

And there it was! Two tiny marks on the inside of his wrist, almost too faint to notice.

How had he smuggled an asp into the infirmary? Who would have done such a thing?

She tugged the sleeve back into place and stood a moment, looking down at the face she might have loved if given the chance.

Tears spilled down her cheeks now, grief doubled, even as she realized how much he had risked, how far he had trod the path alone.

Ah, but you caught a taste of semtu, didn't you, love? It's written on your face, in your eyes, your half-smile. Beloved champion, you rushed to the post before you were ready—before either of us had a chance. For such rash endeavor none dares condemn you, and I can only love you.

She stretched a hand to his face and softly drew his eyelids closed.

Rest now in Inanna's care. Be happy, my Siamun prince.

When she returned to the others, she had regained her composure enough to declare her intention with unshakeable resolve. She addressed Jebbut as master of his house.

"If you would, sir, have him prepared for travel."

"But Uruna, we have a place here for him."

"Thank you, dear Jebbut, but Khufu belongs with his ancestors, with his family who sent him to us. I believe they live in Mennefer."

"Uruna! That's the other side of the world!"

"He managed the journey from there to us, and so shall he return."

Jebbut's dark face grew red with alarm. "Impossible! Send the prince on a sailing ship across the Great Sea? The ladies won't allow it. Too dangerous."

"Indeed, but we owe as much to his family. Please, Jebbut, surely you of all people understand."

Jebbut turned his gaze to the empty doorway beyond which his young kinsman reposed. After considerable inner turmoil, his chest heaved with a deep sigh. "I shall see to it."

The following morning a sailing craft bearing the Egyptian son set out downriver from Nippur, leaving a small party of bereft Nubians standing on shore. Uruna stood in their midst, beset by conflicting emotions. She could only interpret Khufu's death as a sign she had not yet found her mate, which must mean another awaited her. Small comfort. Khufu's loss was too great for her to find any comfort in that notion. As on similar occasions past, she would set aside judgment and await the hand of divine providence, trusting Enshiggu to reveal the next step in its own time.

But today she faced a far more complicated situation than any before. So many factions stood in line, each seeking its own satisfaction at the expense of the others, each relying on prophecy for answers. This first failure was a stunning blow to Lukur pride. Worse, it might shake public faith in temple claims to infallibility.

She must choose rightly at every turn now, for if she did not, if she made a single step in error, her access to Sight would be forfeit. And with it, her vow to the divine that superseded mortal hopes and dreams, including her own.

Most especially her own.

Chapter 35

Temple Dialectics

A life as mundane as a barley shoot now tilted Sumer's fortunes off center and sent its guiding servants spiraling out of control. For certain members of the elect, times of plenty would prove elusive, whereas the rest would immerse themselves in a dark night of self-delusion.

Contrarily, and true to her nature, Uruna found hidden within the emerging calamity the seeds for a people's rebirth.

She might have taken heart at once if she had not accepted in the same breath that Sumer's growing pains would be sharp and the journey to fruition long. Much more so than those in authority anticipated.

Not long after sending Khufu on his journey back to Egypt, Uruna was inducted as a *naditu* priestess in the lowest echelon of the Lukur hierarchy. At twelve years of age, she was the youngest to be so honored in the collective memory of those attending the ceremony. Up to that point, as a *kadishtu* acolyte, she had enjoyed a small taste of autonomy and privilege. A *naditu* was devoted to duty, which was nothing new to the aspiring prophet of Enshiggu.

Thus, her first chance to serve arrived hard on the heels of her "great day" as a new minister.

In the Sumerian world, tradition must be observed, even one so tired as Springfest, an annual gathering of farmers in dirt poor Sikkim. For the planting community, it marked the high point of an otherwise toilsome year. To the Mothers, however, the trek out and back posed an inconvenient interruption not worth the effort and poorly attended by city folk.

Enter Uruna Kumta, *naditu* freshly made, and by virtue of her origin appropriately born to the soil. At least that was the political convenience offered when Uruna received her commission as Springfest priestess-in-charge.

She and a tiny retinue of three reluctant teenage *udalla* anointers gathered on the steps of Ancient Spirits to be taught the festival rites—barely one hour before embarking for Sikkim.

To Uruna, the assignment was a joy.

To the girls with lower aspirations, it was just one more chore piled onto dozens—until Uruna pointed out how the trip offered a chance to escape the grind of daily servitude and the disapproving stares of hall monitors and grumpy matrons.

"We can make of it what we want," she said.

When the girls demurred, she went on. "Two hours on the road to play our favorite guessing games. A town of bumpkins who shower us with flowers and praise us every time we smile. And boys, boys, boys."

And thus did their happy venture proceed, until Uruna's tiny quartet reached Sikkim's street. The dour faces of hard-scrabble planters quickly disabused the young ladies of any notion of "fun."

After the obligatory ceremony before a worn-down outdoor brick altar, Uruna called for a dance to animate their disappointed hosts. The town ladies showed up with a roast pig and trimmings, and things picked up a little. She still sensed a subdued note as she took her place beneath a large awning with the town leaders.

One fellow asked Uruna to say a benediction, and when she finished, the crowd grew silent. Celebration seemed as far from their minds as Nippur.

Zug Abu, the work-worn farmer at her elbow twisted his mouth in disapproval.

"This is all well and good," he said, "but we know better'n to think anything done here'll fix the problem."

"What problem is that?"

"You mean you ain't heard?"

"Why don't you tell me? I'd rather hear it from one who knows."

"It's the rust."

"Oh, no! Where?"

"Wheat caught it over to the other side of the east fork. River runs low back there. Tough enough going when you got flow out to about forty lengths, but we didn't get but fifteen this year. And what's there is shallow."

"So you're talking about a drought?"

"No, not that bad. We gets water down there, but when it's dribs and drabs, that gives the rust a chance to set in on your barley. We noticed right after the seeding. Come outta winter ready to hoe and plant, and there ain't water none."

"Can you keep the rust from spreading?"

"Sure. We cut off Bundug."

"Pardon, but what's Bundug?"

"You don't know? Oh, I forget, you're a young'un. Bundug is that area over yonder from about Rod 120 clear down to the tip of Kuffir."

"I'm sorry, I still don't know. How many hectares?"

"Uruna, you're a nice young lady, you give us more attention than we've had in years. But darlin', Bundug is the whole District

Eight."

"One whole district?"

"That's right. 'Bout half the people come to town today are out of work. That's their homes out there, their save crops as well."

The shock of Zug's words hit Uruna like a hard gust of wind. A save crop was grown on the small patch of land allotted to each farm woman for her family's use. Her husband and sons worked the large fields belonging to the landowner or temple, while the women tended vegetable gardens and grass plots for goats. The loss of a save crop was disastrous. It meant you had to pick up family and livestock, pack your goods on your back, and leave for any place rumor told you had work, and hope you found it when you got there. If you didn't, your children became wards of the temple, while husband and wife were forced to split up and work as drudges. Most such families never got back together again.

The news was devastating. Why hadn't she been told during the briefing for Springfest? Perhaps the Mothers themselves didn't know yet. Or, more disturbing, they knew and just weren't telling.

Uruna got to her feet and beckoned Zug to do the same.

"What's on your mind?" he asked.

"I need a count, Zug."

"We ain't got nothing to count out there. No seed corn, no barley."

"It's not about barley anymore, Zug. I'm talking about people."

With Zug's help, Uruna and her "ministers" marshalled counters of people to go around the town square and tally those displaced or about to be. When they regrouped under the tent, Zug had another question.

"So we counted what, about forty and a hundred folk?"

"Fifty-two and a hundred."

"What you gonna do with that number?"

"Give it to the Mothers at Ekur. They need to know how many

extra mouths to feed and beds to set up. And that's just a start. I want to comb the hinterland, find any others out there needing help."

"Temple can't take care of that many, Uruna."

"These are our people, Zug. That's what we do."

When it came time to leave Sikkim, Uruna and the girls had a difficult time getting through the throng of embraces and hugs. The people had turned from scorn to hope-filled open acceptance. The concern she and the girls had shown for their plight had won hearts aplenty.

On the trek back, Uruna silently rehearsed how she would present her case. The lives involved were too important to waste with an ill-prepared appeal. But that was not as daunting as her overriding concern.

Would any listen?

MINISTRY

Chapter 36

To The Rescue

Twenty leagues upriver from Nippur, just before sunset, the wind died off at the end of young Suba's westward tack. The sail luffed and slackened against the mast like a loose skirt. He muttered a curse at the sky gods and planted his foot on the rudder to make a gliding course parallel to the west bank. He'd hoped to sail another hour before setting up camp. Now it looked like the open desert would be his abode for the night.

Early that morning he had decided to sail another day beyond the target landing set by Nabi Gahn. He enjoyed taking a poke at the irascible hunt master whenever he got the chance. Within the first hour, the younger lads were so far back he couldn't see another sail on the horizon. Solitude suited him better anyway.

Nabi's sailing trials had begun at a place called Babyla, across the river from Kish and north by west another few miles. The point of the exercise was to demonstrate one's sailing skills, along with those for hunting, cooking, camping, and fishing. Suba had tired of the master's harangues and sailed away from the others before dawn. He'd earn a tongue-lashing from Nabi and probably extra duty mending fish nets or some such when he got back to camp.

The embankment was nearly barren of vegetation. No sticks or weeds to tie off to. He brought down the sail and waded ashore with his tow line, hauling the boat behind like a reluctant goat as he cast about for a place to settle for the night.

According to Nabi's reckoning of the distance to Mari town, and his own since passing by that wretched hold, he was beyond Sumer's western frontier by half a day at least. No one could farm the wasteland stretches. Nabi had told him the Bedu wouldn't wander this far north, although he might come across a lion or two stumbling about.

He put a line in the water in case there were fish about. Otherwise, it would be dried tack for the duration. When the light got too dim for the fish to bite, he pulled his line and climbed up the bank to fetch his tuck. At the top, he stopped short.

A man was standing beside the leather bag, staring down at his own feet.

Suba reached for his knife and sidled left past the man. His own sword and spear were beyond reach in the boat, but on second glance the fellow looked harmless. In fact, on closer inspection, he appeared damaged.

Suba decided to attempt a bond. "Do you need help, friend?"

The man looked up slowly, his eyes vague. "They killed Mazla, took my boy away with them."

Uh-oh, trouble.

"Who did this?"

"Nazim. Come out of the western sun. Demons in flying black beards and wild eyes. Took our village. I was away poling my barge, saw the smoke, got there too late…"

His voice faded as his lower lip trembled.

Suba sheathed his knife and extended both hands palms up in a gesture of peace. "I am called Suba," he said.

"I am Set-Om. We call ourselves Tiga, or did. I may be the last."

"Where did this happen, Set?"

The Tiga man nodded over his right shoulder. "Up there. River place had no name, nothing for them to take…except lives."

"When did you last eat?"

Set-Om held up two fingers. Two days without food? No wonder the man could hardly stand.

"I have meat in my tuck there."

"Don't waste it on me. I'm half dead."

"Not if you can stand. Come, sit. I eat better with company."

They both squatted in their tracks and chewed strips of dried beef in the gathering dusk. Suba fetched water from the river in a jar and after sharing a long draught, Set-Om livened up a bit.

"First man I've seen since I left," he said, pointing at Suba. "You got a man's size and way about you, but you look plenty young. Or maybe I've been on the road so long my eyes gone bad."

"How long is that?"

"Three days, maybe four. I was out of my mind with grief for most of it. My family—none left."

"I'm sorry, Set. Can you tell me any more about your attackers?"

"We heard about the Nazim before. Coming out of the west, something bad driving 'em out of their homes. All they know is killing. Can't farm, can't build a fence or a house or even a hen coop. Women folk are just as wild as the men, kill you as soon as look at you."

He chewed some, became lost in thought. Suba was ready to call it a night when the bargeman spoke once more.

"They worship Lamashtu. You heard about that?"

"No, but there's all kinds of gods in the world."

"He's the god of death. What I've heard, they hold that a killing releases the dead to save the living from further death, or some such rubbish. Except to them it's the only sense in the world. You better hope they stay up there where I left. They come down here, you got your hands full."

Death worshippers. The stuff of fireside fable, old wives' gossip. Nabi had explained such beliefs as the curse of ignorant fools, most of them female. But Set-Om was nobody's fool. And his account sounded real enough.

Suba folded his tuck bag and shifted it under his head. "I have to head back in the morning. Got room in the boat for one more. Might do you good to get back with people, get a fresh start."

The next day, with Set-Om on the paddle downstream and a following wind, the return to Babyla took but a single day. The other boys had returned the night before, and now crowded the shoreline, taking in the stranger's dour face, all eager to hear an adventure. When at last Suba caught Nabi's eye, he had no time for the master's chiding remarks.

He pointed at his refugee passenger and spat on the ground.

"Desert tribe took his village."

"Bedu?"

"No, Nazim."

Nabi considered a moment before speaking again. "How far?"

"Three days, maybe four. Less if they're headed this way."

Nabi stared long and hard at his pupil. Then he turned and walked over to his spears.

"Get your weapons."

Chapter 37

Unsanctioned Compassion

By the time Uruna reached the Aniginna gate on her return from Springfest, she had worked up a mental list of the points crucial to motivate any who might listen, provided she found an ear for her plea. Having also concluded that few ranking Lukur, besides Kinar, would grant audience to a twelve-year-old *naditu* acolyte, she surprised herself with her first choice.

Semma Karkhan allowed few intercessors beyond a teenage girl assigned to her quarters to make sure she didn't expire in the night unnoticed. Uruna's first attempt to gain entry was soundly rebuffed by a husky girl in her mid-teens.

"Entu is sleeping. Come back tomorrow."

"What would be a good hour?"

"Depends. She might be lucid, she might sit the day long staring out the window at a tree."

"Who's on morning duty?"

"Dunno. Usually a troublemaker like me doing penance. Changes every day."

Well, that was that for tonight. She might have better luck in the morning.

As she started back down the hallway she met Lubna Seddua coming the other way. The woman stopped her with an irritated scowl.

"What are you doing here?"

"Visiting."

"I told you to stay away!"

"You told me to mind my tongue, and I have. Now excuse me, I must report to Lady Kalumma Dalla."

"What have you got to do with the high-priestess of the *nigenna*?"

"I spent the day at Springfest."

"That waste of time? Better you learned your evensong verses."

"I already know them quite well."

"Don't be brash with me."

"Then stop bothering me and let's both get on with our work, shall we?"

Uruna darted around Lubna and continued down the hall before the woman could detain her further. She'd been given no order to report to Kalumma, but saying so served to remove her from Lubna's clutches.

The confrontation put her out of sorts. She was tired, near exhaustion. She must bide the night and consider the refugee plight with care. That left but one course: prayer.

Before exhaustion could consume her entirely, she went straight to her room, fetched Memet, and wrapped him round her shoulders in their customary approach to the god. She then knelt before her small shrine to Enshiggu and struck a flint to the stubby candle at one side. Settling herself into a deep, long breath, she waited as Memet slid from her shoulder to coil on the floor at her side. The cares of the day eased away, making a place for peace, a place for the god.

Before she could form the first thought of supplication, a voice from the divine rang deep in her soul. And behind it, the unmistakable power of Goddess Inanna.

Beloved, thou art whole.

A soft blanket of peace descended about Uruna's shoulders, soothing, nurturing. She bent forward and choked off a sob as tears welled up and spilled down her face.

Thou art my servant to those who suffer in the land of Bundug.

Get thee downriver to a place with no name. Build there a home of homes. Let thy works there be a balm to raise up victory from failure. Feed the hungry from a new stream in a new land. Abide therein for two plantings, two harvests.

For this task art thou chosen above thy masters. Selah.

The lightest touch graced her heart and left.

She sat still for a long time, savoring the warmth of that moment, feeling its balm sink deep into her soul, replacing every last shred of doubt with rock-bound assurance. She might be just an acolyte priestess, at age thirteen barely a woman. But Great Mother's truth rang strong in her heart. She was chosen for some character yet to be discovered. She would flower as the hand of Inanna opened and extended Her bounty to the world, for Her divine edict superseded all else. Even the call to prophecy.

At her side, Memet rested perfectly still, coils relaxed, his probing tongue withdrawn, eyes suffused with a contented calm she had not seen before. She pinched the candle out and gathered him to her, and he came willingly as she rose from her shrine and crossed the room to her bed.

Before retiring, she carried out what had become her nightly cup-and-spoon routine, the same Mena Ramush had taught her long ago as preparation for prophecy. The cup to milk Memet's fangs, the small oil spoon to reduce the toxin for her own ingestion. After each night's ritual, as she waited for sleep to come, she would ask Enshiggu for one more day without eternal slumber.

Her sleep that night passed in dreamless rest, girding her for the arduous path ahead. Heaven had spoken, though the world no longer listened. And she, still a child of that world, must find a way to use it.

Chapter 38

Mission To Oblivion

Uruna did find a way to prod the worldly into reluctant action. The means, though, came not with a flash of inspiration, but crept into her awareness with the silent stealth of a wily fox.

Her first attempt to gain Council's attention was conceived in the altruistic assumption that these were women of action. Instead, her earliest appeals only demonstrated a pervasive contempt for youthful ideals and an abiding habit of sitting on one's duff.

Of course, Kinar conspired with her to launch a campaign in spite of willful inaction. "We'll spend a lot of time on the river," she began.

"*We*? I only sought your advice—"

"So we'll need swifthulls for people and a barge for supplies. I can provide two fast boats, and I think I know where to find a halfway decent raft. But before we ship goods, we need to go down there ourselves and get a complete assessment of the extent of rust damage, the numbers of people affected, and the severity of their straits."

"Kikki! You have planters of your own to tend to."

"Don't forget I spent nearly a year developing contacts among the farm folk of this very province. People in the Bundug know me and I know them. We'll need their help to organize relief. As for my crops, I have overseers aplenty. Besides, I'm only giving you a head start. We must determine the extent and bounds of the infestation first. And owing to human nature, some planters won't cooperate. I know you mean well, but you'll find there's always a prideful few who disdain help."

"I'll enlist them to help the others."

"Good idea—if you can manage it. But first, let's get a feel for the size of the problem."

They agreed to meet the next morning and set off with two people in each boat. They would add to their own company an *udalla* counter and a construction manager. Kinar suggested girls from her own apprentice group, who would be both eager to demonstrate prowess and physically up to the hardship involved.

"We'll be camping in the open a lot."

Shortly after sunrise Uruna arrived at the quay to find a substantial gathering of people and boats already in place. Kinar stood in their midst, pointing this way and that as she instructed this load bearer and that. Uruna caught her eye.

"So many people to wish us well," she said. "Their support is gratifying."

Kinar shook her head. "They're coming with us."

"Down the river? All of them?"

"These are planter folk, mostly from my holdings, but also some of their neighbors who happen to be in town. We'll probably pick up more on the way down."

"But there must be twenty or thirty people here."

"Well, I might have found more if I'd remembered to send a herald over to Old Town, but there wasn't time. Here, help me with this sack. I can't lift it by myself."

The next hour went on in like manner, with helpful people

coming and going, bringing foodstuffs, extra linens, flints, candles, and piling everything on the quay.

"Where will we find enough boats for all this?" Uruna asked at one point, huffing as she hoisted a bolt of linen.

"It goes on the barge. The boys will take care of it."

"You found a barge too?"

Kinar pointed to a balding man giving orders from the rail of a flat raft.

"Lemdu over there loaned it to us for a week, no more. But I think that's enough for a start. Now, there's a couple back here by the fish nets I want you to meet."

It went on like that for most of the morning. Caught up in the constant flurry of activity, Uruna had no time to stop and marvel at the outpouring of effort. The people on the quay were accustomed to helping neighbors. A healthy constitution born of hard labor lightened everyone's burden, and the air was soon peppered with wry humor and joking banter as young and old alike pitched in.

When Lemdu finally blew the ram's horn to announce departure, Uruna found herself in a swifthull paired with a young woman from Sikkim. Nulla-Sin had journeyed to Nippur immediately after Springfest to visit relatives. When she'd heard of the Bundug plight, and being acquainted with Zug-Abu, Nulla had rounded up her own clan from the city warrens.

"My father is a river rodman," she said happily as they paddled at ease behind the slower raft. "He taught me how to read the waters where we're going. They're not the same as up here."

At one time in years past, the river had touched Sikkim, but some forty years ago the stream had wandered west. Thus, Uruna and her flock would not stop off at the town on their trek eastward. She had no idea where they might establish their first outpost.

Nulla had a ready answer.

"I know the perfect spot. So does Lemdu. His barge can nose onto a mud bar down there just fine, and there's a good footpath from there directly to the river road for offloading cargo. I traveled it often when I was a kid."

Nulla didn't seem much older than a "kid" herself, but she had a few years on Uruna. A girl from the hinterland grew up fast. Her kind also became some of the best temple ladies—until their love of home called them back.

Nulla also knew about barley rust.

"This is the stripe kind. Once it strikes a field, it spreads fast. By the time you see it, it's too late to save the crop."

"How many hectares are planted in the Bundug?"

"Can't say. Most of the southern part is clan Seddua land. We don't go down there. But up here where our people found the rust, we have maybe four hundred in barley, another eighty in emmer. Wheat's mostly scattered fields and some might not have the rust yet. For a total, your counters will have to cover a lot of ground, might need boats of their own."

More resources to marshal, Uruna thought. What manner of work had she set for herself? If she'd had an inkling of the magnitude of effort involved, she would never have volunteered. So much for her adolescent dreams!

Zug met them at the landing. Somehow word of their purpose had preceded them, for several dozen planter folk stood with him, ready and waiting. After a brief round of greetings everyone got busy offloading stores. Uruna and Kinar were so caught up in supervising the effort that they failed to notice the mob marching up the river road toward them. Three men separated from the group and approached Uruna.

"You'll come no further with that lot," said the apparent leader.

"But sir, these have lost their homes. The rust has taken their livelihood."

"Not my problem. Don't need their kind as allowed the rust to set in."

"Have you no care for your neighbors?"

"I care all right. I care that they get far to other side Kissim before planting time."

"Tell me please, what is your name, sir?"

"What matter is my name to you?"

"I would know whose authority sends me and my people away."

"Don't need authority down here."

"I would have your name anyway."

"He's Shurub," said one of the other two. "Son of overseer Mara."

Shurub's pride in his station showed as he lifted his chin to regard Uruna with narrowed eyes and a mouth twisted with disdain. Was that a hint of arrogance mixed with his air of the righteous?

Uruna pulled out a tablet and began poking marks with a wedge-shaped reed stick.

"What's that you're doing?" said Shurub.

"Making a mark for your name. *Shu-rub*. It goes on the left side of this line to remind me who stood against us. All these to the right have helped where they could. So far, yours is the only mark on the left."

"Looks like quail tracks to me, like the one scratched at my door. Had him for supper. Tracks don't mean a thing. I stand with these here that come with me."

"Well, Shurub, now you'll be known for your stand far and wide. Remember this when it's your turn to ask others for aid."

"I take care of my own and always have. Always will, too."

"So did these with us until they lost everything. It's too much for one man to bear alone, just as it is too much for one man to turn away his neighbor in need. Now, kindly remove yourself and let us pass."

"I'll do no such thing. It's plain to see, girl, you work for them Hanza planters. These parts belong to Seddua clan. You take one more step and I'll call you to court for trespass and attempted assault."

Kinar stepped forward. "You brigand! We come from Ekur. This *girl* as you call her is a priestess of the Most High Goddess Inanna. I am *naditu* constable for the nine provinces. That includes the ground on which we stand and that by which you came. There is your authority, sir! Now stand aside or I'll have you tanned right here on the spot!"

Just then a deep voice from behind caught Uruna by surprise. "What's the holdup here?"

Gar's huge shape moved into view, his massive forearms hanging at his sides, fists doubled and ready to strike anvil blows.

Shurub took a step back, his eyes wide and his mouth agape at the sight of the Nord's immense bulk. Uruna was just as surprised. Where had he come from? Certainly no one she knew of had summoned anyone from Na Purna.

Kinar laid a restraining hand on the forge smith's arm. "It's all right, Gar," she said. "This fellow is just confused, is all."

Shurub started to move forward but thought better of it and stood in place. "Very well, threaten us if you like, but the Seddua constable will hear of this and you won't be so sure next time."

He nodded his head once to add emphasis to his claim.

Gar strode forward with outstretched hand and a benign smile. "Easy now, just let these folks through and no one will get hurt."

Using his great bulk to advantage, he ushered Shurub and his group to one side. None resisted, and when the refugees had marched safely past, he turned to Uruna and spoke in a low voice.

"As you know, this won't be the end of it."

"Maybe so," she replied, "but give us time to prove we're good neighbors and all should be well enough."

Gar's furrowed brow betrayed his doubt.

Zug and several elders deemed the landing unfit as a town site, and recommended scouting further downriver. A short trek brought them to a wide bend. Nulla took Uruna aside to explain the site's suitability for occupation. Where the river's arc skirted a knoll of high ground, Nulla pointed at a reed brake stretching into the distance.

"Wouldn't take much to set up some reed buildings, clear a footpath or two from the road."

She bent and ran her fingers through the silt at the river's edge. "Good clay here. You can start a wall to keep varmints out."

"Like Shurub and his crew?"

"I was thinking more like those fellows over there."

Uruna looked where Nulla had trained her sharp-eyed gaze. A pair of jackals watched them from the edge of the brake. True, they were scavengers, but this was their hunting grounds and the intrusion would place extra burdens on establishing a town here. Every Sumerian before them had faced similar challenges.

They set up camp that night in a haphazard array of tents. Uruna stood first watch with Gar until he finally sent her off to bed.

"You need to rest up for tomorrow. Got your hands full."

"Thanks for coming down, Gar, I should have thought to bring more protection."

"Oh, you'll find a lot more you didn't count on. But see, what you're doing makes it worthwhile for others to step in. Don't hesitate to ask for help. These folk around you don't need prodding."

She had no doubt the planter folk were both able and willing to pitch in. As for herself, she had the will, no question. But did she know how to do it?

Chapter 39

Reluctant Benefactor

The first week in the bush sped by in a whirlwind of inspired activity. Everyone seemed to know what to do and simply got busy doing it without being told. Uruna frequently found herself in the way, and so she began offering herself as simply an extra pair of hands and a strong young back.

On the tenth day of the mission, another barge showed up from Nippur laden with barleycorn and clay vessels bearing much-needed oil. Its captain carried word from Lubna Seddua:

Return to Nippur for further instruction.

Uruna was caught unprepared. As she had received no instruction to begin with, Lubna's message wasn't clear. Kinar had returned home nearly a week ago, so wasn't available for counsel. In the meantime, Uruna had learned more about plot surveys and hut building than many temple overseers. People came to her for decisions. Regardless of her importance there, Nippur called the final tune. She was a priestess and Lubna was her superior, and that seemed to be the end of it.

She put Zug Abu in charge—a role he had already assumed for himself on several occasions. She made sure the newly arrived stocks were safely on their way to the new makeshift barn, then set out for the city afoot. She had gone a mile up the river road when Nulla caught up to her in a swifthull. Zug had sent her to make sure Uruna got to Nippur and back in due haste.

With the two of them on the paddle, they reached Nippur just as the sun's last rays colored Ekur's flanks. Once inside the Aniginna, Uruna quickly made for her room in the Gipar to freshen up and grab a bite to eat. She had just finished supping rabbit stew when a *kadishtu* maid showed up to fetch her to the First Minister's chamber.

Niccaba met her in the hallway outside her office, her usual stern expression replaced by a look of amusement.

"Your rescue mission has made quite an impression around here, young lady," she said, "but you might have consulted Lubna before making such a splash. As it stands right now, she's embarrassed and more than a little upset with you. Tut-tut, not to worry. Blame it on your youthful exuberance."

"But everyone involved has volunteered. The cost to the temple is nothing. I don't understand what could make her upset."

Niccaba gave Uruna's cheek a fond pat. "My dear, she needs to feel she's in charge. She must be persuaded that your relief effort was her idea in the first place. If she's harsh with you, just act humble and listen until she's finished. I'll be there as your witness. She doesn't dare stop the flow of goods to your little hold, lest she offend the entire Council."

"Stop the goods? How could she even consider such a thing? That would be—so unfair…"

"She might try, but I don't think she has enough influence with Council."

"Even so, I don't see how any temple woman could be so uncaring."

"Uruna, it's not a matter of care so much as the need to follow procedure. There are ways of doing things, protocols for marshaling temple resources that we all have to follow, or else risk misappropriation of monies and assets possibly already earmarked for allocation. You see—"

"What I see is blind adherence to rules. I took a temple oath to serve the people, particularly those in need, as I believe every priestess before me has done. When the need arose, my attempts to reach those in authority were thwarted. I was forced to take the matter into my own hands, just to begin something, anything, even the small effort we were able to manage."

"Well, my dear, not so small anymore. Half the country has heard about the new town below Sikkim."

"New town?"

Niccaba went on. "They talk about how hundreds have gathered to follow the snake girl from Anshan, how she's leading the rescue of the destitute while temple Ekur does nothing. Now, I know that's not the whole truth of it, but you know how rumor can spread, and that's why we must be sure to start these programs from the top."

A *nadishtu* aide appeared in the doorway. "First Minister will see you now."

Uruna stepped aside for Niccaba to lead the way out of the room, but the aide raised a hand. "Just the girl, madam," she said.

"But this is a Council matter," Niccaba objected. "My presence is required."

"Not so. First Minister Lubna considers it personal. I shall come for you when she's ready. Uruna, this way please."

As she followed the aide, Uruna shot a questioning frown at Niccaba, but received only open-mouthed shock in return.

Lubna stood waiting behind a table at one end of a large room. In the corner behind her, a single oil brazier cast a sullen glow over the far wall. The *naditu* assistant left the room and closed the door behind her. Once again Uruna was left alone with the harridan who had threatened her on similar occasions. She advanced two paces into the room and waited for further instruction.

Lubna idly tapped the table surface with a long fingernail while she gathered her thoughts. A final stab punctuated the silence and she crooked the same finger, beckoning Uruna forward.

"Ah, yes," she sighed, "our wandering minister returns from duty afar. Such sacrifice, such sweet intention, so many favors showered upon the needy. I wonder how long it will be before you receive the nomination."

"I don't understand. Nomination for what?"

"Why, for your highest ambition, of course. Your eye is set on becoming Entu, Queen and High Priestess of Ekur, leader of all that is sacred. That's what you want, isn't it? You've chased that office from the first day you set foot in this place. You can't even wait to come of age before starting your campaign. You would leapfrog dozens who stand in your way by warming the hearts and softening the minds of the common folk. Well done, my sweet. You managed to make me look the fool as no other woman in this infernal bunch of old hags could even imagine!"

She slammed a fist on the table and came around one end, her eyes blazing hatred, her ferocious temper barely restrained, stopping only when she could advance no further without stepping on Uruna's feet.

"Wretch!" she screamed in Uruna's face. "Wicked, conniving street urchin! *Naditu* priestess? I gave you that office! I cast the deciding vote that bestowed honor upon you years before your time. Oh, how your allies revered you. Uruna this, and Uruna that, they said. She must be made *kadishtu* so that she can be made *naditu* and thence serpent seer, and why not queen while we're at it! After all, she is such a beautiful child. And pure. And smart. And just look at her now—giving succor to the common folk, building and replenishing and nurturing those poor suffering farmers, just like a full-grown woman. Why, she's as good as any of us, better than most, in fact. No matter that she's only thirteen years old. She must be special. She must be heaven-sent. Let us praise her name and shower her with garlands, for she is the savior we have sought, lo these many generations."

Lubna seethed. Her chest heaved with furor, her mouth stretched wide in a grotesque mimic of a smile. Uruna stood in place, a strange calm easing her need to respond. So this was the Lubna few others saw, ambitious, vengeful, jealous, and oh, so lacking in human introspection. One might feel sorry for the woman if her wrath didn't make the least shred of sympathy impossible to summon.

But Lubna wasn't finished. "Have you any idea how much work it has taken for others? How much toil and pain to achieve the slightest public appreciation for all that we do here? Then you come along and in one day—just one, mind you—gain the hearts of the rabble. Well, we shall see, young beauty. You may think that by winning the first battle you have won the war, but you are wrong. Not on my watch. Not if I can put a stop to your emotional pandering to the crowd. Not before I get my chance and take it!"

Was she finished? Did Lubna expect an answer to her tirade? Did she even want a word from Uruna? Better to do as Niccaba suggested, and wait it out.

They stood toe to toe for several moments, Lubna's hot breath fouling the air between them, the solitary brazier flickering in one corner. Uruna decided she would stand there the whole night if need be. But eventually it was Lubna who broke the impasse. And not in any way Uruna could have imagined or expected.

The grand First Minister of Ekur choked back a sob, her face screwed into a tormented mask, and she sank to her knees at Uruna's feet. Her hands clawed at Uruna's dress folds, as though clinging for life, a dying climber grappling for a purchase before the final fall.

"How do you do it?" she whimpered. "How do you get people to love you?"

Uruna bent to the uplifted face, searching for guile, uncertain where the sudden turn had come from. Before she could utter the least reply, Lubna sucked in a deep breath, as though gathering strength to go on.

"You won this contest," she said, "and you'll win the next and the next after that. You always know what to do, what to say. You're always so damnably right, every time! Oh, how I wish I knew your secret. If I just could see—if I had your—"

She broke into sobs, still kneeling on the floor. Uruna didn't know what to make of it. Her first instinct was to reach out to the woman, console her, seek the fiery torment that made her so foul-tempered and stamp it out.

But was this another Lubna performance? Another of her infamous contrivances calculated to misguide and deceive?

If that were so, how could such behavior possibly serve prideful Lubna Seddua? She already had power aplenty. She was tacit ruler of all, even without the title. What more could she want, unless she had become acutely aware of her own shortcoming? Had she looked inside herself and found something vital missing?

Uruna hesitated. Perhaps if she met Lubna half way, confessed her own misgivings, her foibles, her fears, perennial doubts. If she revealed how much pain accompanied each triumph, she might prove she was as flawed as anyone else. But so doing might also play into Lubna's hand. Would the consummate schemer then use such information to discredit her avowed enemy?

The quandary came down to faith and trust. Uruna could only be herself—as Niccaba had advised. She must not play another's game.

She reached down and took Lubna's hands and lifted her up to stand once again.

"If I knew the answers to such things I could not keep them to myself," she said. "Each of us is given gifts, some large, some small, according to our needs. Mine have yet to be realized to their fullest, but I trust Inanna to make a path before me, and I try my best to follow it. In the end, that is all any of us can do. Isn't that so?"

Lubna's eyes explored Uruna's face, searching for the slightest hint of insincerity. For wasn't deception the essence of the world in her view? Could Lubna Seddua fathom the concept of a trust so deep that one might risk the pinnacle over a promise?

At once, Lubna dropped her gaze and took a step back, thus ending the meeting.

"You may go now."

Uruna nodded acknowledgment and stepped back herself. "Shall I send Niccaba in now?" she asked.

"That won't be necessary. Oh, and see the purser before you go back out to that wretched hinterland. I set aside a stipend for the refugees."

Uruna started to say her thanks, but Lubna stopped her with a single command.

"Go!"

On her way back to the Gipar after visiting the purser, Uruna considered Lubna's unexpected generosity. Ten Minas of silver! Never in her life had she held so much wealth in her hands. Was it a test to see if she could be trusted with such an amount? Or did Lubna's twisted mind consider it a bribe of some sort?

The stipend might have been Lubna's intent all along, the very reason for her summons, despite the harangue and histrionics.

But her change of heart could just as easily be a tactic to win a political contest about which Uruna, in her outlier role, was totally uninformed.

Either way, and most important, the outcome would benefit the refugees. But whether gift or ploy, the difference meant a great deal to Uruna, not for what it left unsaid, but for the confounding enigma now thrust into her path.

An enigma who would rule as queen.

Chapter 40

Pushed Out of Sight

The next few months passed too quickly for Uruna to dwell on anything but the task of building a town. Lubna's further infusions of money and goods followed at such a rate that the residents came to expect and rely on it. The extent of Ekur's largess became a concern once Kinar made Uruna aware of the subterfuge behind it.

"Your success here plays to her advantage up there," she said.

"In what way?" Uruna wanted to know.

"The longer you're occupied with hinterland problems the better her chances to exert her will on the Council. She's building a following. The urgency for a prophet is gradually fading from Lukur minds."

"In other words, she's maneuvered me out of the way."

"I suppose that's one way to put it. It's no secret she has her eye on the top spot, and would rather get it without a budding prophet becoming a stumbling block."

"Or the lack of one," Uruna added. "Look, Kinar, I'm no closer to the Sight than when I started out. No one knows, perhaps not even the gods, how long it might take or how much effort might be put forth and wasted because of a mistake or misstep. I certainly pose no immediate threat to Lubna. But the way I see it, if she views her career as a contest requiring my absence, so much the better. My presence here allows me to build a community that will last."

Kinar grew pensive for a few moments, then for whatever reason kept further counsel to herself.

Did she know something Uruna didn't? She was Uruna's only reliable tie to temple doings, and thus the sole source of news other than river gossip. If Kinar saw fit to withhold an opinion, then she must have good reason. The needs of hundreds did not accommodate petty political divisions by the few.

The village was coming along nicely. Resourceful planters had already begun preparing new fields for cultivation. Come spring, they wanted to be ready to start a crop of their own and begin their lives anew without further dependency. She had very little to say in the matter, which was best for long-term prospects. Independence was essential to survival.

Somewhere along the line she came to realize she was de facto queen of their tiny realm. She conducted worship thrice daily, settled disagreements, managed finances, recorded trade transactions. Farm folk brought their problems to her, large and small. She could not stop to ponder the right or wrong of their assumption, nor even to enjoy her elevated status. It had become her new life, in which she moved about with free will.

As Zug put it with his earthy simplicity: To this you were born.

As the village swelled with house plots and grain stores, a new problem was brought to Uruna's attention.

"We need to give this place a name," said Zug.

"Great idea," Uruna said. "What have you come up with?"

"We thought it ought to come from you."

"It's their town, and yours. In a short while I'll be gone. Put it to the townspeople and I'll be happy to pass their choice along to our benefactors."

A few days passed before Zug came to her with a result.

"Three names have been put forward and the counters have returned from abroad after much bickering and confusion."

"Yes? So what are the names?"

"Well, I'm not sure…"

"What's the trouble?"

Zug scuffed his toe in the dirt and looked away to the distance. "Uruna, these here are working folk, don't have much imagination, see."

"My friend, just tell me."

"Well, 'No Bog' was the top one. Then comes 'Blazing Face of Utu-the-Sun,' and after that 'Wide Stream.'"

Uruna suppressed a smile. "I see what you mean."

In the end, the solution came from an unexpected quarter. Villagers had been toiling in the heat one morning when a swifthull approached from the south, bearing two Hani boys. It seemed they had been fishing not far away and had learned of the new town going up nearby. They approached the village elder, curious to know more about this *mada ghin*. The elder brought the boys before Zug and Uruna. When asked what they meant, the taller boy gave a diffident shrug and explained.

"It means New Beginning," he said. "Whenever we fish out a place and move to a new part of the swamp, we say the ancestors are giving us a new start, a *mada ghin*."

Uruna looked at Zug, and Zug looked at the elder, who nodded his head once and walked away. Thus did the town of Mada Ghin receive its identity.

On her next trip to Nippur, Uruna made sure the name got passed around among the merchants and barge men. Soon thereafter, Lukur trade ministers picked up on the name and earmarked tokens and bundles with their symbol for the Mada Ghin destination. It wasn't long before the first merchant showed up on Mada Ghin's muddy quay with stocks of cooking pots and charcoal for the coming winter.

Toward the end of the Enten summer season, travelers in both directions were stopping over at Mada Ghin, expecting refreshment, entertainment, and eventually lodging. An enterprising plowman got his neighbors together and erected a *mudhif* lodge of reeds, contracted with a local cook, and assembled sleeping accommodations for twelve. Within a few weeks, the new entrepreneur had saved enough money to build the town's first clay brick house. More abodes quickly followed as word of the town's prosperity spread abroad.

At that point, Uruna's chief concern became whether the town's grain stores were sufficient to sustain refugee families through the Emesh winter and on into spring planting. The true test lay months away. Meantime, more than a hundred families depended on outside relief. Because of the town's success, its numbers had increased, adding new mouths to feed and forcing the town planners to revise their estimates.

But that wasn't all. Winter arrived, and with it a new demand for Uruna's attention.

"You must take a husband to warm your bed," said Zug one day.

When she objected that the idea was preposterous for a girl of thirteen, he reminded her that Mada Ghin was still a frontier town, and its founder would garner increased respect as a married woman.

Accepting that as true, then who would make a proper mate? After all, she was a priestess of the temple, her role as future prophet must not be forgotten. And didn't the legends speak of a consort being essential to the task?

Recognizing that no local lad was suitable, Zug approached Kinar on one of her visits. "We're simple farm folk here," he pointed out. "Uruna's got the makings of a queen, so needs a worthy gentleman of finer station."

Kinar looked around at Mada Guin's muddy disarray of haphazard footpaths and half-finished huts and gritted her teeth in a grimace. She was more inclined to think Uruna needed a finer workplace, an opinion she wisely kept to herself. As it turned out, before she could take the first step toward finding a candidate, one appeared on his own as if summoned by the gods.

One with whom Uruna was already acquainted.

She was seated inside her hut at the small table where she often conferred with village elders. The last woman had just squeezed out the doorway when it was filled jamb-to-jamb with a large male shape. Uruna looked up and beheld Suba's perfect smile.

"What are you doing here?" she asked.

"Nice to see you too," he said, his easy smile still in place.

"I'm sorry, it's just that you startled me. Come in, come in."

Suba found a stool that barely accommodated his size and straddled it like a milker.

"I heard about this place, how you started, what you've been doing, so I came to see if I can help. I've learned to hunt pretty well and I know how to build something besides a shack that needs burning twice a year."

Uruna laughed as she looked him over. Suba was even bigger than before, and just as bold and brash. And there was hardness to his eyes she didn't remember from before.

"Did Nabi Gahn have anything to do with it?" she asked.

"Yes. He struck me for the last time. I haven't seen him since."

"I'm sorry to hear that. You were doing so well there."

"Not really," he countered. "He prefers his glory boy, ran off to the west with him in search of some imagined enemy. The rest of us can blaze in hell for all he cares. Besides, I think I learned all I can from the old scourge."

Uruna felt her former attraction for Suba returning. They hadn't had but a few hours in camp together, yet she felt they had built a close kinship in that short time.

"We can always use another hunter," she told him. "In fact, I guess we don't really have one as such. These folks know the soil and the river. And I have to admit, I'm getting concerned about all the new faces showing up, and us with just a bare minimum of cured meat stocks."

Suba spread his arms wide. "Then put me to work. Mada Ghin is as good a place as any for me to put down. Best of all, you're here."

"I-I don't know what difference that makes."

Suba brought his arms back to his sides and stepped so close Uruna could smell the sweat of his skin, an altogether pleasant sensation. His eyes lingered on her face with a hunger she found unsettling.

"I haven't thought about anyone else since you left camp," he confessed. "And when I heard a rumor that you mentioned my name once or twice, well, that gave me hope."

"Hope for what? Suba, we're stretched very thin here. It's a bare existence right now, with little chance of improving our lot for a long time. You saw the town. Three mud hovels and a gaggle of reed shacks, and nothing but prayers to get us through the winter. Mada Ghin has very little to offer you right now."

Suba shrugged a shoulder. "Considering my condition when we first met, you might call this a palace." He rolled his eyes around the *mudhif* interior until they came to rest again on Uruna. "I like what I see."

Her face reddened beneath his candid gaze. Why was she so thrown by a half-breed bumpkin from a hunting camp? Except his origin wasn't the real reason, was it? What she liked about him was exactly what and who he was—unpretentious, good-humored, confident. She felt safe around him.

Just then Zug's call for a husband-protector echoed in her mind, and she rebelled.

Not now! I'm not ready for that. It's too early and a lot needs doing first.

When she informed Zug that Suba was staying, the headman's first concern was where to accommodate the newcomer with such a large frame.

"Uruna, everyone's cramped as it is," he pointed out. "I'd offer my donkey stall, but that's hardly the way to treat a guest. I think maybe your place, since you have that extra room off the back."

Uruna bridled. "That's my prayer shrine, where I prepare for worship!"

Zug shrugged an apology. "Just a suggestion."

She knew what the old matchmaker was doing. It was hard to come up with a real objection, but when she presented the idea to Suba he gave her an easy out.

"I've been sleeping in the open for three years. I'm not ready to spend an entire night under a roof yet. I wouldn't be good company."

That lasted one night. Within a week he was sleeping on her floor, and in another week, sharing her bed. Whereas a queen might take a consort as mate, an untried temple minion simply chose a husband without ceremony, the same as any commoner. They set a wedding date for the eve of spring planting.

Chapter 41

Under The Eye

Once Niccaba discovered the extent of monies flowing to an oddly-named frontier settlement in the hands of an adolescent *naditu*, she grew alarmed and decided her own mission to Mada Ghin was in order. Brushing aside Kinar's assertions that Uruna's effort required no further Lukur involvement, she concluded that the town deserved closer inspection.

She chose not to divulge the hour of her departure to anyone beforehand. A surprise visit often bore the best fruit. Shortly after dawn she slipped away to the harbor and hired a swifthull and two strong oarsmen on the spot, confident she'd be down and back in a day with no one the wiser.

That notion was blown to the winds the moment she set foot on the mud slick that stood as Mada Ghin's quay. First off, none came to greet her, which although her hope all along, proved inconvenient when she was forced to remove her sandals and wade ashore like a hired scrubwoman.

And the town! Not a mud hole at all. The quay bustled with draymen bearing bundled reeds to and fro, a moored barge loaded with crates and barrels awaiting an unlading crew. The cluster of reed huts Kinar had described a few weeks ago now stood four deep. As she watched, bricklayers added tiers to several clay buildings. A large field adjacent to the town sprouted green as planters tended a fresh crop. In the distance, a crew of men and boys labored to clear a water channel. And closer to the quay, a row of artisan tents ended with a forge. Mada Ghin had its own smith!

The overall effect was of a thriving, established community living under conditions adequate for basic human needs. Niccaba felt her chest swell with pride. Here was the industrious Sumerian spirit at work.

To add to her surprise, her two hired oarsmen had quickly spied what they were looking for and now stood beneath an awning, quaffing beer. Already Mada Ghin sported a beer merchant! Such an enterprise required regular deliveries, and at this distance from Nippur, twice weekly.

She stopped a large young man who looked out of place among the scrawny, hard-muscled planter throng. A small lad skipped at his side.

"Where can I find the woman in charge here?" she asked.

"Oh, you must be the high minister we were expecting," he answered with a pleasant smile.

"Chancellor," Niccaba corrected before she could think. What did the young fellow mean, "expecting?" Was her clandestine plotting for naught?

He spared her further chagrin by explaining. "We post a few lookouts upriver and down as a precaution to be ready for barge traffic." He put a brawny arm around the boy and drew him close. "This one nearly burst his lungs racing ahead of you with the news."

The young man continued to grin as he pointed at a small house of plastered brick nearly lost in the forest of thatch huts. "Uruna can be found there most anytime she isn't away in the fields. You're in luck today."

Niccaba nodded and lifted her hem, already stained with mud. "Thank you, you're most kind. And who should I say referred me?"

"I'm Suba."

"The lad from the hunter camp?"

"Yes, but I left there a while ago. Made a pretty good home right here in Mada Ghin. I'm *galla* constable for the town."

"Under whose commission?" she demanded.

An amused smile played over his face. "Temple Shar-kalla."

"Never heard of it. Where is it?"

Suba jerked a thumb at a clay brick obelisk jutting up from the edge of the quay. "That's the name Uruna gave it. She does Morning Call and a bunch of other things there. Got plans for something with a roof someday."

"I see, thank you."

Niccaba moved on, thoroughly rattled now. Great gods! How had she missed so many developments? A temple *and* a constable? Or was the young fellow toying with her?

It was obvious the clay hut he pointed out had been constructed in haste, and probably not with any great skill. Niccaba stepped over the door sill carefully before she rapped on the hollow clay knocker hung from a peg.

Uruna looked up from a pile of tablets stacked on a bench and dropped her stylus. Her eyes widened with surprise and then a wide smile lighted her face.

"Niccaba! What a delightful surprise!"

Uruna got up quickly and embraced Niccaba in a warm hug. She seemed taller, as if she might have added an inch of height, as well as a woman's full bosom. Her hair was pulled back in a practical bun and her apron was spattered from making her own tablet clay. A healthy glow about her face told Niccaba she was happy with her lot—or was it more? Had young Suba told the whole truth? Had Uruna so soon chosen a mate on her own?

"Please come sit over here," Uruna said, moving several pillows and an eating dish from a nearby chair. Niccaba noted it was the only chair in the room besides Uruna's.

Mada Ghin's unofficial priestess leaned close in earnest excitement. "I want to hear all the latest, but from your lips. Kikki only gets down here once a month, if that, and then she's gone before we have any time together. You look well. Would you like some tea?"

Niccaba realized she really could use refreshment. "That would be nice."

Uruna crossed the room and fetched a pot from the window sill where it still caught the late morning sun. "How did you find me in this maze of huts?" she said as she poured.

"That young constable, Suba. Is he the one you met at Nabi Gahn's camp?"

"Yes, we're to be married soon."

"Oh, my heavens! Don't you think that's rather hasty?"

"Not really. After all, I was here three whole months before he even showed up. Of course we can't have a proper courtship. Neither of us has time. Anyway, he's everything I could hope for in a husband."

"But what about Serpenthood? What about the promise of prophecy? And what's become of your snake—what's his name, Mem-something?"

"Memet is quite content here. Right now he's out in the garden catching the sun. Or a mouse or lizard. The neighbors have gotten used to him, although they keep their distance most days. Ha-ha!"

"Hah, yes, of course. Most days."

Niccaba cast about for some sort of distraction. Somehow the situation has escaped her control before it started, and realizing so made her uncomfortable. Still, she had to admit the tea was quite good and Uruna a gracious hostess. She must at least make an attempt to gain the upper hand.

"Tell me what you were doing when I came in."

It came off more demanding than she intended, but Uruna seemed not to take offense.

"Oh, I was just checking the counters' work. We have two of them now, you know. Got in our first seeding just last week. Everyone's so helpful and willing. To be honest, I sometimes have little to do, and so I go out in the boat and look for someone to bother. Sort of like an everyday housewife, I suppose."

"You seem happy. Even with all this work and so many to look after. Kinar says you're doing a marvelous job by yourself. Says that's to be expected."

"Perhaps, but enough about me. Tell me about the ladies. All I know is Lubna still rules while Semma continues to dance in the raw, scaring the children in the park." Uruna laughed at her little joke, then sobered as she realized Niccaba wasn't laughing.

"We have...concerns there," Niccaba began.

Was this the appropriate time and place? She hadn't really intended to reveal her misgivings to anyone yet, least of all to the chief contender for the job, and by the look of things around her, already the most capable. She had dropped her guard by coming unannounced. Oddly, though, she felt no regret.

"You have doubts about them both," Uruna said with customary insight.

Gods! The girl—no, the woman, she corrected herself. Uruna still knew everything before it happened. How disarming to find oneself in the presence of a woman as capable and intelligent as any temple matron of thrice as many years.

She rules with intelligence and fairness, Kinar had told her. *Every bit the queen already. You should see for yourself.*

Now Niccaba did indeed notice Uruna's comfort with the burdens of responsibility. The young lady had carried out every aspect of public administration, albeit on a small scale, a frightening prospect in any hands but those of the earnest young woman before her. All the more reason to allow the youth to flourish in this garden of opportunity.

"Let me be honest here," Niccaba said, surprised by her own words. "I came down intending to chasten you, admonish your impetuous waste of resources, haul you back to Nippur and put an end to this foolish notion of a frontier settlement. This is not easy for me to say, Uruna, but, well, I was wrong. You have carved out a home in the wilderness, made a place for these people to survive without burdening others. The strength of your conviction is evident everywhere here. Mada Ghin? Is that how you pronounce it? Not a mud hole but a triumph over adversity. The temple fold would envy the extent of your achievements here, if they saw for themselves what you have done."

Uruna's wide gray eyes grew even wider as she stared at the venerable Chancellor of Ekur. "I would thank you, Niccaba, if I believed we were even halfway to success," she said. "But we won't know for another year if it worked. Real proof, reliable evidence that we know what we're doing, may take longer. Until we've pulled at least one harvest, stored and saved it successfully, and started the second season without rust or some other dire setback, Mada Ghin will continue to be just one more attempt to master the wilderness. As you know, the stories of failure abound in our lore."

Niccaba regarded her young apprentice with new eyes. Uruna not only understood how to plan and execute, she had a sensible appreciation for the magnitude of her undertaking, saw the need for patience and practical expectations. The waif from Anshan was gone. In her place stood a woman wise beyond her years.

Uruna drained her tea and set the mug delicately on the tray. "I suppose you'd like a full accounting of our expenditures."

"Thank you, but I really don't have time. I have to get back to

Nippur for an evening meeting."

"As you wish, but I have it right here. It will only take a few moments for you to check. I was working on last week's sums when you arrived, but everything up to that point is in order."

"Are you quite sure? I mean, it usually takes Ku-Aya several days to reconcile accounts."

"Oh, no trouble at all, I have the first three months stacked here on the shelf." Uruna walked over to the opposite wall and removed a stack of dried tablets. She set them down before Niccaba and stood aside. "I hope you can read my hen scratches."

"Read them? Heavens, Uruna, your scribing is perfect! Where did you learn—never mind, I know the answer already."

She bent to the brief task. It was one of her favorite chores to review the meticulous work of a practiced counter—a talent Uruna seemed to have absorbed in her sleep. Was there anything the young woman could not do?

"What gives me a lot of trouble is cooking," Uruna said, as if reading Niccaba's thoughts. "Luckily, my neighbors prepare excellent dishes and are happy to do so. We eat quite well, thanks to Ekur's generosity."

At that point, Niccaba had come to expect only the utmost perfection from Uruna—in any endeavor. She quickly checked the first two tablets, then, satisfied by what she found, handed all three back to Uruna.

"I shan't need to do this again," she said. "Nor will any other Lukur, if I have a say in the matter. We shall be only too happy to continue supporting your efforts here. If you need more don't hesitate to ask. I'd rather the funds go to capable hands than where they usually end up. I quite enjoyed the tea, dear, but what pleases me most is to see you thriving and happy."

She rose from the chair and realized in her heart that she would rather stay. How odd, when she had been so anxious to get back to

Nippur just a short while ago. The prospect of facing dour old women with stubborn dispositions was far from pleasant. Certainly not as uplifting as the last hour.

As she left Uruna's humble little abode, she met Suba coming up the path toward her. Before she realized what he was doing, he wrapped his great arms about her and drew her close.

"You honored our little community," he said with sober face. "Please convey my personal gratitude to the ladies and assure them we intend to do right by their generosity."

As well said as any practiced consort. These young people grew up so fast!

When he released her, Suba extended an object in his outstretched hand. Niccaba looked down and beheld an amulet of amber clasped in gold wire and suspended from a woven leather thong.

She shook her head. "Suba, this is far too fine a gift for me."

He answered with a wide grin. "I know, but it's all we could come up with on such short notice."

Niccaba spluttered her heartiest laugh in months and reached up to tweak his cheek. "You take care of our girl," she said in a voice husky with emotion.

"Always my first duty."

Back in Nippur that evening, Niccaba did not regret missing her first temple meeting in recent memory. Her mind was still mulling over her pleasant interlude at Mada Ghin when she finally dropped off to sleep, the amulet clutched in one hand.

Very much like a child with a precious keepsake.

Chapter 42

Victory, Then Capture

Mada Ghin survived its first year with modest achievement. Certainly the harvest offered little cause for celebration, but the planters deemed it a triumph that not a spot of rust appeared.

The local townspeople were quick to credit Uruna and her "magic" with each kernel of progress. She was just fourteen, but she accepted their praise in the understanding that she had become the human symbol of their new identity, though the planters' collective memories, and not her own, had served them throughout the meticulous rituals of planting and irrigating.

Harvest was another matter. The yield barely fed the town, swollen now with outsiders attracted by a new market in their midst. Farm folk farther out would have to rely on save crops from their own plots to carry them through the winter ahead. But those meager vegetable rows had been planted and tended by children while their parents doubled their labor in the communal fields. The youngsters did their best, but the disappointing results proved that splitting up families was a desperate measure not worth repeating.

Thus, when Zug Abu brought an ebullient delegation before Uruna, she quickly dispelled their mood with a practical assessment.

"One season does not promise a second in like measure," she reminded them. "We've more work to do."

Zug reluctantly agreed but was eager to keep spirits high, though the townspeople would continue to rely on temple subsidies of seed corn and other day-to-day necessities.

Despite Uruna's misgivings, the second year proved better than the first. Uruna's first objective of a rust-free harvest was met. Her second, for Mada Ghin to slip loose from the yoke of dependency, would require further diplomatic effort, particularly with the First Minister. She and Lubna hadn't had direct dealings for more than a year, and she did not look forward to another contentious round of verbal sparring. To make matters worse, she hadn't heard from Nippur at all for quite a while—several months, actually. The harvest counts and distributions had taken her full attention, as well as three new settlements erected in the swell of optimism.

She was returning from giving a benediction to the nearest hamlet when an excited boy ran up to her about a mile from Mada Ghin. She recognized him as Reza, one of Suba's lookouts.

"Six fast boats!" he exclaimed breathlessly. "Two men each, all armed. Bound up Suba. Tied him to Shar-kalla altar. Came to take you away!"

His voice trailed off in a tormented wail.

Uruna started to pull the lad to her, but he bent over double to catch another breath.

"Did they harm anyone?"

A shake of his head. "Suba says run. Run!"

She had no chance of outrunning a swifthull fleet.

"Who are these men?"

"Soldiers—Nazim war...warriors. Sent from the big temple."

"From Ekur?"

The lad nodded and bent again.

Why send an armed troop to fetch her, when Niccaba would do? She had never heard of any *galla* regiment called Nazim. Maybe if she asked the boy? No, he wouldn't know.

She reached for Reza again, hoping to reassure him with soothing words. He yanked his arm free and scowled at her.

"These men are killers!" he shouted. "You must do as Suba says."

"We'll go back together and see what this is all about."

"But Suba said—"

She resumed her walk, with the boy reluctantly tagging at her side.

"Tell me what the men look like," she said.

"Dark skin, black beards, some wear leather armor. They're all mean and smelly."

"Not our *galla*."

"No, worse."

Uruna looked twice to see if the boy was joking, but he plodded forward like a drayman pulling a load. For years the deplorable state of Nippur's besotted police had caused concern, but lately it seemed they had worsened under ongoing temple neglect.

She looked ahead as she neared the town. A squat, brawny soldier waited at the end of the quay, hands on hips, feet spread apart to declare his domain. Beside him stood Shurub, the Seddua troublemaker from her first day of the rescue mission, a sly grin of satisfaction splitting his grubby countenance.

The soldier twisted his frame as she approached and with quick hand gestures ordered two of his men to take Reza over to the lodge. Uruna assumed Suba was in there as well, and prayed he'd suffered no harm.

"I'm Captain Umaki," the soldier announced. "These men report to me. First Minister Lubna commands you to return at once to Nippur to face criminal charges at Hall of Laws."

"Charges? For what crime?"

"Didn't say. You'll find out when you get there."

Shurub stepped in. "I warned you about trespassing on our lands. Now you got yourself in big trouble—"

"Silence!" Umaki made a cutting thrust with his hand, and the farmer backed away as Umaki turned his attention back to Uruna. "Into the boat with you."

"I have just a few things to fetch first—"

Umaki grabbed her arm and pulled hard. "Now!"

She stumbled and fell to her knees in the muddy shallows. Umaki hauled her up by both elbows and pushed her over to a swifthull where two oarsmen sat ready. She stood in awkward confusion, unsure why he acted so rude.

Umaki shouted at her again. "Sit!"

As she struggled for a seat, he reached in and twisted her arms behind her. Another man appeared at his side and bound her wrists with coarse lading twine. Umaki grabbed her by the hair and yanked her head back, then pressed a blade to her exposed throat.

"I'd as soon do you right here, but there's worse waiting for you in that temple of yours. I'll be right there to watch it myself."

He gave her chin a hard twist and beckoned the boat into the channel.

"Make speed!" he hollered to his men. Then, to Uruna, "We'll take good care of the big fellow for you. Got to save him for the sacrifice."

The journey to Nippur was mercifully quick but she arrived in a great deal of pain. The ropes had rubbed her wrists raw and her sodden clothing chafed her buttocks. Her spine was stiff from sitting with her hands behind her back. Months in the open had saved her skin from the sun's worst assault, but when the boat finally made shore, her limbs were weak and she ached all over.

At the quay, more rough hands hauled her out of the boat. Her legs failed to support her and she stumbled again. Her handlers dragged her up the mud slope to the footpath, where they prodded her in the back until she fell in a heap on the sand, utterly spent and unable to move. To a man, the Nazim seemed to delight in adding to her pain and humiliation.

"Back on your feet!" one shouted.

She rolled into a crouch, trying to find the strength to stand. Another lout hauled her up by her hair and pushed her forward. She tottered on weak legs and fell headlong into another, who wrapped her in a bear hug and held her tight. His beard reeked of stale beer and sweat. Another ripped the fellow's arms away, grabbed for her bodice and missed. They were enjoying her misery. Soon the harangue would turn into sport.

A loud male voice broke through her torment. "Enough! The queen wants her able to stand for the ritual."

It was Umaki! Back so soon from Mada Ghin? Did that mean Suba was nearby?

Umaki wasn't finished dealing with his men. "Put her on a litter and carry her the rest of the way."

The man nearest to her bared his teeth in something resembling a leer. "Got no litter. She can make it on her own just fi—"

The Nazim captain's fist crashed into the man's mouth, shattering teeth and lips. He went down hard and rolled onto his back with blood spurting from his mouth.

Umaki drew a flashing sword and pointed it at two other men.

"You and you. Find a litter, do as I say or taste my wrath like this one."

He then glared at Uruna. "You see what you make these men do."

"I did nothing."

"Witch! You bedazzle them with your beauty. They fight

among themselves for your attention, challenge my orders. I have enough on my hands without dealing with your infernal charms and spells."

To argue with the superstitious would be futile. She might use talk to play for time. "Where were you told to take me?"

"Hall of Laws, to be tried and sentenced—"

"Better send another two along to watch their backs."

"Your *galla* sots are no threat."

"Careful, Captain. You have enemies in my city you cannot see."

A litter arrived just then, and before Umaki could issue another order, she plopped down on it and crossed her arms over her face. Without another word from Umaki, the bearers took up the poles and started off.

Uruna closed her eyes and took three deep breaths. For the first hundred paces or so, she used the bouncing rhythm to concentrate on first-stage *semtu*. Almost at once strength began to return to her limbs. She relaxed to the swaying motion and matched her heartbeat to the pace of feet pounding beneath her.

Restore my spirit, gird my soul, she repeated to herself.

She considered her captors. Steeped in fear, the simplest of them could not move without direction from higher authority. The slightest resistance invited a vicious response. Blind obedience carried the day. Lubna must have grasped their superstitious nature and seized the opportunity to take command and hold their primitive minds in thrall.

Two hundred paces from Nanna Gate, she was feeling well enough to address her bearers.

"Take me through Uruk Gate. It's closer to the Aniginna entrance and the *igiggi* won't bother you there."

Four jogging paces to absorb and respond.

"Who are the *igiggi*?"

"Demons who dine on mortal innards. But usually only at night. If you'd rather use the moon gate, I think we'll be safe."

The lead bearer angled away to follow her suggestion. It was a meager victory, but her spirits lifted as they passed between Uruk Gate's stone lions.

Her mood darkened, however, when she saw the empty boulevard ahead. Not a soul ventured forth on Street of Abundant Life, usually teeming with humanity at this hour. The sun shone bright overhead, supping hour was a distant hope, when her Nazim bearers turned left and trotted up the avenue toward the Aniginna enclosure.

A new palmwood gate had been erected to block the arched entry. The crude affair stood only waist high, a mere obstacle rather than a defense. A Nazim soldier had replaced the usual *galla* sentry.

Her bearers stopped just inside the gate as a Nazim squad approached bearing swords. The leader exchanged a few words with the bearer pair, who lowered Uruna to the ground and stepped aside. One soldier sliced her bonds and used the tip of his knife to prod her onto her feet. As soon as she stood, he poked her buttocks with the tip. She winced and bucked, causing the lot of them to laugh.

Her escort marched her off to Laws without further humiliation. The empty commons belied the afternoon brilliance. Not a soul dallied at the reflecting pond. She scanned the government buildings surrounding the open silence. Every hall of government was guarded by a pair of Nazim sentries. The Aniginna crouched under silent siege.

Her escorts stopped at the foot of the broad staircase in front of Laws. A woman in loincloth and leather breastplate emerged from the shadows and stepped into the bright sunshine. Her face and body were daubed in saffron-colored paint, arms and legs overlaid with sinuous indigo designs resembling serpents. Braids the color of wine twisted about her crown, and from her ears hung clay discs fashioned into striped coils.

At first, Uruna failed to recognize her. But when the woman beckoned toward the darkened doorway, the flesh of her arm gave her away.

"Come inside out of the heat," said ancient Semma Karkhan. "Our prophet has waited long enough."

CONSPIRACY

Chapter 43

Sentence

Uruna might have enjoyed the cool wash of air inside Hall of Laws, had her confusion not been so complete. A flood of questions tumbled through her mind. If Semma truly had abdicated, what was she doing at court? And why the bizarre costume? Was she party to the charges Lubna had cooked up? Or was she simply the tool of Lubna's ambition?

And why were either of them in league with the Nazim?

She followed Semma through a few twists and turns until they passed through the double doors to the Grand Court chamber. Inside, a dozen women stood waiting—young women ripe with health, beyond adolescence but callow. Other than Semma, not one familiar face greeted her—until Lubna Seddua glided in through a side door.

A drab gown of gray linen reached her ankles. Her neck and arms were unadorned, locks of dark hair hung straight from her crown. The contrast struck Uruna dumb, as if Lubna and her grandmother had swapped roles. On the surface the transformation made no sense. So blatantly artificial—it had to be another of Lubna's inventions. Placate a doddering queen by pandering to her gods, and therewith appropriate both her office and religious following. But Semma's four senile old dears were not present. Where had the congregation come from?

Semma moved to one side to yield attention to her granddaughter. Without further ceremony, Lubna got straight to the point.

"We'll dispense with Niccaba's usual flowery introduction and explanation of law. Uruna, everyone here knows you practice serpent rites that are an abomination to our Lord Lamashtu, a proven failure for as far back as anyone can recall. The truly faithful among us know that a fortnight ago Lamashtu anointed his First Prophet with sacred foresight. To worship the other god, whose name cannot be uttered under penalty of death, invites the wrath of our master and his followers.

"Therefore, we appeal to you, Uruna, to renounce the usurper of sacred Sight and be restored pure. If you do not, you must suffer the ordeal from which no mortal can survive. What say you, Uruna?"

It was a clever twist on an old stratagem, this switching deities to vanquish political enemies and launch a new power elite. Mena had described it at great length, Nashi had mentioned it in passing, and Uruna saw evidence for herself in the incredible array of deities populating the Sumerian pantheon, accumulated over generations of theo-political maneuvers. Lost again and again in the secular melee was the spiritual essence that had inspired the original faith. More disturbing was the unbroken pattern of religious appropriation that had marched down through the ages to taint the present.

Lubna understood all this, but she also understood Uruna's unwavering commitment to Enshiggu. She had just condemned her adversary to an ordeal of death, whatever form it was. No doubt the Nazim had contrived an atrocious, life-ending torture for the purpose.

Before her imagination started down that course, Uruna recalled Mena's words from their first hour together: *You will never be tested beyond your ability.*

There stood her answer.

"Madam," she said, "you pretend to give me choice while in truth you offer none. May you be forgiven the lie. May you and these who have lost their hearts be forgiven their maddening fear. I cannot disavow my god Enshiggu, I gladly say his name before this sham court, for Enshiggu brought me out of the mountains. Enshiggu appointed me to serve this great land. I accept the consequences of my choice. Sigah, Selah, Selashum."

The court erupted in a clamor of outrage. Lubna was pleased to let the cacophony roll on without restraint. When it looked like the more fevered might break ranks and resort to violence, she raised a hand and held it until the noise abated.

"For your transgressions, Uruna Kumta, you are remanded to custody in your quarters until the pit is sufficiently prepared for your walk of penance."

To Uruna's puzzled look, Lubna waved a finger in a little theatrical gesture of recollection. "Oh, you weren't informed. How careless of me. In your 'special tutelage' were you told about Damuzi's punishment?"

"The old legend about Inanna and her consort."

Lubna turned to her grandmother and bade her come forward. "Mother Semma, if you will."

Semma reached for a staff held by one of the young "faithful" and brandished it at Uruna like a club.

"Describe it!" she spat. "At least what you think you know of it."

This fuming harridan was a Semma she had seen only once—as she traded epithets with Lubna over family treasure. Uruna struggled for calm as she recalled her learning.

"Great Mother leaves Damuzi behind while she visits her sister in the underworld, but she can't come back without help from the other gods. They take pity on her and help, and Inanna finally escapes. But *igiggi* demons come for Damuzi and drag him back to pay penance in her place."

"Is that all?"

"Damuzi runs away and hides. Inanna and her sister search all over and finally find him and bring him back. But as part of the bargain, Damuzi must stay in the underworld for half of every year."

"Yes, that's one version. There is another."

"I was told there are many. I was also told one cannot know the truth except by penance, sacrifice, and prayer."

"Yes, that's the best Sumerian interpretation. The Nazim have another."

"I thought your god was Lamashtu."

"We have many gods. And we have legends, one of which accounts for the rise of Lamashtu over Inanna."

"Let me guess. You know it to be the one true account."

"Did any of your conniving mentors tell you about *danu lim baraqu?*"

"Test of a Thousand Strikes? Sounds like a barbaric lashing, but no."

"Pity. A serious flaw in your upbringing. According to Nazim lore, Damuzi was unfaithful while Inanna was away. On her return she learns of his infidelity and accuses him. Damuzi denies it, so she works out a test. She will send him down into a pit of asps, then bring him up. If he was faithful, he will live. If guilty, he dies. For one so blatantly unfaithful as you, the test applies."

Uruna kept silent. Her senses picked up the rapt awe of the young acolytes in the gallery. Nothing would be gained by provoking them further. Semma continued, enjoying the attention she had gained.

"The ancients who built the Old City had a temple dedicated to Serpenthood. Ages ago the river destroyed it. Today, it lives on as a great pit in the ground, offering cool shade to the creatures who wander there. At last count several dozen asps were caught at the bottom. They can't climb out. Voles and mice fall in. The snakes feast on them and multiply."

Lubna returned to Semma's side to take back control of the proceedings.

"The Test is simple. Your Lukur friends will gather at the pit's edge to witness your death and the end to Serpenthood. They will watch you descend by a rope to the pit floor, watch you walk the length of it. If you reach the other side alive, we will haul you out in whatever condition the serpents have left you. If you die, as I'm sure you will, Serpenthood prophecy dies with you, confirming ages of Nazim tradition. If you live, we Nazim will leave to find another home for ourselves and our god. I will step down as First Prophet, and Serpenthood will be free to proceed on its tottering old legs toward its inevitable doom."

Lubna stepped closer until she monopolized Uruna's entire field of view. With a toothy smile as false as her heart, she uttered a bitter parody of Uruna's blessing.

"May you die. May you be wretched. May you endure eternal suffering."

Uruna simply stared back, for the latch of her mind had just lifted and then shut again. A blink, then gone, but enough to reveal a streaming flash of the eternal. Enough to recall an astonishing truth she had forgotten but would never forget again.

She had faced all three curses before.

And not just once. Many, many times over.

Chapter 44

Stealth and Resolve

Suba spat blood from a cut lip and fought the urge to retch. The Nazim warrior had jumped him from the shadows. He had responded by instinct from years of practice, his reflexes faster than his vaunted foe's.

Now the man lay dead at his feet. The second killed by his hand.

He wiped his blade clean and stole away through the shadows beneath the Kirisha Uru wall bordering Nippur's great central park, grinding his molars as he went. There would be more killing before the night was through. He could only hope he might have a choice the next time.

The Nazim had found Mada Ghin deserted, its people having melted away into the reed brakes after being forewarned by lookouts. Suba was not so lucky. He'd stumbled into a Nazim patrol on his way home, and had taken down two of them before four more set upon him. Thereupon the Nazim captain had beaten him with a palm slat while two soldiers held him down.

They were worse than animals, just as Nabi had warned at camp. When Suba couldn't move, they tied him to a post in Zug

Abu's barn and left. With one eye swollen shut, he spent fruitless hours sitting on the floor, fretting away at his bonds. One moment he was alone, the next Nabi Gahn emerged like a wraith from the barn's shadows. Nabi had made quick work of the ropes, gave no explanation for how he'd found his former apprentice or what had brought him to Mada Ghin.

Once freed, Suba stepped outside into total darkness. Nabi's swifthull lay ready and waiting, spears and knives in the bottom. Not a word passed between them, as neither of them knew if more Nazim were about. Following Nabi's hand gestures, Suba armed himself with two spears and a knife. Nabi shoved him into the forward paddle position and they slid into the water without making a ripple. They made Nippur before first light, reached Nanna Gate by circling around Nazim patrols.

Nabi told him how it would be, fighting in Nippur's streets.

"In close quarters, in the dark, you don't have time to think. You kill your opponent, drag him out of sight, and move on, ready to meet the next enemy."

Suba reminded himself that these men had already killed and would kill again without a thought. Nabi Gahn counted such men less worthy than any beast of the field.

"Be the survivor. Live to save your family from these devils."

Suba shuddered. Each kill tore at him, leaving him with grinding remorse he could not shake. He recalled a saying that a paid killer was a man without a soul. Now he understood. If you kept it up, at some point you had no soul left to lose. He could only hope that hadn't happened to him yet.

Farther down the street, a figure darted for the shadows between two houses. He dashed forward, looked up just in time to watch Nabi disappear over the top of the Aniginna wall. No explanation, no plan. Suba had told him about the captain's remark. Was Nabi headed for Hall of Laws on his own?

The wall was too much for Suba's heavier frame—he'd never done well at wall climbs in camp—so he dog-trotted through the streets, searching for a break but keeping to the shadow of the Aniginna's perimeter wall. If only that pigheaded Anu hadn't left camp and run off to that swamp town. He could use a good fighter right now. Anu had gristle to endure the carnage and a grown man's muscle to match. But that was water over the dam.

A whippoorwill called in the darkness, like the signal for the hunt taught at camp. He answered with his own imitation, then waited, trusting Nabi Gahn's assertion that the Nazim didn't know one night bird from another.

When the noose dropped over his head, Suba remembered his own warning to himself months ago: Nabi didn't know as much as he claimed.

Chapter 45

Suba At Large

Suba came to his senses in a darkened chamber with four windowless brick walls. His abductors had kept him conscious and on his feet only long enough to walk him blindfolded and bound through a maze of alleys to some appointed room deep inside a large building. Probably somewhere in the Aniginna compound, judging by the lengths of hallways and countless turns.

Now the blindfold was off and his hands were untied. He lay on a bunk shoved against one wall. A small taper lit the wall beyond his feet. He sat up and placed both feet on the floor. A familiar scent reached his nostrils.

Gods, could it be Memet?

The cobra hood rose suddenly right before his face, three feet off the floor. Memet's dark irises regarded Suba with the intensity he had grown to know so well. They had shared a household for nearly two years. He should know the serpent's moods by now, but this was different. As Memet's eyes caught the lamplight, they flashed anger, an animal warning not directed at Suba but intended to put him on guard.

Well, of course, their lady was in danger. They were

surrounded by enemies, men who would kill at a command.

How had the Nazim brutes managed to transport Memet all the way from Mada Ghin? Did a serpent handler live in their midst?

None of that mattered. The point was that the Nazim had gone to considerable trouble to bring Memet alive to the Aniginna. They had a purpose in mind for him as well as Suba. Maybe Memet already knew it, but Suba would have to figure out both for himself.

He turned again toward Memet. "Do you know why I'm here, Memet? Can you tell me what to do?"

At once, the cobra turned away and moved across the floor to stand before the door. He waited there, facing the door, without another glance at Suba.

Did he expect someone at the door? Was Suba supposed to understand the significance of the door?

Maybe it was just dumb animal behavior. "I need out, the door is out." Memet was like a house cat in many ways. Would not soil his home, took himself outside through a small door Suba had fashioned to go about his business. Kept his "food" outside too.

No, probably the dumbest animal in the room right now was Suba.

He tried to imagine what Memet thought of the men who had brought him here. Would he attack if one of them came through the door? Did he know how to evade a handler's hook-and-rod? If he was a menace to the lot of them, then who had placed him here?

Suba got up and edged past Memet to the door and pulled the handle. The door didn't budge. Barred from the other side. No surprise there.

He turned back to the room. Empty but for the bed and a brick table built into one wall. His shirt hung from a single peg, a basin in the corner served for his personal hygiene.

Memet now left the door and moved back to the bed. Stood there staring at it without moving. Was he pointing at something?

Pointing with his nose, like a jackal to its hunting mates?

Suba went to the bed, lifted the cover. Just a tick mat beneath. What else?

Memet continued to point.

Suba lifted the mat, saw an ordinary bed frame with webbing to support mat and sleeper. Nothing else there, nothing beneath, but Memet didn't move.

Peg.

The image arose in his mind, dissolved like salt in a water pot.

The webbing was secured to the frame with pegs. Nothing unusual about that. He turned to put a question to Memet and discovered the cobra had moved back to the door again.

Peg.

Door.

What?

Suba crossed to the door and ran his hands over the surface. It was just a wooden door, oak slats held together with a pegged oaken frame. Was there some connection between the pegs in the door and those in the bed?

His hand found the frame's crosspiece. The copper latch lay at the same level on the other side.

And beneath the crosspiece, a peephole.

Small—the size of a peg.

"You sly devil!" he said to Memet.

His serpent companion moved aside, his conspiracy complete.

Suba knelt by the bed and went to work. By twisting and yanking on the webbing, he managed to work a peg loose from the frame. A little more work and the thing came loose and tumbled out onto the floor. He picked it up, saw that its length matched his hand span.

Back to the door. Was a sentry posted on the other side? He shot a look at Memet, but the serpent kept his eye on the door.

No one there.

Suba had to wiggle the peg a few times before he felt the latch lift above its catch. A gentle nudge, and the door opened a crack. He pushed again, and Memet was immediately at his side, a signal to move swiftly.

He pushed the door all the way open and checked both directions. The corridor ended abruptly a few paces to his left, extended a good twenty to his right before it intersected with another. He considered going back into the room for his shirt, but Memet had dropped to the floor and was already on the move, slithering off at a fast clip.

At the intersecting hall, Memet rounded the left corner without pause and sped on, his low profile and brown-green color blending well with the clay brick walls. With such camouflage he himself might easily slip past a guard, but he would not lead Suba into trouble.

Suba almost stopped as that thought passed through his mind. Was the notion his or Memet's?

Memet seemed to have a destination in mind, for he took on the maze with clear intent. As Suba jogged behind, he remembered that the snake had ridden Uruna's shoulders through these very corridors every day for years. They were as familiar to him as his Mada Ghin domain—probably more so.

After several minutes of pursuit, Memet slowed at a crossing and hugged the right corner. Suba flattened against the wall and waited.

He heard voices echo from that direction. Two sentries talking?

Memet lay perfectly still. In that moment, Suba wished to be a snake.

The men continued their talk, something that sounded like "she won't last long down there" as they moved away in the other direction. Suba watched Memet for the signal to proceed, and when the trunk rose up to full height again, he knew something was up.

Memet rounded the corner without caution, sped ahead, and stopped abruptly before a closed door. Suba caught up with him, sent a silent question as he placed a finger under the latch. Memet stayed on point, so he lifted the bar lightly and pulled the handle.

The room inside was completely dark, but Memet raced forward and disappeared in the interior. Suba quietly closed the door and paused to let his eyes adjust to the faint ambient light.

He stood in a large space, a good four times the size of the one he'd left. He heard the rustle of fabric from the far wall. A light *Oh!* And then an eerie whisper.

S-s-s-sah!

A flint scratched in the empty silence, followed by the muted glow from a tiny oil dish.

Uruna's face bloomed into existence, her eyes widened as she caught sight of her husband.

"I felt you nearby," she said, and raced into his arms. "I felt you and hoped I was wrong. Quickly, we haven't much time."

Chapter 46

Heartbreak

Uruna clung to Suba through long moments, none long enough. He kissed her scalp, her face, her neck, ran his fingers through her hair as he murmured his relief in her ear. He smelled of sweat and blood, and his raw power drove her giddy with elation. Her Suba was alive!

And yet, the remnant of some terrible ordeal of pain and anguish lingered behind his loving gaze. A brush with death had added years to his features. He had suffered greatly, yet his indomitable spirit lived on. He had come back to her.

If only that could be the whole of it.

"I should have been there," he started, but she wouldn't allow it.

"You were right where you were supposed to be, love. Let's put that behind us and turn our thoughts forward."

"I just want to hold you a while longer. Tell me what's going on."

She hardly knew herself, so she struggled to explain the strange transformation overtaking the temple, the change in Lubna

Seddua, her twisted interpretation of ancient lore, the Lukur's astonishing capitulation.

"I don't know what's become of any of them," she told him. "Lubna wouldn't say, just told me to forget them and save myself."

"They've filled a pit with vipers?"

"The vipers have been there for years. Nobody can figure out how to get rid of so many without dying in the process. Lubna just decided it would make a good arena for spectacle. She intends for a huge crowd to watch from above. You're to be sacrificed for some trumped up infidelity."

"She sounds deadly ambitious. Her scheme is almost too elaborate for belief. Has she completely captured Nazim loyalty? I've already…dealt with their kind."

"Two squads will come for us at dawn. You must be gone by then."

"I belong at your side."

"Not for this. I may not survive, but at least I have a chance. You would have none."

"I don't understand. Why are you sending me away again?"

So she explained the Strikes test, Suba's role as Damuzi, the ritual death assured by vipers driven mad with rage.

"She wants you to die, but more than that, she wants me to watch you suffer. What she doesn't know, what I must tell you now, is that my chance lies with a rite I've kept to myself since the age of nine. Kept from you, even in the deepest privacy of our home."

She took a deep breath, having never expected so dire a situation to drive the secret from her. Still, Suba was her husband. He deserved to know.

"Cobra venom swims in my blood," she said. "Every night I drink a potion that prepares my body for the Sleep of Serpents. If I'm stung in the pit, there's a good chance I can still reach the far side."

Suba released her arms and stepped back with an uncomprehending stare. "This is lunacy! Lubna Seddua, Semma Karkhan, the Nazim, they're all as crazy as bats! I can get you out of this mess, but we'll have to act fast. There's got to be a way to reach the rooftop. From there we can—"

"Suba, no! That would only postpone my death, and yours, and everyone else in temple service. Lubna must be defeated before her own following. I can do it. You must trust me, Suba."

"Trust you? In this? I want us to live together, Uruna. The rest of these people haven't shown a gnat's eye of loyalty to you. They're all hypocrites interested only in themselves."

"That's not true, my love. You can't lump them all in the same stew. They're all worthy of saving, but especially you. I have to send you out once more. It tears me apart to do it, but I don't want to lose you to these unfeeling beasts. You've already seen what they can do. If I let you stay, I'll have to watch you die. That's senseless."

"There has to be another way."

"Suba, when it's over, when I march out of that pit with victory, we'll be back together again."

"No, that's not how it will be."

"What do you mean?"

"I've seen an end coming. You're moving away from me. Have been for some time. I just didn't realize it until now. We've been drifting apart, you on your path, I on mine, and it breaks my heart to say it, but you…you're growing so fast! Far faster than I can run. I didn't want to admit it, lied to myself to keep things going at my pace, but I'll never catch up with you. I shouldn't try. I'll only hold you back."

It was happening again. She was losing the man she loved, just like all the others. Gudamma, Mena Ramush, Khufu, her mother and father. Now Suba would either drift out of her life or die.

"Please don't say that," she begged. "I love you, Suba."

"I know you do. And I love you deeply. But I'm getting a better look at things tonight. I've...done some things, seen some things...I can't bring them into your life. If I do, it will destroy the life you're building. And I don't want that to happen, can't let it happen."

He placed one foot on the window sill to peer down, and she lost sight of him behind a curtain of tears. The next moment he was sitting on the sill, dangling his feet outside and making faces at someone below.

"Well, what do you know, the old weasel came back for me after all."

"Weasel? In the garden?"

"Nabi Gahn's down there in the bushes with a coil of rope. I guess he wants me back to nursemaid his camp babies."

A grappling hook snagged the sill just inches from his leg. Suba grabbed the rope and slipped into the air like an egret, dropped from sight for a breathless heartbeat, then called back from below.

"Would you be so kind as to pull it loose when I'm down."

"But not before," she said, trying to make her voice light.

"That would undo everything we've worked so hard for."

A moment later, he waved up at her in the light from the window, and she unhooked the grapple and tossed it out into the night.

"Auf, my poor toe!" Suba joked.

"Knock a few heads for me."

"Gladly. Until next time!"

It was too much. She spun away from the window, unable to keep the banter going, and threw herself on the bed.

"Next time," she mumbled into the pillow.

When the soldiers came, her sobbing had stopped.

Chapter 47

Grit Meets Greed

Four soldiers took Uruna through a maze of corridors, out of the Gipar, across the Aniginna commons, and into Hall of Ancient Spirits. Why Lubna had chosen the repository for the dead made no sense unless she sought to impress her new following with a macabre ritual.

But instead of stopping there, her escort passed through the main hall and out the north side to House of Safekeeping, where the Lukur warehoused religious artifacts and relics. The significance eluded her.

Lubna stood in the main hall with a dozen or so women of rank, Niccaba and Kinar included. Both kept silent counsel beneath severe expressions. She caught a flash of relief on both faces as she entered, then the hard masks dropped into place again.

They were there under duress—Umaki's duress, as he leered back at Uruna and brandished his sword.

Lubna had no interest in their plight, and began with Suba.

"I suppose you had nothing to do with your husband's escape."

Uruna decided that with this woman she could dissemble as

well as any.

"Last I heard he was on patrol outside Mada Ghin."

Lubna's expression told the room she disbelieved that account. "No matter," she said, "he'll be found soon enough and punished according to Nazim tradition. I believe that entails the removal of the accused one's head."

She sought Uruna's reaction and, finding only bland disregard, added. "In a public square."

Suba had already eluded several Nazim attempts at capture. Uruna also suspected he had taken a life or two from their ranks. He would repeat the insult at every opportunity.

It was then that Uruna realized the Entu was missing. "Where's Semma Karkahn?"

"We had a disagreement over certain property. She became belligerent, we were running out of time. She—fought me. Umaki had to step in and use force. I believe the effort was too much for the old crone."

"You killed Semma? Your own grandmother?"

"I did no such thing. She brought about her own death."

Uruna seethed. Lubna was too careless with other lives. Ambition was one thing, but murder deserved swift and lethal punishment. Would the law find a champion amongst the faithless?

Lubna was anxious to move on with her plan. "There is a pit in the desert," she said. "About an hour's walk from the Old City's west gate. The river used to run out there at a place time and the gods forgot. Demdua—in homage to the Flower Goddess. Story goes that a temple full of treasure was lost when a great flood buried the town in mud. High priestess had to abandon the treasure and shift the city east to the new river course—now Old City. Or as best we can tell.

"Now, no human soul knows exactly how the pit formed, but

everyone knows the river god is a fickle woman, moves on a whim. Some say the river, or a branch of it, returned to Demdua at one point, scoured out a cavern, then left again, and hasn't returned to this day. Semma knew we would find the treasure in that cavern. She wouldn't tell me outright, but I know Demdua's the place.

"So what are we to do? Just march down to the cavern and haul out the gold? Not that easy. Fate, or the gods, added a further obstacle: guard the treasure with a host of deadly vipers. We had a look, found the place crawling with vipers and their prey. Umaki wanted to burn them out."

She noted Uruna's cringe with a smirk.

"But I asked him, 'How do you know you got the last of them?' Because one sting in the right place can kill a man. Then Semma made up a story that stopped those superstitious bastards cold. She said the cavern is the entrance to the Underworld. Crawl back in there too far, and you meet up with Pazuzu's legion of demons. Well, they all went bug-eyed at that. Then someone mentioned the serpent girl from Mada Ghin, and everyone else smiled.

"So here you are, the answer to our prayers."

"You want me to climb into a nest of wild desert asps and find your treasure for you."

"Yes, and then attach a rope to it so we can haul it up and put the gold to proper use. We'll haul you out, too, of course, if you get that far."

"Promise?"

"Would I lie to you?"

"At every chance. And if I refuse? Or, if I agree but don't make it alive?"

"Then every Lukur priestess from top to bottom goes down to do the job until it is done."

"You would really send each one to her death, wouldn't you."

"I'd rather not have to go that far. You could prevent such a drastic outcome, you know. Or at least die trying."

"You already have one death on your hands. Probably more by Umaki at your bidding."

"Do try to focus, Uruna, and save your concern for the living."

"When does this fool's errand begin?"

"What difference does an hour or a day make to you?"

"Time for prayer might mean I'm spared long enough to satisfy your greed."

"We've prepared the pit for our use. You'll descend with a rope and hook. A path cut into the walls will lead you as far as my men dared to go. Torchlight to see by and keep the snakes at bay as best we can. I want you to succeed, Uruna. Nothing's to be gained if you add your bones to the others."

"My bones?"

"We discovered skeletons at the cavern mouth. Have to assume the unlucky fools died from snakebite, but they might have killed one another for any number of reasons. Suffice to say, we're making your effort as safe as humanly possible."

Spoken by the least human woman in Uruna's world.

"I'd like a look beforehand."

"That won't be necessary."

"It might give your plan at least a gnat's chance in hell."

"Again, not necessary. You're going in tonight."

Suba pressed flat against Safekeeping's outer wall and hugged its shadow to let the Nazim patrol pass. Once they were gone, he turned to the figure across the gap between buildings and signalled all clear.

He and Nabi had left hiding immediately after overhearing Lubna's plan and stolen outside through an unlatched window. High Priestess Lubna had gone rogue, and her reckless disregard for life changed everything.

The Aniginna was bad for him right now. He and Nabi were heavily outnumbered, easily spied in broad daylight by any Nazim with two eyes. Any kill would attract swarms of the bloodthirsty warriors to his trail. But if he slipped out of the city now, he might find cover near the pit and pull Uruna from Nazim clutches before the worst happened.

Nabi crossed the pavement to his side. As usual, he knew Suba's unspoken thoughts.

"We are *not* going there," he said in a hoarse whisper.

"She's my wife!" Suba spat.

"Hence my reason never to wed."

"A flaw for which every woman in Sumer can be thankful."

"I could stop you, rabbit."

"I know. But what would you gain by it?"

"Besides satisfaction, maybe an able fighter for later."

Suba checked the surroundings. Another patrol was crossing in their direction. Time to go.

"Can't stay here," he said, and slipped deeper into the shadows before Nabi could react.

According to earlier plan, they split up. Suba's size made him an easy target, so he took a short route to a potter's storehouse that held two secrets. It was unoccupied, and it contained a hole to the catacombs under the city. He'd explored Nippur's underpinnings as a boy. His main concern now: size again.

The doorway was still where he remembered, behind a stack of urns. His strength made quick work of moving the huge containers, and his luck held as he squeezed through the gap and dropped into the old house whose roof was now the storehouse floor.

He was amazed how quickly he recalled every turn and obstacle. Old Shutu Gate lay halfway across town, but he emerged at the river shortly before sundown, with the Nazim rabble none the wiser.

Now to find weapons in the Old City and make his way west to the pit.

He ought to eat first, though. He didn't have Nabi's sparse frame and lean appetite. Such appetite as he did have would suffice for Nazim blood.

Chapter 48

Death Times A Thousand

By the time Uruna reached the cavern mouth, she doubted she would last for the interior. Her mouth was dry, her senses all seemed far away, her legs felt enormous and leaden. She had dodged several vipers that hissed at her passage, only to be stung twice by asps. The nasty little critters were utterly beyond the reach of her serpent senses, enraged by her intrusion and driven to terror by torches arrayed along the pit's walls. Her own torch flame drove back most of them, but one or another would skitter out from shelter for a desperate stab.

The cavern floor was higher than the pit bottom—a good eight feet by her estimation. To get to it, she had to climb through a field of boulder-sized clay lumps. The effort sent the venom racing through her system. An ordinary person would be half-dead on the ground by now, but her nightly potion ritual was giving her an edge.

So far.

Adding to her burden were two ropes, one a safety line tied round her waist, the other Lubna's link to anticipated treasure, coiled about Uruna's shoulders like Memet, only heavier.

Once at the top of the incline, Uruna realized further advance was futile. The roof of the so-called cavern sloped downward and met the floor some four or five paces from the mouth in a wall of compacted dried clay. Anyone at the top could see as much for themselves, but Lubna had ordered the team to press on.

The cavern receded to her right in a hollow as opaque as the back. But as her torchlight erased the shadows, she saw a small wooden box shoved out of sight.

"I may have something," she hollered out.

"I knew it!" Lubna crowed from above. "What is it?"

"A box, looks like cedar, very small."

"How small?

"Length of my forearm, maybe. A handspan deep."

"Send it up!"

"Shouldn't I open it first?"

"No!"

Uruna shoved her torch into a crevice and secured it. Then she crouched on her haunches and withdrew the box.

The cedar had cracked with age and faded to a dull gray beneath a thick coat of dust. The lid was intact, but the cracked leather hasp that once had clasped a wood button hung loose. It would easily open to her touch, but she wanted to end this nightmare as soon as possible, so she pulled the coil from her shoulders and went about fashioning a rope cradle for the box.

She was forced to stop several times as her vision blurred and her benumbed fingers fumbled the knot. When she was done, she picked up the box in her arms and, as prearranged, gave the rope two tugs to take up the slack. When the box was hanging from a taut line, she gave it a single tug and watched the box ascend up the pit wall. When it had disappeared over the rim, she gave her own line a tug and waited for Umaki to hoist her up.

And waited.

And heard a blasphemous scream from above. Lubna's head loomed at the pit's rim as she railed at Uruna.

"The box is empty!"

"Sorry, I'd like to come up now."

"You tricked me!"

"Lubna, I didn't have time to trick anyone. Please haul me up. I'm sick."

"Well, you can stay sick, for all I care. Send up the treasure you took from the box."

"I took nothing. There's nothing left and there never was to begin with. The whole cavern is nothing but nothing! Haul me out of here!"

"Lies! You took it from the box so you can come back for it later!"

The woman's tirade was worse than a spoiled child's. Uruna decided to appeal to saner minds—if there were any.

"Umaki, pull me up and we can talk like adults about this."

The rope tightened, and Uruna stuck her foot in a loop fashioned for it and immediately rose a foot from the cavern floor, then two, then three—

The rope slackened and she crashed to the ground.

Lubna stuck her head over the edge again.

"Not until you send up the gold, you little weasel. There's gold down there and I will have it!"

Uruna had had enough. She loosened the knot at her waist and tossed the rope on the ground. She snatched the torch and without a word to the watchers above, strode out of the cavern and stomped down the talis slope. To every fanged head she brandished the torch, heedless of whether she burned them or not. She felt nothing for the little fiends, she felt less than nothing for her tormentors above.

She reached end of the pit floor, tossed her torch at the last hissing viper, and climbed to the bottom stair, where she began her ascent. Angry determination drove her past danger, as hand-over-hand she clawed her way up the steps cut into the side, heedless of clods tumbling into the abyss, her only interest the next handhold.

She was near the cliff top when her hand met with a foot.

Umaki's foot.

Semma's Nazim killer stood boldly in her path, his sword tip inches from her face.

"No, no, little princess, there's more work to be done."

"Or you'll what? Kill me here? No one else will get as far as I did."

"We'll find a way. This is as far as you go."

He drew his sword back for the plunge, but never followed through.

An arrow hissed through the air and struck his chest—precisely between the two armored breastplates. Umaki screamed and grabbed the shaft, pulled it out and threw it aside. Roaring in agony, he staggered back, caught his heel against the stair step, teetered off center, and plunged into the abyss.

Uruna heard his scream all the way to the bottom. Heard more screams as the serpents fell upon him. Heard the snap-snap-snap as serpent fury granted the killer a quick death--too mercifully quick.

Uruna looked up, scanned the rim for the archer. Was it Suba? Nabi Gahn?

The spent arrow lay nearby. She picked it up, prepared to throw it into the pit after its victim, and stopped as the weapon caught the torchlight.

The symbols cut into the shaft just behind the head. She'd seen the same before. But where? And when?

An image loomed in her mind, of a search for a boy, herself

standing alone in a narrow draw formed by river mud, steep sided like the pit she was in now. Two lions sizing her up, then dead on the ground, felled by an arrow.

An arrow with strange markings like the one in her hand.

The Hani hunter? Here at the Demdua ruin? Sparing her life again?

A quick jerk of her head brought her too close to the stair's edge, and she drew back and flattened against the cliff face. She stole another look at the rim, but found no hunter, no Suba, no Nabi Gahn.

Only a woman on a rope, lowering herself down the cliff.

Lubna!

Lamashtu's would-be prophet, bowing to insatiable greed, determined to see the cavern for herself, was risking death in her own Test of a Thousand Strikes. But unprotected by cobra immunity.

"Lubna! No!" she called out.

Lubna slipped, caught herself, and turned in the direction of Uruna's voice, a knowing grin splitting her face, and continued her descent.

Kinar's voice rang out from above. "Uruna! Forget her and keep climbing. We'll help you at the top."

Below, Lubna had reached the bottom stair and was gathering herself for the descent onto the floor. They were separated by only twenty yards so they no longer needed to shout. Uruna urged Lubna back.

"There's no gold to be had, Lubna. Either someone already took it, or there never was any in the first place. You're risking your life for nothing."

"You'd like me to believe that, wouldn't you? I have never doubted its existence, despite Semma's lifelong attempts to hoard the trove for herself."

"You'll die finding nothing there, and that's so unnecessary."

With a vigorous shake of her head, Lubna stepped off the last stair and grabbed the twisted clay for a purchase. As Uruna watched in horror, she placed one foot on the pit floor, then another. Miraculously, not a serpent head appeared.

Lubna looked back over her shoulder at Uruna, a triumphant grin lighting her face. "You see? I am blessed. This is my dest—"

Her face contorted as the first fangs struck. She shook the asp loose and started a fast walk through the narrow alley of clay boulders and rubble.

Another asp struck, and she stumbled forward, stifling a scream of pain.

Uruna could imagine Lubna's anguish. Her plan wasn't working. The snakes were crawling out of their hiding places, infuriated, terrified, maddened by this new invasion of their domain.

They struck again. And again.

Lubna had now reached the foot of the talis slope. She fell forward and scrabbled a few feet, slid back, and lay there. The venom was working on her limbs. Soon it would paralyze her lungs and she would struggle for breath. In minutes she would suffocate to death.

Uruna started down.

"No!" Kinar screamed from above. "Uruna, you've done your job. Lubna made her choice, you can't risk more venom. Turn around and come back up the stairs now."

Lubna continued lying supine on the slope. Her eyes were half closed, her breathing shallow. Her expression had changed from arrogance to resignation. She was as good as dead and knew it.

Uruna paused at the lowest stair step and looked down. Umaki's swollen carcass lay directly below. She would have to step over his outstretched body and again walk the gauntlet of vipers to reach Lubna. There was no way to find out if she was pushing her luck with more venom. They might both die here in the next few minutes.

What would Gudamma say if she were present? Or Mena, or Nashi? Save yourself for prophecy? Render the dead to eternity?

Or would they say, Be true to yourself?

Without another thought she dropped neatly beside Umaki's corpse. Immediately, she was mired to her ankles in serpents. She struggled for solid footing, desperate to keep erect. Her left heel slithered over somebody's tough, coarse scales, and when another twined its neck around her ankle and began to climb, she looked down.

Umaki stared back with the vacant stare of the dead. His cadaver was no longer of interest to the serpent masses. They sought the warm-blooded flesh of the living. Now both she and Lubna were in trouble, caught beyond right and reason in a hollow pit where death pressed in from all sides.

Uruna turned her attention to Lubna and received a shock that locked her in place. Lubna stood erect on her feet.

They locked gazes, Lubna's eyes once again full of scorn for her avowed enemy, Uruna's searching, probing for a glimmer of life. As she watched Lubna's face, hatred gave way to panic, as the invading toxin reached Lubna's senses and wrenched her body with excruciating pain.

Uruna was herself enveloped in serpents—but to an altogether different effect. The feel of their flesh was nothing like Memet's, but the sensation failed to frighten her. What was this sudden change?

Back to Lubna—and another transformation, panic transformed into—what was it? Curiosity?

Lubna now stood only two paces away. Had she moved? Or was Uruna advancing toward her, unaware of her own stride?

She extended her arms toward Lubna, her muscles constrained

by a dreamy slowness. Lubna's lips parted and her jaw dropped in an effort to speak, but no sound came forth. She tried again, trance-like, her limbs no longer entwined with reptiles, but the poison in her system already doing its work.

Uruna spoke to her. "Give it to me," she said quietly.

Lubna frowned, the familiar obstinate resistance still in place.

"Or would you rather cling to your death?" Uruna finished.

"What do you mean?" Lubna demanded. "Is it my crown you desire? You would wear my crown now that I'm dying?"

Her eyelids fluttered as she began the final turn inward. Uruna had seen it before, had saved some from death's thrall, had lost others. But she felt tonight must be different. She must hold Lubna's gaze or lose the moment.

Now Lubna lifted her arms to meet Uruna's groping hands. Was it an act of resistance, or a plea for help? Or something else altogether?

Moving with fluid grace, Uruna reached outward with a part of her that went beyond flesh, felt more solid and infinitely more powerful. An extension of will, a ribbon of pure light expanding from her very core, instantly in place as though it had never left, but had lain forgotten for this vital moment.

A part of herself stepped into the light and watched as Lubna released immobilizing fear with a monumental upheaval of denial, regret, pain, anguish. An inky essence separated from Lubna's body and floated in the space between them, as loose and aimless as smoke drift. The stuff then caught sight of its next target, gathered new purpose, and made a vicious dash for Uruna's heart.

Where it encountered its own death.

Cobra death.

The evil thing strove mightily for a hold, contended with its master for a painful bout, and in a burst of light, lost the battle.

Uruna reeled backward, realized she was still on her feet, and watched Lubna ascend on the rope up the cliff face, as though borne on wings, her foot planted in the stirrup, firm and strong as she continued upward to a cluster of outstretched hands.

She was free! Lubna was alive and free!

Uruna's knees buckled and she felt coarse earth beneath the palms of her hands.

The rope descended again, and as if in a dream, she watched her foot find the stirrup, felt a brush of air as she swayed over a forest of upturned serpent heads. And then she was at the rim, afloat on a cloud of bliss.

Strong arms hauled her over the rail onto solid ground. The crowd jostled her, as the cavern walls reverberated with jubilant cheers. In the pandemonium she looked aside and saw Lubna enveloped in a cloud of Lukur robes. Lubna looked up and shook herself free of grasping hands, stumbled toward Uruna, and lurched into her arms.

"I felt him! I felt his touch!" Lubna exclaimed in a rush. "What did he do? I thought I knew how it would be to die. I felt the venom and I was so sure I was ready for death, but then...I went someplace else, and I came back, and...it's so much more. Such... I can't..."

"It's love, Lubna. Love of the godly kind. Therein lies the gold you seek."

Lubna pulled back and searched Uruna deeply. "Do you think I can become worthy?"

"You were always worthy. Now you hear of it as well as I."

"What do I hear?"

"The answer that has no question."

A gaggle of ladies begged Lubna's company and began to draw her away. Lubna glanced over her shoulder once more at Uruna, aware now of the bond connecting them, connecting All, her face still tinged with confusion.

Uruna felt a settling peace inside. Some were touched by the divine as they left the womb, others not until nearly the end of their time.

"Thus it begins," she said to herself, echoing Gudamma, Mena, Nashi, and a host of others. "May it never end."

She then turned and gave herself over to an adoring crowd.

Chapter 49

New Soul

Lubna surprised a great many Lukur when she refused to submit her name to the Entu election board. She also excused herself from the board itself with what she hoped would be the last lie of her life, a plea for much-needed rest, despite feeling uncommonly vigorous. In doing so, she spared the ladies the uncomfortable alternative of trying her for crimes committed while in office.

She paused on her way to Morning Honors and leaned against a column to ponder that night once again. An experience of tremendous moment had graced her life, but she couldn't comprehend the whole of it. It was like she had simply stepped into a magical room for a short visit, and come back with the dust of that place still clinging to her. Too soon she was forgetting some of it, and the loss was painful.

She could remember returning from that other place and being vaguely aware of a clamor overhead, of women cheering and crying out in triumph. The noise got louder and invaded her pleasant space. Then the serpent song faded altogether, and the sense-tingling exploration stopped.

She had felt distanced from the commotion above. Calm and undisturbed, like Uruna, because the singing she had heard was more important. Only the Other presence was capable of doing. She was merely a vessel. The Other had made room for something precious and important. But that would take place later.

She sent her mind back to the pit rim.

…Uruna stood facing her, watching her closely, the serpents gone from her arms, as from her own. The others hoisted her up to safety.

When she got to the top, several ladies swung her into a forest of waiting arms. The touch of human hands felt strange. After that, everything got confusing, as she was jostled and squeezed and smothered in teary praise.

For just an instant, Uruna stepped close and gently touched the parts of Lubna that remained in the other place, and she felt a ringing deep in her soul. Then, as she stood in a daze, four matrons wound a white cloak about her naked body. She didn't remember having shed the last of her clothing, only that the soft linen fabric felt luscious.

One thing she would surely never forget. As the Mothers made a ragged attempt to restore order, Uruna's voice broke her reverie.

"Now you know."

And truly she did. She was no longer a hostage to fear. She was…empty…open…

Lubna pushed away from the temple wall and headed outside and across the concourse toward the Aniginna gate. From there she would take the road to her house in the *nigenna*, for she no longer had purpose here. She had already reached the high point of her life. Nothing henceforth would compare to it.

She slowed as she gained the river road and began an easy walk to conserve her strength. Serpenthood. She was too new to its effect to understand the rush of meaning that engulfed her. For the present she was a bundle of emotion, happily swept along in a tide of bliss.

But Uruna's parting remark stood out from all the rest. Rock solid, full of promise.

"You have tasted the infinite. You will thirst for more."

The two-fold pit victory struck an astounding blow to the Nazim spirit. By dawn the next morning, Nippur lay empty of insurgents. The fierce legion had fled without a fight. Their champion lay dead. Their queen had renounced their god. A nomad's life called them back to the wilderness.

The resilient Sumerian spirit recovered in quick order. Uruna joined a small cadre of priestesses in a belated celebration of Morning Honors led by Niccaba Seddua. Council wasted not a moment second-guessing the reason for the Nazim exodus. Too long idled by Nazim interference, they set forth restoring temple works and laying up depleted stores. Merchants forced earlier to camp outside the walls were welcomed inside and dealt with as quickly as the ladies could manage.

Uruna pitched in, lending her prodigious accounting talent to the task of acquiring and storing goods left long in short supply. When the pandemonium reached a crescendo, she stepped forward to organize and expedite the flow. The results caught the attention of overworked Lukur matrons, and by day's end they were coming to her for counsel.

She was completely caught up in her work, tallying bolts of linen, when Kinar approached with a wedge of cheese and dried fruit.

"You haven't eaten yet, have you?"

"I'm not sure, I suppose not."

"Stop what you're doing and eat. You can't keep going like this."

Uruna pocketed her stylus and tablet and sat down on an upended keg. Only then did the fatigue of the day catch up with her. She took a deep breath and laid into the cheese. Kinar proffered a goat bladder of water.

"Have you had any drink either?"

Uruna shrugged. No, she hadn't, and that was foolish. She put on a look of apology and hoped it might work. Kinar was having none of it.

"You were pushing yourself again," she said. "You know you don't need to prove yourself anymore."

"I'm not pushing, but there's so much work to be done."

"Yes, and plenty of hands to do it. Just sit a few moments and relax."

"But Shu-alla needs my linen counts."

"Her figures can wait 'til morning. Eat."

Spoken like a mother. Kinar was enjoying her role.

The cheese was good, the prunes marvelous. Perhaps she was quite hungry after all.

When she had stuffed her mouth so full of food she couldn't speak, Kinar sprang into the void.

"You heard what I said, didn't you? About proving yourself?"

Uruna took a few moments to swallow. "Oh, Kikki, I'm not quite a sage yet. Still working on it." She hoped the joke might lighten Kinar's mood, but it just encouraged her to continue.

"I don't think you realize what's going on right now. Everyone in temple service, from bottom to top, is in a thrall over you. Don't roll your eyes at me, I'm serious. Word of your work in the Bundug has spread like a grass fire. It's Uruna this, and Uruna that, and did you know she started this and finished that. You created quite a stir before you returned, and then the Nazim business with the snake pit, and rescuing Lubna. Now today they can see firsthand what you're made of. No more doubt, rumors dispelled. They consider you a prophet already."

She realized what Kinar was doing, building up to whatever she'd had in mind by showing up.

"What is this about, Kikki?"

"Come with me, I've something to show you."

"I haven't finished my prunes. I'm resting, as I was ordered."

"Bring them with you. This is just as important."

"More important than my health?"

"Not at all. It's all about your health."

Kinar took her along city streets, past the Aniginna gate, and through the Gipar maze to Uruna's own room. She opened the door and beckoned Uruna ahead of her.

"See for yourself. "

Uruna took two steps and stopped in total shock.

On the floor before her sat Memet. And directly before the great cobra sat a small girl. Her head was topped with a mop of red hair, and as she turned at Uruna's entrance, her blue eyes shone with eager intelligence.

"They've been like that half the day," Kinar said. "I came to fetch you after *dissiku* and there she was, Arn Gar's baby girl, Retha. You know her of course. I didn't dare interrupt them. I-I don't have a way with serpents."

Uruna could only stare dumbly at the sight. The child was in no danger of offending Memet, not after an entire afternoon. He was fascinated, the dark orbs of his eyes filled with an emotion approaching adoration. He saw something serpently in the girl, a nascent essence not yet fully formed but recognizable to his practiced senses.

Uruna stepped closer and spoke to him. "Are we finished here now, Memet?"

The slightest change in his attitude affirmed completion of his task.

She then turned to Kinar. "Do you have any idea how she got in here?"

"Why don't you ask her yourself? She's a big girl now, aren't you Retha?"

The girl turned away from Memet and held up three splayed fingers. "I'm this many. He says you were six when you met the faraway lady."

Uruna brought a hand to her mouth to stifle a choke. A tear squeezed past one eye and spilled down her cheek. She squatted on her heels and opened her arms, beckoning the girl to her. Retha uncrossed her legs and stood, but kept her eyes on the serpent lord.

Did she hear the god's voice? Had she spent half a day attuned to the godly? Could it be Enshiggu had begun his dialogue with another?

Uruna heard no voice confirming or denying, nor did she see any sign or feel any stirrings. But there was no denying the god had just allowed her to witness another miracle.

Now Retha came to her, and she took the girl up in her arms and cradled her there. She glanced over at Kinar, saw the shock there, and was moved to explain, when the child spoke for both of them.

"He says we have to forget today. I want to remember, but he says when I'm older I shall. Is that what he told you?"

Uruna kissed the ruddy cheek, afraid her voice might falter. "Yes, darling," she managed as a torrent of memories rushed forth and threatened to drown her.

Exactly the same words.

QUEEN

Chapter 50

Queen's Election

The marathon convocation had no precedent, so none present could explain the extended absence of Ekur's chief temple ministers for three days and three nights. Council remained sequestered behind barred doors throughout, leaving singly for physical needs and returning in utmost haste.

Uruna could imagine no explanation for such a lengthy caucus except that the election of Semma Karkhan's successor must be mired in controversy. The circumstances of the Entu's death certainly warranted careful negotiation. And Lubna's recent abdication and self-exile had brought considerable change to the regime.

Then there was the broader issue, a universal desire to avoid repeating the previous election's folly. The ladies would seek a ruler with her wits about her, proven administrative acumen, and a good grasp of the law. Uruna thought Niccaba would emerge victorious, although the woman had consistently declined her own nomination, citing her previous brief service in that office as disqualification, as well as her own conviction that she was better suited to an advisory position.

When the council ladies at last emerged from Hall of Laws, the streets outside were alight and a river breeze had cooled the night almost to a chill. Uruna was exhausted from her vigil with the forty Uzba members and various *naditu* priestesses seated and standing in the *legatium*, a large room just outside the entrance to Laws and open only to the privileged and powerful. She owed her own presence to her newly won renown as Mada Ghin's founder and the *de facto* leader of Bundug Province.

When at last the doors opened, weary bodies got to their feet and stood as the exhausted Council filed out—shoulders bent, faces drawn by fatigue and frustration. Without a word, the lot of them proceeded past the Uzba gallery, down the hallway, and on to their homes.

Kinar marched past Uruna at a quickened pace with her eyes focused straight ahead. Her inscrutable expression betrayed neither satisfaction nor disapproval, but a white-knuckled grip on her baton of office showed she had weathered fierce conflict. That much was a given. The outcome itself was yet to be revealed.

Uruna thrilled to the possibility Kinar was to be the next Entu. If only it were so, temple affairs might return to normalcy.

Niccaba alone lingered to address the gathering.

"The vote was final, the decision will be announced at Morning Honors after everyone gets a much-needed rest. Good night to you all."

To a clamor of objections, she turned abruptly and left for her own home.

Chapter 51

Queen

The knock on Uruna's door came before dawn's first light. She struggled into a dressing gown, still groggy from sleep. Probably an early call to Morning Honors to prepare for the great announcement.

To her surprise, Kinar stood in the hallway.

"We're gathering the Council ahead of time. Thought you ought to join us."

"But I'm not a member."

"Well, if you'd rather sleep in and miss the whole thing, that's all right with me."

"No, no, I'm coming."

She quickly pulled on a white dress, and was struggling with the shoulder clasp when Kinar stepped close and took it from her.

"Here, let me do it."

"Kikki, I can manage."

"Not today you can't."

Uruna craned around to see what she was doing and jumped. The clasp was gold.

"Am I being promoted at the same time as Entu?"

Kinar simply nodded. "You could say that. Let's get going. I haven't eaten yet and it's going to be a long day."

Uruna gave her no argument.

On their way to the Gipar dining hall, Uruna got several cheery greetings and bright smiles—more than the usual, she thought. Everyone must feel as relieved as she that the choice had finally been made and the new Entu would soon normalize Ekur's activity, missing for far too long.

She and Kinar wordlessly dined on dates and flatbread with honey. Uruna skipped the cakes as too filling. She asked Kinar several times with her eyes who was queen, but got ignored. Maybe once Kinar was crowned she intended an office for her young apprentice. She would keep both secrets to herself, of course, but the anticipation cut short Uruna's appetite. She finished her tea just as Kinar stood up.

"First, let's check in with Niccaba, see if we can help her with the arrangements. I think she'll be over in Laws by now."

Kikki was making a game of it for Uruna's sake. It was clear by now that she was trying, and failing, to hide her own excitement. Uruna was thrilled for her.

Two galla sentries stood watch at the doors to Hall of Laws. Each pulled a handle and drew his door aside for the two ladies. Their usual severe expressions were replaced by broad grins. So they must know already!

Uruna started down the broad hallway ahead, but Kinar took her arm and angled right. "The dressing room is this way."

"Oh, Kikki, I'm so excited!"

"So am I."

The vaguest hint. Uruna fought for composure. The youngest *naditu* must approach Council with aplomb. A coronation was certainly not the place for girlish giggles.

Ahead at the hallway's end, another pair of doors, carved with ornate scrollings, stood closed. Uruna followed behind Kinar as they approached. Kinar grasped both handles and pulled, then stepped in ahead of Uruna.

"Here she is!" she announced.

Well, that was a little unexpected, but Kinar deserved to be full of herself.

The Council ladies stood in an arc facing the door. All were dressed in their finest linens, badges of honor proudly decorating bosoms, instruments of rank in hand.

Uruna put on her best smile as she followed. Oddly, Kinar did not stop in the center of the gathering, but turned and backed off to one side. Her maneuver left Uruna smack in the place of honor. She started to drift in Kinar's direction, but Niccaba stepped out from the rank with a golden staff clutched in her stout hands. She pushed the staff at Uruna, as if to indicate she should take it.

Was she to have the honor of presenting it to Kinar?

"Uruna Kumta, beloved sister, keeper of hearts and healer of souls. To you as Entu of Ekur, I am pleased to present the Staff of Lasori."

Uruna's legs nearly failed her. This must be a mistake! Or else a bad prank. But the words—the words spoken were the same she had heard at Semma's invocation.

Suddenly, Kinar was at her side. "The vote was unanimous. We want you, Uruna. We need you and we trust you."

Niccaba's face broke into a grin. "Take the thing, please, Uruna, it's getting heavy."

Uruna took the staff in her hands and raised the gilded oaken symbol of the highest office in the land.

Niccaba turned about and swept her arm to include the entire room. "Behold your Council, madam, whose good pleasure it is to serve you and support you, in Inanna's name."

Immediately the room erupted in a cheer. The women stamped

their feet in a round of applause, then Kalumma Dalla started the queen's anthem, and all sang praise to Uruna's long-lasting reign.

A flood of tears blinded Uruna in that moment, for the love that poured forth exuded more affection and good will than she had felt in a long time.

Someone broke out a jug of wine and another brought a mug to Uruna. The ladies grew silent and turned to face her. She was but sixteen years of age, yet they regarded her as a woman worthy of their trust. They expected a response equal to their profound commitment.

"You have honored me beyond my wildest imagination. You..." She choked back a burst of emotion. "You, the keepers of our songs, the judges of our actions, the hearts that heal the sick and poor, have entrusted to me the sacred devotion that keeps this land great. I promise to each of you that I shall match that devotion with every drop of my soul. I will call upon each of you for advice, for your wisdom born of years beyond mine. I cannot act alone. Working together we will keep the bounty Great Mother bestows and continue to build. Thank you for your confidence. May Inanna bless us all."

Another hearty round of stomping feet and mugs raised to cheers. A voice from the back called for a toast to Serpenthood, and when it was done, one of the younger women spoke.

"How can we be assured of a prophet now that you will be busy as Entu?"

This would be a continual concern, Uruna realized. Best to declare her stance on the matter.

"Nothing is changed, my devotion to serpent Sight remains steadfast. Truth to tell, I feel even closer to it with your support here today."

Niccaba stepped forth to close the happy ceremony and instruct everyone on the day's forthcoming events. As she finished, tiny minister Ku Aya stepped forward with her hands behind her back.

"Entu Uruna," she announced, "to thee we present this emblem of our esteem and love."

She drew forth a gleaming golden tiara surmounted by the golden head of a cobra. Eyes of deep red carnelian gleamed with a light astoundingly akin to Memet's. The artisan had applied considerable care to obtain a faithful likeness.

She bent her knees for Ku Aya to reach her crown. Again she had to blink back tears. To think how much thought had gone into such a gift, one had to believe several had chosen her long before the election. She sent a thankful glance at Kinar, who smiled back through tears of her own.

The rest of the day was a whirlwind of ceremonies, hymns, feasts, and a public announcement from Ekur's platform. The streets were jammed with celebrants far into the night, for, as the Lukur had surmised, Uruna's popularity had been crowned as well. She hadn't a moment to herself until after the midnight call rang out.

As exhausted as she was, upon reaching her bed chamber her first thought was for Memet. She gathered him into her arms and spoke to him in their silent discourse. His eyes gleamed with pleasure as they sat together before the shrine to give thanks to Enshiggu.

Before they began, Uruna looked down at the small offering block and saw placed upon it a white stemmed rose. Her erstwhile anonymous benefactor had heard the news and found time in her busy chores to leave a reminder.

White, for the pure in heart.

Chapter 52

Verbal Joust

Suba awoke once more in captivity, again bound at the wrists, but this time with open sky overhead and a reed mat for his back.

He sat up, and at once realized he was not alone. A woman reclined against a palm trunk a few paces away. Her eyes sought him out from the shadow of a cowl as she spoke.

"Pray the blow to your head did not addle you further."

Suba checked his senses, found them mostly intact. "I seem to remember the scent of goat manure just moments before the attack."

"Perhaps a ram in rut mistook your hind parts for his mate."

"Why are my hands tied?"

"To keep you from committing further folly. Faith of the gods, Suba! Clad in leather armor and bearing a foolish amount of arrows? Off to rid the world of that Nazim scum? What were you thinking? Oh, I forget—you weren't."

"Well, it's nearly dawn. I suppose the worst has come to pass and I've lost my wife."

"Uruna isn't your wife, she's bride to an entire nation."

"I was afraid you'd say something like that. Is she safe?"

"No thanks to you, more than safe. She's queen."

"Impossible! She's only in Nippur because she was forced here. Or there. Where are we?"

"A stable outside the Old City. Your Nord cousins live just over there. But as to Uruna, I'm afraid you must come to grips with the truth, which was announced yestermorn."

"They made her queen! I've got to find her, congratulate her. I was consort, you know."

"For about an hour—and never confirmed."

"Infernal spirit! I remember you from before. Always meddling, always so sure of everything. Appearing at the worst times. Do you have a name?"

"I have a thousand, none worthy of repeating, every one forgotten. Get on your feet."

"Hard to do, tied up like this."

"If I were a Nazim lancer, you'd find your feet quick enough. Come now. Up, up!"

Suba kipped up onto his haunches and stood. The woman was just as quick, and went to work on his bonds.

"Where are you taking me?" he asked.

"I'm not taking you anywhere. You'll use your own feet."

"What makes you so sure?"

The cape fell away from a face weathered by time but graced with undiminished perfection. Suba caught his breath as eyes of purest blue regarded him with the first hint of affection.

The twine fell from his wrists as he beheld the woman who had given him life. He was free to go wherever he might, do whatever he would. But his only wish was to stay and never leave.

"Mother," he said.

Chapter 53

New Legacy

A song wafted into her dream and Uruna sat up in bed, quickened by the sense of another presence in her room. Memet's coiled form lay on the floor, deep in slumber. Soft light from the brazier in the hallway showed the royal bedchamber to be otherwise empty, but she couldn't shake the feeling of "other."

The song continued, its melody familiar, yet just beyond her ability to give it a place. How disturbing that she was unable to recall a memory of it.

Or was she hearing something greater—?

Gudamma!

"Oh, Nana! I feel your heart now," she burst out loud.

The song stopped, and a face blurred before her, then resolved into the merest essence of human shape. Uruna found herself speaking as she did with the god, thoughts alone doing the talking, ideas without words bridging the gap.

And Gudamma was there for her.

Share my joy! Feel my love for you! Tonight begins the life I sought for you, built for you, and which you have served so faithfully.

Uruna felt a soft caress, not a mortal touch but a loving stroke that spoke of enduring care, protection, unqualified satisfaction with the play of events that had led up to this moment.

Uruna paused to reflect.

Each pain had brought new meaning. For every love lost, another had risen in its place. Not a moment of travail had been for naught.

Each step of the journey—from their first encounter at the well in Shagri to her coronation as Entu—had imbued her with purpose. She was endowed with a bulwark of assurances that would carry her forward endlessly.

Rest firmly assured, said the voice in her head, *that your place in Heaven is secure, your unswerving devotion has brought about the end with which we both were tasked. May the child brought out of the wilderness endure, even as the woman chosen this day is cherished. As in Heaven, so on earth, we move as one soul, one spirit. Selah.*

Hours later, on her first day in office, Uruna was on her way to Morning Honors with her aide Lakti in tow, when two cleaning drudges stepped into the hallway ahead. One glanced up, then looked away quickly.

Uruna stopped.

"It's Tula-sin, isn't it?" she said.

Tula kept her eyes downcast as she muttered a reply. "Yes'm."

"You're the one always left a rose bud in my chapel room."

"Oh, that. Sorry, but couldn't find better on my way—"

"Hush." Uruna turned to Lakti. "Take this woman to the florist and see that she's given work there."

"The *temple* florist?"

"Yes, at Ekur. She has an eye for color." With a gentle finger she lifted Tula's chin to gaze at eye level. "Haven't you, dear?"

The woman who was old enough to be her mother pressed her lips together and answered with a silent nod.

"Tomorrow can't be too soon," Uruna finished and strode away.

The two maids paused before resuming work to admire Uruna's receding form.

"She's a real beauty, that one," said Tula's companion.

Tula sniffled and flicked a tear from her cheek, recalling years ago her harsh treatment of the girl who'd been so sure she would be queen.

"Aye, but it's her forgiving heart makes her precious."

Chapter 54

Peace In Turmoil

In an odd twist of fate, the second summer of Uruna's reign found her one night far from Nippur on a delta mud flat called Ur. She had traveled there to meet a suitor proposed by a rich landowner, but the fellow had run off before the first offer could be made. It seemed the least mention of serpents involved in the arrangement drove off even the stoutest of men.

Her small retinue huddled on a low rise. She hadn't bathed for three days, her hands and nails were filthy, and by her dirt-stained garments she belonged more properly behind a plough. Campfire talk had receded to grunts and short replies when she heard a sound at the light's edge and looked up. A human figure in rags, besmirched like so many southland peasants, wanted the fire but seemed afraid to ask. Uruna looked closer, saw it was a woman, and beckoned her over.

"We've meat aplenty," she said.

The woman crouched a few feet away but would move no closer to take the food offering. She kept her face averted from Uruna's view. Was she scarred, perhaps? Diseased?

Uruna pulled a hank of ham and, keeping her eyes on the fire to respect the woman's wish, shifted closer with her hand extended.

The woman sniffed at nothing in particular and angled her face toward the fire.

"You look like hell," said Lubna Seddua.

"Oh, gods!"

Uruna dropped the meat on the coals and grabbed for Lubna's hand.

Felt the connection.

Heard the song.

Fell in thrall with the wry humor exuded by her erstwhile nemesis.

"Did you know I'd be here?" she began.

"Not so much as knew I would."

Uruna tried to figure that puzzle out and failed. "Where have you kept yourself?"

"Dilmun. Or close to it. Just red rock and sea."

"I'm told it's a harsh world down there."

"Suits my nature. Penance for my excesses."

She hadn't said 'crimes.' Did that mean she had forgiven herself? The first step was always the hardest.

"Do they treat you well?"

"They're hardy souls, too often caught up in tribal conflict. I try to provide a guiding hand. Sometimes they take it, sometimes not. Often enough they appreciate it, so I stay."

"You could come back, you know."

"Yes, I suppose, but to what purpose? No longer my place or time. Maybe never was."

"It may sound strange, but we miss you. All of us."

"That's your problem. Mine are being solved elsewhere."

"It seems you have found a home, Lubna."

"Could say that."

"Have you also found peace?"

A single heartbeat before answering. "Never lost it, only thought I had." Her lips parted in a sidewise smile, and she turned full-face for the first time.

Silver-grey eyes gazed back at Uruna.

"But this you knew before asking."

Lubna got up and moved off to merge with the darkness without another word or a backward glance, leaving Uruna to stare into the fire.

No farewell was needed between souls locked for all eternity.

Chapter 55

Morning Honors Retrospective

The view from Ekur's roof garden always inspired Uruna to long moments of reflection. Having just finished Morning Honors and put away her vestments, she paused at the top of the stair to take in the surrounding sights. Utu had risen quickly above the flat desert horizon, heralding the lengthy brilliance of summer. The light washed the tops of the highest buildings with gold, and across the city to the west, Enshiggu's spire gleamed white above the river's sweep.

What a blessing to be alive! Her greatest fortune was to witness each new beginning right here, from Sumer's highest pinnacle. She, once an impoverished orphan, was queen for a nation, respected, a lady of position, a woman who could call an entire city her home, whose allies at Council followed her lead. She had learned to persuade, to bend the minds of many to her cause if needed. Political power no longer posed the confounding mystery that once had thwarted the child-queen of the past. She now coped with it, wielded it herself, understood the necessity for its existence as she ministered to thousands.

But could she rule without The Sight? Others had succeeded

without it for generations. Sumer would always prosper. The Lukur's ongoing obsession with prophecy was evidence of a fixated hope clinging to lost tradition. She, the lucky one, had been chosen for the purpose by mortals, and the gods had shown their approval. Prophecy was within her grasp. Surely Heaven would see to it.

She could rejoice in all if not for one loose end: Memet had ceased talking to her. As unsettling as it might appear, such a lapse was not the dire omen she would have feared years ago. Rather, it posed a rare chance to exercise dominion, to assert her own mastery of serpent lore won from travail and doubt. She was free to search for and find a serpently man—one such as Khufu nearly was and might have become, had he lived. A man with Suba's stouthearted loyalty. The lives of those two proved such a mate could exist—even waited for her.

Just then Kinar caught up with her at the top stair and hooked an arm through Uruna's elbow. As the two friends began a slow descent to the street, Kinar surprised her.

"You see it, don't you?"

"What, the river?"

"All of it. The sweet beauty of our land, our city, our people. I watch you up here after prayer, and at court and temple, and I count us blessed to follow your lead, even as you are blessed to be that servant."

"For heaven's sake, Kikki, I'm only eighteen."

"Yes, and you carry the wisdom of a sage. Once you apply that to your saintly purpose and attain The Sight—"

"I shall need a man for it, as you well know. And none has come forth. Not the right one anyway."

"Have patience, love. It's early yet."

"Sometimes I wonder if I'm listening to my own voice."

"You will be given a mate for your purpose. The god has prepared a place for him at your side. It may take years…"

"Oh, Kikki, not like that last one, I hope."

"Do you question the god's wisdom?"

"No, I can only trust that we'll hear correctly."

"We, Uruna?"

"For a quest of such magnitude we must marshal our very best. All of our wills, all of our minds. Didn't I tell you so years ago?"

"How could any woman forget such a moment?" Kinar said.

Uruna turned and found her most trusted ally gazing at her with wide-eyed intensity.

So there lay Kinar's commitment. With such steadfast devotion on her side, she could not miss the mark. Who else but Shua Kinar was so attuned to the gods, so keen to perceive truth hidden in the human spirit, so uniquely qualified to guide her queen to the rightful mate?

As Uruna's first footfall struck the street, a light warmth kindled a spark at her center and she lost sight of the friend on her arm, the temple wall, the early risers trudging to work.

A whisper, and a rush of wind…

Old comfort in a fond, familiar voice of welcome…

A settling peace, as at last doubt's ceaseless shuttle came to rest and left her locked in bedrock assurance.

Her heart lifted as she turned her thoughts outward to greet a wash of purest love.

He was out there, somewhere ahead. A mate waiting to take her soaring to Sight's utmost pinnacle. He belonged to her, and she to him, with a love none could put asunder.

She would search the world as long as she had breath, no matter how many false steps or how many failures lay in her path.

And by the gods, she would find him!

Ready for more Uruna?
Her story continues in...

EDEN'S BRIDE

SUMERIAN CHRONICLES I

DANIEL PHALEN

Under the watchful eye of a deadly cobra, empath queen Uruna risks her life and mankind's future to foresee an alternative to war.

The world is about to turn from rule by women to the age of kings and wars. Nippur's high priestess Uruna is tasked with preserving the matrilineal culture by prophecy. Her final recourse is her lover, a renegade lion hunter who must perform flawlessly with her in an arcane ritual no man has lived to finish.

But the regime's lack of an armed defense opens the door for a power-mad priest to impose his occupying army of insurgents, remove women from office, and confiscate their lands.

Torn between her longing for love and her pledge as bride to a nation, Uruna risks death to pull humanity back from the brink of chaos--even if the cost is more shattering than her worst nightmare.

Now available in softcover

Creston Hall Press

Please visit www.danielphalen.com

GLOSSARY

Since we can count on the fingers of one hand the number of humans literate in Sumerian, a glossary might help your understanding of this book's who, what, and where. If your e-reader permits, feel free to bookmark this page and bop back and forth as you read Uruna's story.

Places

Nippur	(ni-POOR) sacred city of Inanna; capital of northern Sumer
Ekur	(eh-KOOR) Nippur's temple
Aniginna	(ah-nuh-GHIN-uh) Nippur's enclosed administrative center
Euphrates	(yoo-FRAY-teez) one of two main rivers through Sumer (Iraq); Sumerian *buranun*, Akkadian *ipurattu*
Tigris	(TIE-griss or TIGG-riss) Sumer's other main river; Sumerian *idiglat*
Ghana	(GAH-nuh) the Great Marsh, swamp, river delta where Tigris and Euphrates rivers meet the Persian Gulf; refuge hold; wilderness
Uruk	(OO-ruck) Sumer's largest metropolis, civic center, Enguda's headquarters
Eanna	(eh-AH-nuh) Uruk's temple
Kish	small city upriver from Nippur, Nazim quartering nearby

Gods

Inanna	(ee-NAH-nuh) supreme goddess, mother protector; Great M
Enshiggu	(en-SHIG-oo) god of Serpenthood prophecy
Lamashtu	(lah-MAHSH-too) pagan god of death
Utu	sun deity

Nanna	moon deity

Terms

disikku	(di-SICK-oo) midday worship ceremony
Emesh	Sumerian god of summer and personification of summer; brother of Enten, god of winter. Depicted as a farmer.
Enten	Sumerian god of winter who watched over the birth and health of animals during the cold, rainy season.
gipar	(ghi-PAR) women's temple dormitory
kadishtu	(kuh-DISH-too) acolyte priestess
meh	a power or ability conferred by a deity; god-endowed strength, talent, right, custody, possession
mudhif	(moo-DEEF) large communal house of the marsh people; guest accommodation, gathering place for weddings, funerals, etc.; constructed with bundled and woven reeds.
naditu	(nah-DEE-too) caste of businesswomen; temple order who conducted commerce with traders from abroad
napishtu	(nah-PISH-too) a sacred rite; a woman of sacred bloodlines
nigenna	(ni-GHEN-uh) temple-owned farm lands
swifthull	slender water craft with upswept prow; Sumer's speediest transport; paddled like a canoe or with a long pole
Uzba	(OOZ-bah) group of forty elected landowners who lobby with temple authorities over entitlement, seed allotments, and price-setting

NOTES ON THE TIMES

Uruna's Sumer was Iraq 5,000 years ago. To this day the rivers wash the desert with silt each year, transforming the topography over time. Modern-day Basra once lay deep under the Persian Gulf.

Whereas the *Sumerian Chronicles* trilogy begins and ends around the Great Marsh at the Tigris-Euphrates river delta, Uruna's beginnings as Misha place her in the Zagros mountains east of the Tigris. That region has endured under various names including Elam. Her supposed birthplace at Anshan was on the Persian plateau and didn't figure in history until thousands of years later.

Sumerians were industrious, assertive people of round skull, beaked nose, black hair. They were assimilated as a race by Semitic Akkadians c. 1800 BC. Sumerian firsts include the wheel, writing, a code of law, schools, and the first love song (by a woman, of course, Enheduanna (2334-2279 BC).

Sumerian cuneiform writing didn't coalesce as a unified body of texts until 3,000 BC. Their invention of the wheel coincided. Earliest cuneiform tablets recorded kings and their victories in war.

The Sumerian pantheon contained more than 400 gods and goddesses, for all types of human situations. Thus, the story's characters speak of gods the way we might say "I think" or "what a coincidence" or "how did that happen?" They spoke to anthropomorphized deities they believed lived and died and ate and drank and magically flew and all sorts of things. I tried not to go all Fantasy with this notion because I want the story grounded in realism.

Ziggurats! The most famous is of course the semi-restored monster at Ur, which American soldiers brought home in still image and video. It didn't exist in 3200 BC. Those temples barely rose above 10 feet in height. The platforms weren't finished.

Sumerians built one on top of the other. Leonard Woolley in 1921 dug at Ur 40 feet below surface to find streets and houses under 5,000 layers of silt. I stretched fact a little with Ekur (at Nippur) and Eanna (at Uruk).

AUTHOR'S NOTE

Thank you for taking the time to read *Eden's Promise*. If you enjoyed it, please tell your friends or post a short review. Word of mouth is an author's best friend and much appreciated.

Visit my website at **www.danielphalen.com** to learn about current and future projects. You'll find some interesting illustrations and facts about Uruna's world and where it stands in the annals of human history.

Dan Phalen

www.ingramcontent.com/pod-product-compliance
Lightning Source LLC
Chambersburg PA
CBHW020659110726
47901CB00001B/244